Unleashing the Spirit Within

Valerie Sells

Copyright © 2017 Valerie Sells
All rights reserved.
ISBN: 9781549681271

Contents

Chapter 1	1
Chapter 2	11
Chapter 3	13
Chapter 4	17
Chapter 5	21
Chapter 6	30
Chapter 7	40
Chapter 8	50
Chapter 9	59
Chapter 10	70
Chapter 11	78
Chapter 12	86
Chapter 13	93
Chapter 14	102
Chapter 15	112
Chapter 16	120
Chapter 17	129
Chapter 18	143
Chapter 19	150
Chapter 20	159
Chapter 21	170
Chapter 22	178
Chapter 23	188
Chapter 24	198

Chapter 25	204
Chapter 26	216
Chapter 27	224
Chapter 28	233
Chapter 29	241
Chapter 30	254
Chapter 31	264
Chapter 32	274

Chapter 1

Crazy. That was the only word Anastasia Addams could find that would adequately sum up the man in front of her. He simply had to be insane to the point of lunacy! Of course, when she'd first walked in he'd seemed perfectly normal. Sitting there in his finely cut suit, hands clasped on the desk behind the shiny name plate that told everyone he was Robin Bryant, high-class lawyer guy. To be fair he was also now looking at her as if she were the crazy one, and given what had just happened, Annie couldn't argue that she might seem a little eccentric.

Again, Anastasia tried to focus her eyes on the piece of paper she'd torn from the lawyer's hands, almost ripping it in two in the process. The printed letters seemed to jumble before her eyes, but as soon as they settled she realised that perhaps telling Mr. Bryant to shut up might have been a little thoughtless.

"I'm sorry, but this makes no sense," she told him, re-reading the words that stunned her every time. "Where would my grandmother even get a house like this?" she shook her head in amazement.

The lawyer visibly squirmed and cleared his throat before explaining.

"Apparently, she, er, won it," he said, feeling rather ridiculous. "In a poker game, no less."

Annie coughed and laughed at the same time at that comment. Her grandmother? Poker? The little old lady - who disapproved of her darling daughter marrying an American and emigrating - was a gambler at the age of seventy-something, and for stakes as high as this?

"Grandma Rachel... played poker?" Annie repeated slowly, trying to make sense of it. "She won a freakin' mansion, and now... now it's mine?"

Unleashing the Spirit Within

"Exactly". The lawyer nodded once. "Along with all her other worldly goods, which alone are worth several hundred thousand dollars. It seems her gambling paid off in a big way."

Anastasia started to laugh again. She seemed to have no control over her own reactions any more, but all of this was so crazy and not at all what she expected when she came into this office. Sure, she knew her grandmother had died and that something had been left for her in the will. Annie wasn't ready to hear that everything was now hers, or that 'everything' included an English mansion house!

"I'm sorry," she apologised when Mr. Bryant sighed at her outburst and she waved her hand as she tried to get her breath and calm down. "It's just, my life is not exactly what you'd call great right now. I work six days a week at the local supermarket, and two late shifts at the corner store on weekends just to make rent on my apartment and pay back the loan from college. My Mom's in the Caribbean with a guy whose reputation could probably keep you in business for the rest of time, my Dad is dead, and I only actually ever met my Grandma Rachel like four times that I remember."

"Well, it seems she had more affection for her absentee granddaughter than anybody else," she was told, "because, as I said before, she left everything to you."

Annie just blinked, finding the information she was being given just did not fit in her head no matter which way she sliced it.

"I know it's a lot to take in," the lawyer sympathised, "and you don't have to know what you want to do about all this right now."

He took the paper from her hands and pulled an envelope from the desk drawer, tucking the document and a few others into it.

"Take these with you, think about what's happening and come back and see me if you have any questions." He smiled, pressing the envelope into Annie's hand. "I hate to hurry you," he continued as he got to his feet, "but I do have another appointment..."

Annie just stared at him like an alien from outer space. This guy had just told her she was rich, beyond anything she'd ever imagined. Her dreams were to be able to pay the rent on time each month, to get a big enough pay rise at the mart so she didn't have to work two jobs. Then there was the one involving Jump Street era Johnny Depp and a family size tub of strawberry yoghurt, but that was a whole different issue entirely. Anastasia Addams was not prepared to be told she owned an English mansion or that she had enough cash to live a life far beyond that she was accustomed to.

"Miss. Addams?" the lawyer prompted her eventually. "I really do have to ask you to leave now."

"Uh-huh." She nodded absently, rising from the chair. She snapped out of her trance at the door and shook hands with Mr. Bryant.

"Thank you," she said almost looking through him. "I'll probably call you soon."

With that she headed out of the office and got halfway down the hallway before she squealed with apparent delight, holding the envelope in her hands tight to her chest. Her life had just been turned around in the most wonderful away, and yet the first person she told would not be her parents or one of her friends. It would be her boss at Robertsons Supermarket. She'd waited a long time for this.

Annie grinned to herself as she hurried from the building and down towards the bus stop. She was practically bouncing up and down on the spot for the entire ten minutes she had to wait before boarding the vehicle that would take her just a few feet from her home. She was sure her fellow travellers thought she was insane, but she could afford to be a little weird in public now. Hell, she could afford to be anything she wanted to be and she planned on being just that.

For the first time ever, it didn't bother Anastasia that her neighbours had left smelly bags of garbage on the steps of the building, or that she had to pull and push her own front door six different ways before the key and lock would work in harmony and let her inside. It didn't matter that the couple next door were enjoying their lunch break so much that their headboard banging against the adjoining wall made every trinket on the shelves jump rhythmically, or that the water in the bathroom would not run at any temperature but freezing cold. Today was one of the last Annie would spend in this apartment, in this town, in this country! Her life was about to be turned upside down in the best way possible, and whilst it was scary as hell if she actually thought about it too much, the idea of going back to her country of origin and owning enough cash and property to make a really decent life for herself thrilled her beyond words.

Anastasia dug in the back of her closet, grinning when he found what she was looking for. She changed out of the fairly smart skirt and jacket she'd worn to visit the lawyer, and into what could only be described as Grade A slut-wear. She only had the skirt because of a party Janine had dragged her to last Christmas. One of the easiest costumes they could make themselves without a whole lot of expense was St Trinian's school girls and the pair had kept the left-overs of their outfits to wear again if they were ever invited to a similar occasion.

Valerie Sells

The top she pulled over her head was fire engine red and clearly at least two sizes too small for the expanse of her chest, but it'd been something Annie really wanted and she'd purchased it with money from her first ever pay check. Sentimental value would not allow her to part with it. A pair of spike-heeled knee-high boots added three inches to her height and a grin to her face as she caught sight of herself in the full-length mirror that adorned the wardrobe door. It was so far from her usual attire, but it was perfect for what she had planned. Grabbing her make-up bag, she over-applied shadow to her eyes and colour to her lips before heading for the front door, hips swinging all the way.

Annie had never been more glad that she worked just a few yards from home as she was reminded all too painfully why she never wore these boots any more. As she rounded the final corner though, the smile was soon back on her face and she came through the front door of the supermarket grinning widely.

"Annie, I know things are rough," the woman on the first checkout called to her, "but don't tell me your white skinny ass has sunk as low as the red lights, girl?"

"No way, Shanice!" Anastasia laughed as she walked by. "This is just a means to an end," she explained, gesturing to her outfit.

Several female customers looked at her with mixed jealousy and distaste, whilst a man in the freezer aisle almost fell right in!

"Where are you going dressed like that?" asked a familiar voice, as a hand landed on Anastasia's shoulder.

"Don't worry, Mikey," she said, patting his hand. "I'm just going to see Darryl."

She referred to her boss, the famous womaniser whom she'd foolishly dated for two months when she'd first taken the job there, not knowing what he really was. He'd been trying to get her back ever since.

"Don't do anything I wouldn't do!" Michael yelled behind her as she headed for the staff only door.

Annie turned around and winked at him.

"Leaves me with plenty of options." She smirked as she disappeared from view.

Darryl was so going to get what was coming to him today. He was good-looking, there was no doubt about it, but he knew it altogether too well. He was arrogant and selfish and expected every girl to fall at his feet when he snapped his fingers. Usually they worked out what he was and dumped him, but by that time he already got what he wanted, the same thing every guy seemed to want from a woman, with the exception of Michael and those that rode his bus. It was all about sex, and what really got to Darryl was that Annie never actually slept with him before she dropped him like a hot brick. He'd been trying to remedy that little problem ever since, and everyone knew she was his golden girl at work. He came close to firing her so many times but never quite followed through, and now Annie had the chance to quit in the most spectacular fashion. People would talk about this exit in league with Antigonus, though Annie didn't plan to be pursued by a bear.

"Hey, Darryl," she said seductively, posing in the doorway to his office and making the most of what she had.

The manager looked up from his paperwork and smiled in filthy fashion as his eyes raked over her form.

"Anastasia. I didn't expect to see you until late today."

He smiled and she faked a laugh as she strutted over to the desk. Hands flat on the surface, Annie leaned over towards him until she was fairly certain he could almost see her toes via her top.

"Well, y'know, I thought we should figure out that little misunderstanding we had yesterday," she said softly.

"Misunderstanding?" he said, swallowing hard.

This was not how Annie usually behaved, and whilst Darryl wasn't about to request that she stopped any time soon, it was throwing him off his game intensely.

Annie tried not to smile too much at his reactions as she walked around the desk and sat down on the edge beside him, crossing her legs and making her skirt go impossibly high as she leant her weight back on one hand. He was too busy studying her assets to realise her fingers had hit the switch to the public address system. From that point forward, everything said inside the office could be heard by every employee and customer within the store.

"Y'know, yesterday? When that guy 'accidentally' grabbed my ass and I sort of hit him a little bit," Annie reminded him, ducking her head like a naughty child, ashamed of her actions. She felt quite the opposite, of course, but it was all part of the plan.

"I should have fired you for that, Anastasia," Darryl told her, eyes unable to fix on hers but travelling everywhere else instead.

"You say that a lot," she said, leaning towards him. "Like that time after we broke up when you said I was fired if I didn't sleep with you."

"That bastard!" Shanice yelled when she heard her friend's voice over the PA.

Whilst the silent listeners all around her were a little shocked by the outburst, they whole-heartedly agreed with her sentiments, most especially the women that were present.

"You didn't follow through then," Annie continued back in the office. "I wanted to be certain you wouldn't this time."

"One might think, Miss. Addams," said Darryl, smirking. "That you were trying to use your, er, assets, to bribe me in some way?"

"Oh, Mr. Grant!" She faked a shocked expression, before asking; "Would I be the first? I mean, so many girls must want a piece of you," she said, reaching out to straighten his tie, "and most of them need to keep their jobs so..."

"Annie, you know you mean more to me than any other woman I ever met."

He was giving her the usual line and Anastasia couldn't help but grin. She knew for a fact he'd used the same one on almost every young woman that worked in the store, and some of them had yet to figure out that he was stringing them along. They knew now, as the smashed eggs and dented tins attested. Several shop assistants got angry, upset or both at the realisation they were being used, as Annie knew they would.

"I know," she said, finally answering Darryl in a seductive whisper as she stood up, pulling on his tie and bringing him up with her. "That's why I wanted you to be the first to know..." she said softly, as he leaned in ever closer.

"Know what?" he asked, swallowing hard.

Annie's smile was wide as ever as she shoved him away from her roughly, sending him sprawling into the filing cabinet.

"That I quit, you perverted moron!" she told him with all the attitude she possessed.

"You can't quit!" he yelled angrily, getting to his feet

and grabbing her wrist as she turned to leave. "You need this job, and you know it!"

"Screw you!" she said, getting angry herself and snatching her arm from his grasp. "Not that anyone with two brain cells ever would!"

She picked up her purse and turned towards the door. Turning back right before she left, she smiled the sweetest smile.

"And Darryl, baby? I think you left the PA switched on," she told him before pushing the strap of her purse higher on her shoulder and strutting back out into the store.

"Anastasia, you are crazy!" Michael said in amazement as his friend appeared through the Staff Only door once again.

Darryl could be heard shouting obscenities as he fumbled to turn the PA system off again.

"You go, girl!" Shanice called from her station.

Annie laughed.

"Seriously, Annie, how can you afford to just quit like that?" Michael needed to know, looking like he might explode if she didn't tell him right now.

"I can't hang around right now, sweetie," Annie told him with a shake of her head as she realised the whole store was staring at her. "But meet me at Vivacity tonight and I'll explain everything, okay?"

With a confirming nod from her friend she headed out of the store, shaking the whole way but determined not to let it show. Annie had waited too long to bring scum like Darryl Grant down. In fact, she'd waited too long for a lot of things. Now it was all about to change, a new chapter in the life of Anastasia Addams and she was going to enjoy every minute of it. After all, you never knew when your time might be up.

Unleashing the Spirit Within

Chapter 2

It was dark when he woke, but then, what else was to be expected at such an hour of the night? Or should that be morning? His mind was too foggy to remember, though he was fairly certain he'd only had four beers. A good night out usually consisted of seven or eight and then maybe a bottle of vodka before his body finally gave in to the beautiful oblivion of unconsciousness. Hangovers were frequent but never like this. His head felt too light, his legs too unsteady for his symptoms to be caused by over-consumption.

Stumbling towards the window, he caught hold of the sill with his hands before his body had a chance to collapse completely. He squinted out into the darkness. Figured he had to be on at least the second floor, though he had no recollection at all of climbing the stairs.

Dropping to his knees, he concentrated on remembering the events of the day before. The drive up from London to this overly grand house. The time spent talking with his cousin, his friends, and others he'd never met. The alcohol, the card game, the talk of re-forming the band, and then... Nothing stuck in his mind beyond that point. Not a single word or picture, just darkness, the one thing that still remained now, even with his eyes wide open. The near-full moon lit just one edge of the room, leaving the rest, including the door, in thick gloom.

A hand reached up to rub his eyes as he tried to focus on the less visible areas of his surroundings. He scanned the walls for a switch that might turn on a light of any kind, but there was nothing. His head swam badly as he pulled himself to his feet once again and dragged his body around the room, hands constantly searching the walls.

Unleashing the Spirit Within

A sound near the door caught his attention, but startled him enough to knock him down before he had a chance to turn. With his legs in a useless tangle beneath him and his back to the entrance he had no way of knowing someone stood behind him now.

The first he knew of the blade in his back was a rush of heat and the strange sensation that came with looking down and seeing the tip of a sword coming out through his chest. His whole body convulsed as blood seeped from both wounds. The pain only seemed to kick in when the weapon that skewered him was pulled free once again.

The feeling as if he were being pulled inside out lasted just a few moments before he fell into blackness again. This time, someone was there to make sure he would never wake up.

Chapter 3

"That's insane!"

"For God sakes, Mike, could you stop saying that!"

Annie laughed into her electric blue cocktail, narrowly avoiding getting the umbrella and fruit decorations up her nose.

"When the boy's right, he's right," said Shanice definitely. "You just told us you got yourself a damn mansion, girl!"

Anastasia couldn't help but laugh all the harder at her friends' expressions. The pair of them had been in complete awe from the moment they'd arrived at the club and she'd explained what had happened with her grandmother's lawyer a few hours before. Actually, they weren't the only ones to be shocked by the news.

"When she told me, my first words were... Well, let's just say they're not even repeatable in polite society," said Janine with a nod, before downing the rest of her drink and chewing a piece of pineapple off a cocktail stick.

Anastasia found the whole thing so amusing, mostly because this was her fifth highly alcoholic drink in the past couple of hours and she wasn't entirely used to it. The fact was she could barely afford a couple of beers once a week usually, but knowing as she did that she had just come into serious money, she was in the mood for celebrating - big style! Of course, she needed her friends for that, and the only three people she could really give that title to were here right now.

Shanice and Michael she had met from working at the supermarket. Both had been there much longer than she had, and Shanice was easily ten years older than Annie, whilst Mike was a couple of years younger. In them, Annie found an older sister, possibly even a mother figure, and the near-perfect man with just one small flaw that prevented Annie from marrying him on the spot - he liked guys as much as she did.

Janine was Annie's best friend from high school, and they sat together in all their classes, studying together and hanging out at all other opportunities as well. Tonight, however, was far from study night. It was a total celebration, though Annie knew the real reason she was knocking back so many drinks was because of what she had to tell her friends next.

"So, when you sell Castle Addams or whatever, how many millions will you have to spend on us?" Mike giggled, shoving his friend slightly to get her attention when she seemed a little dazed.

"Er, that's kind of the point I was trying to get to," Annie admitted. "Or maybe I was actually trying to avoid it," she added under her breath, finishing her drink in one gulp and setting the glass down on the bar.

She took a deep breath and looked at her three friends in turn before choosing the floor as a good place for her eyes when she finally spoke.

"I'm kind of not selling it," she said, almost too quietly. "I'm kind of going to go see it and maybe live in it for a while?"

Mike and Shanice shared a look as Janine's mouth opened and closed like a recently landed fish. Yeah, those were the reactions Anastasia had pretty much been expecting.

"But, you're coming back, right?" Mike asked her.

She shifted uncomfortably before daring to look him in the eye.

"I don't know," she admitted, hating the pain she saw on his face.

"Well, sweetie, I think it's great." Shanice painted on a smile as fake as her nails. "You get out there in the world and be young and free," she told her with an encouraging pat in the back. "You deserve it, honey!"

"Thanks." Annie swallowed hard to avoid the onset of tears that seemed set to follow her previous fit of giggles. "Y'know, it's not like I wanna leave you guys," she promised them. "You're my best friends, my only friends, and I wish it were easier for me to stay but..."

"It's okay, Annie." Janine managed a brave smile too. "We get that you want to do this, that you have to."

Her encouragement only served to make Anastasia feel worse.

"I just think there has to be something else to life, y'know?" she said, voice wavering with emotion. "I think I wanna go and find it. When am I ever gonna get a chance like this again?"

"You're right. You gotta go for it, sweetie." Mike nodded, leaning forward to hug her close. "I'm just going to miss you so much."

"And I'll miss you too," she assured him as they held each other, "but we can call and write, and you can even come visit me, maybe?"

"Try keeping us away, honey," said Shanice, with a smile. "I wanna get me some handsome English prince or whatever so I can play at being a Lady of the house too." She laughed when she said it, but it didn't help. Annie was fighting tears as she moved to hug Shanice, grateful that her friends were so understanding of her leaving.

It made sense for her to go, but it did mean starting again - new friends, new experiences, and in a new country too. Still, Annie was quite determined to do this. She needed to just as much as she wanted to. Her grandmother thought she was the best person to give her worldly possessions to, the least Anastasia could do was use them as intended. It seemed wrong to leave a big, beautiful mansion standing empty, she knew it the moment she saw the picture of the house amongst the documents the lawyer had given her. Such a place should be enjoyed by people, and filled with laughter and joy all the time.

Chapter 4

"So now you know everything. Why he wanted rid of this place," he said, as he stood by the door lighting a cigarette, the flame from the match lighting up the darkness only marginally and yet the two could see each other as plain as day.

"I knew before I came here." She smiled in the blackness. "I knew before I took my seat at that table."

He looked surprised.

"You did it on purpose," he realised, blowing out smoke. "Makes you stupider than I thought," he scoffed, pale hands going into the pockets of his jacket where they spent most of their time, since he had little else to do with them.

"I would say you ought to respect your elders," the woman told him, "but we both know how inaccurate that would be."

She smirked, an expression that didn't quite fit on her weathered face, and even he could not hold back the smile that tugged the corners of his mouth upwards. Still he tried his best to look annoyed. A rebel to the end, and beyond.

"Doesn't change anythin', y'know?" he said, shaking his head. "This is my place. I'm not goin' anywhere, you hear me?"

"This is not your place," she reminded him. "You know that, the same as I do."

"What the hell do you know about it?" he snapped, throwing down his spent cigarette and storming away into the darkness that he had become accustomed to these past years.

"More than you would think, dear boy."

Unleashing the Spirit Within

The old woman sighed, fading quickly out of sight.

The ringing of the telephone awoke Anastasia with a start. It was two weeks since she had found out about her inheritance from her grandmother and today was the day she ventured across the pond to England where she would take residence of Bennington Hall for the foreseeable future. With a groan, she rolled over and reached for the telephone, the harsh ringing of which still assaulted her ears.

"Hello?" she said groggily, rubbing at her eyes.

"Morning, Starshine!" said a chirpy voice on the other end of the line.

"Hey, Mikey!" Anastasia smiled. "What's up?"

"Clearly not you, sweetie. You sound half-asleep."

"I only just woke up," she admitted. "I had the weirdest dream, and my grandma was in it. There might have been a guy, but I have no idea who he was."

"Was he a hottie?"

Annie laughed. It was always his first question whenever men were the topic of conversation!

"That's not entirely the point," she said, stretching her free arm above her head. "Honestly, I didn't really see his face or notice anything about him that matters. I was more wondering how come I'm suddenly dreaming about my grandma. I guess just because I'm moving into her house today," she rambled a little as she mulled it over, ending with a large yawn.

Anastasia wasn't entirely awake yet and half of what Mike said, at super-speed no less, was completely lost on her semi-functioning brain. She managed to catch the gist though, that when Janine drove her to the airport, he and Shanice would be coming along to wave her off with appropriate amounts of hugs and tears.

After agreeing to the suggestion and exchanging goodbyes with Mike, Annie hung up the phone and dragged herself out of bed. She looked around the dismal little bedroom with its peeling wallpaper and damp patches, and she smiled. This was the last day of waking up in this hell hole of an apartment. From here on out, it was four poster beds and chandeliers for Anastasia Addams.

She smiled as she rifled in the drawer and pulled out the picture and description of her property once again. Bennington Hall, less than two miles from Bennington Town, and surrounded by beautiful English countryside scenery. It was so far from her cramped and dirty little apartment, six floors up from the filthy streets of the big city. It was almost too much to dream, and yet this was no fantasy. This was happening, and today, no less. Anastasia would be on a plane in just eight hours' time. Goodbye old life, hello to the new!

* * * * *

"Well, this is it."

Anastasia smiled and cried at the same time as her flight was called and she hugged all three of her best friends in turn.

"You have a great life, honey. You deserve it all and then some," Shanice told her as she squeezed her almost too tight.

"Oh, sweetie, I'm going to miss you every day forever," said Mike tearfully as he took his turn at saying goodbye, "but I love you, and Shanice is right, you deserve this so much!"

"Thank you, guys, and you know I'll miss you too,"

said Annie, trying to dry her eyes, "but I'll call and write, and when I get the place straight you have to visit, really."

"Like we'd ever not want to come see you." Janine cried openly though she forced a smile through her tears and hugged Anastasia to her.

"You take care, Annie," Shanice told her, trying not to blub, "and you meet any hot English guys you make sure you give them my number!"

"I promise." Annie nodded, tears streaming down her face as her flight was called for the final time and she knew she really had to go. "Bye guys," she said shakily, with a little wave as she was forced to leave them standing there and pass through the gate to get on the plane.

It was all a pipe-dream, the promises of her friends to come visit. It was clear to them all that they would never afford it, and there was nothing to say how things would turn out for Anastasia once she got to England. This might be the last time she saw any of her friends in the flesh. She felt sick as she walked through the gate, still crying like her heart would break.

Annie knew she was making the right decision, deep down she was sure of it.

"You think she'll be okay?" Mike asked as they watched their friend's back disappear around the corner.

"Ain't got no doubts," Shanice told him definitely. "She's a smart girl, don't take nobody's bull. She'll do just fine."

Chapter 5

Anastasia was exhausted after all her travelling, to the point where she was half asleep in the cab that ferried her from the train station to her new home. It was mostly dark outside. The sun had just set and the moon was steadily rising beyond the trees.

"See your house from here, love," the cab driver told her.

Anastasia forced her eyes open and leaned towards the window. She was amazed by the sight that met her eyes. The photograph hadn't done the house justice, not at all. They called it a mansion, and that was certainly the correct description.

"Wow!" she gasped, the only word she could find to say as the building loomed in the distance.

It might have looked even bigger and grander in real life than it ever had in the pictures she'd seen, like something from a fairy tale, she thought. Anastasia had to pinch herself just to make sure this wasn't all a dream. It was at least the seventh time she had done so since the lawyer told her about her inheritance. Once again, the action proved she was indeed awake. This was real, this house was hers now.

"Might look alright from here," said the cab driver with a smirk. "Can't say as I envy you livin' there though."

"You know something I don't?" Anastasia frowned as she sat back in her seat and waited for a response.

"'S only rumours but..." he paused before continuing, "well, they say nobody who lives there is ever exactly alone. Know what I mean?"

"What?" She chuckled at what she thought he was saying. "Are you trying to tell me that house is haunted or somethin'?" she checked. "'Cause that might be the funniest thing I've heard so far in this country, 'cept for the guy at the airport who told me it was his birthday and asked if I wanted to blow out his candle," she considered, shaking her head as she recalled the drunken idiot at the gate, and the satisfying sound of his girlfriend slapping him round the face when she heard what he'd said.

A haunted house! Like Anastasia was ever going to believe any of that crap. Sure, she had heard all the stories, read the novels, seen the movies. There were a hundred and one theories about ghosts, spirits, and such, and all of them were as dumb as each other, she reckoned.

As the cab driver continued to insist that there had to be something in the rumours, Anastasia let his voice fade from her ears. She focused on the house growing larger as they headed on up the driveway. It was big and beautiful, maybe not in the best of conditions, she supposed, but she had money to fix it up, and it wasn't as if she needed all of it to live in anyway. A few rooms would be fine, and she could take her time making the rest habitable, then maybe sell it off and get herself something more suited to her situation.

"Ought to take notice, love," the cab driver warned her as he pulled up in front of Bennington Hall. "Anything goes bump in the night, consider yourself warned."

Anastasia laughed, noting he was trying to hold in a smile himself. Fairy tales and ghost stories. They had them back home in the States just the same. She supposed there were more in England, just because there were a lot more older buildings here. The country had a bigger history for that kind of thing, it was to be expected. She didn't know all the details yet, but hey, there was a chance this very house was older than the United States itself.

The cases and bags were dragged from the back of the car. The driver offered to help her inside with them, but Anastasia insisted she could manage.

"After all, if you come in, the ghouls might not let you leave!" She winked at the driver.

He rolled his eyes, accepting the fare she handed him. Before long the cab was driving away, the only real source of light going with it. Anastasia squinted in the pale moonlight and fumbled with the front door. It wasn't even locked, which seemed a little weird. Of course, if the haunted house rumours were well-believed, she supposed nobody would want to break in. Besides, the nearest town was all the way back down the hill, a far enough distance, it would be quite the trek to even get up here to Bennington Hall.

Pushing her way inside, Anastasia pulled one bag in after another and piled them up in the hall way. If she thought it all looked incredible from the outside, she was no less overwhelmed by the view from inside. Sure, the place needed cleaning up, a lot, in point of fact, but it was still incredible. High ceilings, grand staircases, old paintings on the walls, and thick curtains hanging at every window. It was like walking into a movie set, and she was in awe of it all, even in the dark.

Anastasia reached for the light switch. She assumed there had to be electricity, but it sure didn't seem to be turned on, since flicking the switch made no difference to the dark. She shivered, because it was cold in here too, somehow even colder than outside had seemed.

"Ow!"

She stumbled on something she couldn't see, cursing as she looked closer at the floor. Picking up what she must've tripped on, she turned the envelope left and right until the moonlight from a crack in the curtains caught it just so. Her name was typed on the front, possibly with an actual typewriter, no less! Anastasia ripped it open and tipped a large key into her free hand. There was a letter too, and from the words she could decipher in the semi-dark, she figured it was from a lawyer or what the British called an estate agent maybe. Anyway, it seemed to be confirming this was her house and giving her a means to lock the door. That all had to be good news, she supposed.

Anastasia considered pulling her luggage up the large staircase to rooms unknown and quickly decided against it. It was late and she had felt tired in the cab from all the travel, from plane to train to car. Now she was here in the house, her new home, the new adventure she'd been craving, sleep didn't seem to appeal any more. She wanted to take a look around, investigate her new surroundings and see what she had to work with.

Quite deliberately, Anastasia took off at a run, giggling like a child as she bolted from room to room, daring to rush up one particular staircase without a care. This was her house, she could do whatever she wanted. Sure, there was the slight concern she might fall through the floor or inhale so much dust that she choked to death, but she wasn't scared. Anastasia vowed never to be scared of anything anymore. If she could leave everything she knew behind to come here, then she could do anything. After all, she had spent her life doing what she had to in order to get by. For once, it wasn't a case of just surviving. She could finally live.

She was upstairs now, tearing around the first floor of the building, whooping and calling like a crazy person. Anastasia figured she didn't have to care when nobody would be able to hear her.

Valerie Sells

Reaching for the door handle on the next room, a shudder ran through her, stopping Anastasia in her tracks. She backed up slowly, one step then two. Before she knew what was happening her back was against the banister rail that creaked in protest. She turned sharply, afraid of the whole thing giving way and plunging her back to the foyer too fast.

Something was wrong here. It just felt wrong, that was the only word in Anastasia's head. She felt sick. The hand that had reached to open the door felt as if it burned somehow, and she shook it to relieve the sensation.

Breathing rapidly Anastasia stared at the door a second more, then took off up the next set of stairs and onto the second floor

It wasn't long before she stopped worrying about what happened before. It was just a locked door in a dark and dusty house. The cab driver had put dumb ideas in her head, that was all. She was freaking herself out for nothing, Anastasia told herself, as she soon discovered a lavish bathroom bigger than her entire apartment back home had been and then back downstairs to ballroom with a chandelier. She was laughing and smiling within moments as she went up and down and around the house, discovering all its hidden treasures. Everything was beautiful, illuminated by the moonlight creeping in around the curtains, and Anastasia never flinched at any sound or movement after that.

* * * * *

The sound of her laughter was like music through the house, the kind of sound that hadn't been heard here in as long as he could remember. She was prettier than he expected somehow, giddy at the prospect of a new beginning, it seemed.

Her happiness came from what she saw as good luck, he supposed. A big adventure in a foreign land, high hopes for the future she could build. Beautiful and rich, the things that women like her would always crave. More importantly, she seemed so child-like, so innocent and naive.

She wouldn't last long.

* * * * *

Anastasia woke with the sun in her eyes and a taste in her mouth like mothballs. It took her a moment to find her bearings as she lifted her head off an age-old blanket and shielded her eyes from the bright light flooding in through the window. This had to be some kind of master bedroom. She had thought so when she came rushing into it last night and it proved itself by the light of day. The four-poster bed was amazing and she had bodily throw herself amongst the pillows and blankets. It was the first room in the house that looked as if it might actually have been inhabited in living memory, and just didn't seem as dusty and old as the others. It was so easy to fall asleep on the shockingly comfy bed. The jet-lag had caught up to her, Anastasia supposed, and she had slept for hours. Now the sun was up, and she could get a better look at this place she was quite allowed to call home.

It didn't look all that homely, Anastasia noted, as she wandered out of the room and back down the large flight of stairs to the ground. They were incredibly steep, and the childish urge to ride the banister to the bottom was almost overwhelming. She might've done it, but literally shook her head when she recalled how much the rails creaked and groaned just from a little light leaning. She needed to get this place structurally sound before she did anything else, that was for certain.

Anastasia doubted the money her grandma had left her would be enough to fix up an entire house this size. In the harsh light of day, she had to be realistic. It was a shame, but it just wouldn't be possible, she supposed.

"Then what did you expect me to do, Grandma?" she asked, turning her eyes heavenward as she descended the last few steps. "I mean, I love that you cared enough to leave me everything you had, but... well, this is crazy!"

She laughed out loud and the sound echoed in the emptiness.

In the main foyer, Anastasia was met by her own luggage, haphazardly dumped right inside the door. She had no idea where to start in unpacking or putting anything away. She supposed she would need to pick a bedroom, preferably not the one she slept in last night since even one floor up those steep stairs dragging her cases was a little more than she was prepared to deal with right now.

"Okay, priorities," she said to herself, kneeling down on the floor by her bags.

The zip on the case opened easily and Anastasia flipped the top open, rifling through her belongings. She got together her wash bag, a basic change of clothes that were not going to matter so much if they got messy, and then trudged off to look for a bathroom. On the ground floor alone, she found three, and though the electricity was definitely not working in any way at all, she did seem to have water - cold water, but it was better than nothing.

Once cleaned up and changed, Anastasia went back to her case and looked for a notebook and pen. She started a To Do list, all in block capital letters, and the first items were hot water and electricity. She started to wander around the house again, pulling back curtains and checking each and every room on the ground floor. Most of them probably hadn't been used or even looked at in years, maybe decades. Anastasia knew nothing about anyone living here, she wasn't even sure if her grandma had been here herself, though she supposed she must have. If she had another home, it hadn't been mentioned.

The To Do list grew, with everything from 'find out more about the house' to 'fix broken window'. Anastasia had covered six sides of paper before she hit the final room on the ground floor and gasped at the sight that met her eyes.

This was it, this was the room her grandmother had lived in. There was fresh wallpaper, a vase of long dead flowers, and a small bed in the corner all made up with pink and white linen. It was a big room, and it seemed as if Grandma Rachel had made it her own little corner of the world. An electric heater stood in one corner, a standard lamp in another by a huge armchair. This had been how her grandmother was living, alone in one little corner of this massive house on a hill, all by herself. Anastasia couldn't imagine how she coped, and the shock of realising just how lonely she must have been made her hand shoot up to her mouth and tears come to her eyes unbidden.

"I'm so sorry, Grandma Rachel," she cried, words muffled by her hand and wavering from the emotion. "I should've come to see you, I should've..."

Tears overtook her, until her body shook hard with every sob. Anastasia sank to her knees on the hard, wooden floor and cried like her heart was breaking. It was as much the stress and shock, the long flight and all, as it was the sadness of seeing how her poor grandmother had lived, all alone like this.

With her eyes closed and her mind occupied, Anastasia didn't realise she was no longer alone, until suddenly a hand gripped her shoulder.

She screamed.

Chapter 6

"Good God, woman! Are you crazy?"

Anastasia didn't know what to say as she looked down at the man she had pinned to the floor of her grandma's house. He didn't look like a burglar or any kind of sexual deviant. She wasn't exactly sure that they had a uniform or anything, but he really did seem pretty normal. Sandy hair and dancing green eyes filled her vision as she looked down. He was pretty cute too, she noticed, even if he did look far from happy. It was then that Annie's brain caught up with her wandering eyes and she realised what she was doing.

"Oh, I'm sorry," she apologised, shifting her weight and trying to find the best way to stand up without making matters worse.

Her hands pressed down a little more than they should on the chest she'd been leaning on as she levered herself up from straddling the stranger. It was only now she let herself wonder at the way he was built, fairly solid and not exactly uncomfortable to be on top of. A hundred dirty remarks flew through her mind, many sounding as if Mike and Shanice were saying them. Anastasia bit her lip and hoped she wasn't blushing - it didn't seem likely, but she still hoped.

"Not quite the welcome I was expecting," said the stranger, straightening out his jacket and shaking his head a little.

"I'm better at the welcome when I hear the knock," said Anastasia, just a little put-out by his tone.

After all, this guy had come barging into her house. She owned this place, legal and binding. Maybe jumping on top of the man was a little OTT, but she knew the kind of things that happened to young women in

America. She couldn't imagine nobody ever got jumped in England, and this house had such a creepy air, she just reacted without a thought in her head. She couldn't really be blamed for that.

"It wasn't entirely my fault," the mystery man said then. "You had left the front door unlocked, and in actual fact, I did still knock three times, and called your name before I let myself in-"

"Woah, woah, hold up a sec," she stopped him, waving her hands in a 'slow down' kind of a gesture. "How were you calling my name? You don't even know me."

"No, that is true." He smiled then. "But I know of you, Anastasia Addams," he said smartly, reaching into his inside pocket and producing a document that he immediately handed to her.

Annie reached out for the papers and pulled them into her own hands. Legal documents, copies of the papers she signed in the lawyer's office back home. Now it was making at least a little sense.

"You're a lawyer," she said, a statement not a question as she looked the mystery man over one more time.

Cute he may be, but she wasn't entirely interested if he was that type, and it must have shown on her face given how he reacted to the look she cast his way.

"We're not monsters, you know." He rolled his eyes. "Unlike some I could mention. You know I almost thought you'd dislocated my shoulder when you threw me down like that," he complained, holding his right arm with his left hand, rolling the joint over and over.

"I'm sorry, Mr...?" she prompted for a name, looking anything but apologetic in this particular moment.

"Thomas," he answered easily. "Richard Thomas."

"Like, Bond, James Bond?" asked Anastasia with a smirk. "Nah, I guess not," she answered her own question. "I wouldn't've floored you so easy if you were a secret agent."

"Well, maybe I let you do it," he replied quickly, the look in his eyes coming as a surprise, until it disappeared as fast as it arrived.

Anastasia bit her lip as she watched him try his hardest not to blush. Suggestive remarks were clearly not Richard Thomas' forte. He tried his luck in the heat of the moment, but they both knew that he already wished he hadn't.

"I'm sorry," he said then, shaking his head. "I didn't mean-"

"Hey, it's fine," she assured him easily. "Neither of us are coming off too well in all this so far, so how about we start over?" she suggested, sticking out her hand for him to shake. "Hi, I'm Anastasia Addams. Welcome to Bennington Hall."

"A pleasure to meet you, Ms. Addams," he replied, all politeness, as he took her offered hand and shook it gently. "Richard Thomas, at your service. I must say, whilst I do appreciate the welcome, I have been here before. I knew your grandmother."

"Oh, okay." She nodded as she considered his statement. "You were Grandma Rachel's lawyer?"

"Not exactly," Richard explained. "My uncle was her preferred point of contact. I work at his practice."

"Nice," she replied, though her heart wasn't entirely in the sentiment.

Lawyers were dull, at least she always thought so. They had to be smart, that was for sure, and they made a pretty penny, Anastasia knew. Still, she couldn't imagine wanting to spend copious amounts of time with a guy like Richard Thomas. She had nothing against the British, but this guy seemed particularly old fashioned, stiff upper crust and all. That coupled with his stuffy profession, well, back where she came from he'd be branded a nerd in thirty seconds flat, and not in the cool Zach Levi kind of way either!

"Um, I'd ask if you want a cup of coffee... or it's usually tea here, right?" She smiled amiably. "Unfortunately, I'm not really organised yet. I was somewhere between figuring out what I'm going to do with this house, and wondering where the best place is to find food," she admitted, feeling her stomach lurch and hoping the growling sound wasn't as loud as it seemed in her head.

"That I might be able to assist with," he told her with a grin. "I live in town, that is, the nearest town. Unsurprisingly, it is called Bennington Town."

"Imagine that." Anastasia smiled, trying not to let out a laugh along with it. "Um, you couldn't drive me back to this town of yours, could you?" she asked then, bold as brass as per usual. "I mean, I know that's kind of forward of me, but I don't have transportation yet. I really don't have much of anything, including electricity..."

"Ah, now, that you do have," Richard corrected her. "Actually, it should've been back on last night when you arrived, but there was a mistake made and... Well, the long and the short of it is, you should have electric now, as well as water, and even gas, I hope."

"Right. Well, that's something," Anastasia considered. "But I still need to go to town so, how about that ride? Please?" she added the politeness like an afterthought.

It wasn't that she was a rude person usually, just a little thoughtless sometimes. It wasn't really Annie's fault. Her mother hadn't been the greatest of parents, her father had died when she was so young she barely remembered the guy. There was her step-father, Ted, but he was way more interested in Anastasia's mom and their new daughter than he ever was in Annie herself. Nobody had ever really given a damn about her, and she learnt to live with the fact without being too bitter about it. Of course, it seemed Grandma Rachel cared a whole lot more than Anastasia ever could've guessed. She had left her everything she owned, and it still floored her every time she let herself think about it.

"Ms. Addams?" said Richard then, waving a hand in front of her face - Anastasia hadn't even realised she had zoned out until then.

"Annie," she answered like a reflex, then off his confused look she explained. "You should call me Annie. Ms. Addams makes me feel old, and I pretty much only ever get called Anastasia by cops, or my mom when I'm in trouble," she said, rolling her eyes. "So, yeah, Annie is good."

"Then you must call me Richard," he replied easily.

"I was going to." She smiled back, walking past him out of the room.

Richard took it as read that he was expected to follow and so he did. After barely five minutes of knowing this woman, he could already tell she was a force to be reckoned with. Richard hadn't known Mrs. Wickfield, Annie's grandmother, all that well, but enough to know she was a tough old lady. Clearly, Anastasia Addams was no shrinking violet, she had the spirit of her grandma in her, and Richard told her as much as they went out to the car and he politely opened the passenger door, ushering her inside.

Anastasia thanked him, for both the compliment and the door, stopping a moment to take in the view before she slipped into the car. The countryside seemed to roll on for miles in all directions but one. Down the hill atop which the house sat, there was a town. They had driven through the edge of it last night, or so the cab driver had told her. Now Annie was going to see Bennington Town properly, and that was kind of cool.

She supposed that years ago the owner of her new house would've controlled the town below. Those kind of set ups were things of the past, but it was funny to think about, all that money and power. It was such a shame to know that the house was in much worse shape now than it would've been then. There would be an awful lot of work involved in setting it right, but Anastasia was determined. This she told Richard as he drove them down into the town.

"Quite the undertaking," he commented, not needing to concentrate too hard on the empty road before them.

The weather had cleared up since last night. No more storm clouds or heavy rain. Everything was clear and bright, sunny as an English spring day ought to be, or how Annie imagined it should be in her head. She liked it a lot.

"This must be very different to your home, I suppose," prompted Richard, wondering if Anastasia was ever going to speak again.

He had left gaps enough for her to do so, and she certainly didn't seem like the kind of woman that held her tongue if she had something to say. Richard was coming to the conclusion that perhaps she just didn't want to speak to him, when suddenly she did so.

"It's so empty," she said at last. "Not in a bad way, I just... I mean, everywhere is so open and green. It's beautiful." She smiled a giddy kind of a smile, like an over-excited child maybe. "Don't get me wrong, I love New York, but it's so crammed in. Everybody on top of each other, like sardines in a can," she explained. "This is so different, but I think I can learn to love this too."

"That's good to hear," he agreed happily. "You should find the town is welcoming. There's quite a bit of excitement about the mysterious American coming to take over the hall," he told her. "Your grandmother wasn't well known, she spent a great deal of time up there alone, but those that spent any amount of time with her - my uncle in particular - they all spoke well of her."

Anastasia felt strange to realise tears were welling in her eyes at his glowing commentary about Grandma Rachel. People liked her here, but she was ultimately lonely. It made Annie wish she had come here sooner, even if just for a visit, not to stay. Why her grandmother left her everything when she had made so little effort to be a good granddaughter, she just couldn't understand. She would love to be able to say she deserved everything bestowed upon her, but she felt terribly unworthy.

"I'm sorry, what?" she asked, suddenly realising Richard had been speaking again and she had completely zoned out on him.

"I said welcome to Bennington Town," he repeated, frowning a little as he glanced from the road and noticed a tear streaking down his passenger's cheek. "Are you-?"

"I'm fine," she snapped, wiping the back of her hand across her face and forcing a smile. "So, this is... a very small town," she said with a look of surprise.

Annie wasn't sure what she had been expecting exactly. Nothing like New York City that was for sure, but something a little larger than this. Rows of quaint little shops and houses, friendly people who were mostly staring in her general direction. Anastasia had a feeling that far from the ways of her home town, a place where people passed by each other without so much as glance, Bennington was going to be one of those homely little places where everybody knew everyone else's business. That could be annoying, but at the same time, Annie couldn't help but think it might be fun too.

"I'm the talk of the town, huh?" she said, paraphrasing what Richard had already told her on their journey down here. "That's... different."

"Nobody means any harm, Ms. Ad... Annie," he corrected himself, practically blushing when she looked at him. "They're just curious. Most people who live here are 'born and raised' as I believe you Americans say. Very few families have moved here from elsewhere," he explained. "Besides, the old hall has always been a source of enough gossip to keep the rumour mill running non-stop."

Anastasia laughed at the expression on his face when he said that, the way he rolled his eyes so dramatically. Gossip and rumours were sometimes quite amusing, but clearly Richard found it all kind of pathetic. It made her wonder what exactly he thought about her old tumble-down mansion. No way to know apparently, unless she out-right asked, and that was exactly what she decided to do as he parked the car around the very next corner.

"So, what about the rumours I already heard?" she asked. "The cab driver was giving me the full haunted house speech on the way here. Very Stephen King. You know anything about that?"

Richard laughed then, a genuine hearty laugh that made Annie want to join in just because. She resisted the urge as she waited for his answer to her question.

"Why is it large old houses always bring on talk of ghosts, vampires and spirits?" he asked eventually, leaning back in his seat and looking sideways at her.

"I don't know." She shrugged, mimicking his position. "I mean, it's all crazy, I know. No such thing as all these supernatural beings, but... but something weird did happen last night," she said, her smile fading as she suddenly remembered the moment she was speaking of. "There was a locked door, which I know isn't weird in itself, but I..."

When she trailed off, apparently completely lost in the memory, Richard started to frown. It wasn't so strange. After all, Annie had zoned out once on the way into town and completely missed what he was saying, but to break off in the middle of her own sentence was a little odd.

"Anastasia?" he checked, reaching out to tap her shoulder.

His fingers didn't quite make contact when suddenly she shuddered violently and shook her head.

"I felt strange," she said, and he honestly wasn't sure if she meant now or if she were carrying on with what she had been saying before. "Like something or someone just didn't want me in that room."

Richard stared at her and Anastasia stared back. It was a full thirty seconds before either moved or spoke again.

"The door was locked," he said eventually. "That usually means somebody actually is trying to keep you out, though I highly doubt it was anything... other-worldly," he said, finding her a smile.

Annie smiled right back.

"I know, you're right," she said, sighing then. "It is all a crazy concept, ghosts in my house." She rolled her eyes. "So, putting that weirdness aside."

"Yes, indeed," said Richard, catching a hold of himself at last.

The pair got out of the car, and Anastasia took a moment to look around. The sun was shining on old-fashioned streets, red brick houses, and curious little stores. It looked like a painting or a tapestry in some little old lady's living room. Annie couldn't imagine ever truly belonging here, a city girl from the other side of the pond, and the other side of the tracks, truth be told. Still, this was her mother country, and damn if she wasn't going to try to be a real part of it.

She followed Richard back around the corner, only half listening as he talked of the town amenities, mostly the café he was taking her to for breakfast. Annie stopped at the side of the road and glanced up the hill towards her new home. She couldn't see much from here, but it made her smile just knowing it was up there, and that it belonged to her.

Chapter 7

Anastasia had never seen a place like this before. Obviously, there were cafes and restaurants in New York, but in the neighbourhood she had called home for years now, most places were a little grungy, the staff more than a little coarse. A cute little English countryside town was a world away from NYC, and this homely cafe was so different to anywhere Annie had ever been.

Richard watched her from across the table, just a little amused by the way she looked around, eyes lighting up like a child at Christmas. It was as if she never saw a place like this before, and it belatedly occurred to him that she probably never had. There was no way anyone ought to mistake Anastasia Addams for a native. Dressed in an over-sized black T-shirt that was falling off one shoulder all the time, some band logo scrawled across the front in neon pink, and the tightest jeans he'd ever seen in his life, her hair was swept up in a scruffy ponytail, the tie on which was threatening to give up and fall down at any moment. Anastasia wasn't classically beautiful, certainly no marble statue or Mona Lisa type, but she was pretty, very pretty, especially with that smile on her face.

"What?" she asked when she caught him staring. "Am I a total embarrassment to be seen with or something? Just 'cause I'm kinda bowled over by the serious amount of quaint in this place-"

"If you were an embarrassment, I wouldn't've brought you here," he told her easily, glad to be able to say anything even remotely clever right now.

The truth was, he did feel embarrassed, but it had nothing to do with her behaviour, just her presence. Richard was the shy type, and it was the one thing he hated most about himself. He was trying to overcome it, to be more open and forthcoming. He had his moments, but there were still times when he quite despaired of himself. Maybe it was easier to find his own boldness with Anastasia just because she was constantly more out of her depth than he was here. She knew nothing of this place or the ways of its people. For all the similarities between England and the United States, there were plenty of differences too.

"Good morning, Richard!" said a booming voice then, making Annie physically jump. "Oooh, and this must be our newest neighbour. How do you do, my love?"

It took a moment for Anastasia to wrap her head around the stranger's thick accent. She vaguely remembered reading something about those who lived in the north of England speaking differently, less defined, more easy, much like the Deep South back home. Richard didn't talk that way and it hadn't occurred to her it was weird until this moment. Of course, she was now too distracted by the large smiley woman before her now to ask what was up with that.

"Miss. Anastasia Addams, this is Miss. Eva Crowley," he introduced one to the other. "Our newest neighbour, meet our oldest resident. No, that didn't come out right," he said, blushing furiously.

Annie bit her lip as Eva laughed heartily, clearly not at all offended by the accusation that she was old. From here, Annie would guess at least fifty, maybe more, but not old in any way, just older. It was clear Richard hadn't meant to imply she was anything else, no chance he was being rude. After such a short acquaintance, Annie was already pretty sure he didn't know how to be offensive, just cute and awkward.

"Oh, now don't you worry, Richard," Eva told him

kindly. "What he means to say, my love, is that my family goes way back in this little town of ours," she explained to Anastasia. "'Course it all started with the Benningtons who owned your lovely house, but the Crowleys wasn't far behind. All the way back to my great-great-great... You know, I'm not even sure how many greats grandfather, but they reckon right back to 1800, maybe before," she said, smiling widely, extremely proud of her heritage, it seemed.

"Wow, that is really something," Annie replied, feeling genuinely impressed.

"As is your new home, Anastasia." Eva smiled still. "You must let me call you Anastasia, and you must call me Eva. I can already tell we're going to get along like a house on fire, my love."

"Oh, then you should call me Annie," she insisted. "Really, all my friends do."

Her smile faltered the moment she said the words 'friends' and it was hard not to notice. Richard and Eva both looked at each other and then back at Annie.

"Sorry," she apologised when she noticed how concerned they suddenly seemed. "I'm just... I left all my friends behind to come here. When I'm busy and thinking ahead, I'm fine, but just for a second I remember that they're not here. Weird, huh?" she said, forcing a smile, even as she suddenly felt stupidly emotional.

Mike, Shanice, Janine. Just a few days ago she was sat in a bar with them all, telling them about this great adventure she was heading into. Now she was here in a cafe in England, making new friends, which was great, but it also reminded Annie of what she had left behind.

"Oh, my dear, don't you worry! You'll make new friends here," Eva promised, throwing a chubby arm around Annie's back and hugging her tight to her ample chest, "and those from back home aren't going anywhere. They'll stay in touch, if they're worth the knowing." "Yeah, I know," said Annie with a genuine smile now. "Thanks, Eva."

The cafe owner was called away by one of her staff. There were other customers to serve and much more to do than stand around and chat all day, Annie supposed. Left alone with Richard, she took a moment to sniff back tears and straighten herself up in her chair.

"Are you sure you're okay?" he checked.

"Sure," she replied immediately even though she still didn't look entirely right somehow. "Weird day. Weird life, right now, actually," she admitted with a laugh. "So, what's good to eat here? I'm starved!" she declared, reaching for the menu.

Richard took a moment to watch her then picked up his own menu and began to advise her on what she might like to eat. She was quite an extraordinary young woman, like no other he had ever met. He hoped she liked it enough here to stay, give him a chance to get to know her perhaps. Maybe they could be friends, maybe more than friends. Richard blushed just considering it and hated how easily that happened. So much for being a man, he felt like such a boy when it came to women sometimes. A psychologist would tell him it was the lack of a father that made him so shy. His mother had always said that women liked a man that was in touch with his feelings. All Richard knew was that he wanted to be different, to be stronger, to be the kind of man women went weak at the knees for.

Trying not to laugh at his own ridiculous internal monologue, he forced himself to concentrate on Annie's questions.

"And this black pudding stuff, what exactly is that?"

she asked curiously.

He bit his lip and tried not to smile too much.

"Ah, probably not something you'd be interested in eating."

* * * * *

After so many years, he ought to be used to it. The forces trying to pull him in six different directions, the darkness that he lived in. Still, sometimes he watched from the window, the rolling fields and the bright sunshine, and he tried to remember. What the warmth felt like, what it was to run free. Society tried to stifle him, but he hadn't understood then what suffocation really was. The enveloping dark that can sweep down when you least expect it and swallow you whole. It hadn't entirely captured him yet, but it also wouldn't let him go. Caught in a moment you can't get out of, he'd heard that said, sung maybe, but he couldn't be sure. Time held no meaning and words were all but useless to a man that wasn't really a man at all. Still, this was his place. A person, a creature, whatever he was supposed to be, everyone and everything deserved a place to dwell, a home. He hadn't exactly chosen this place, but it was his own now, and always would be. She wasn't taking it from him. She had no bloody right!

* * * * *

"Well, what do you think of our little town?" asked Richard as he drove Anastasia back towards Bennington Hall.

She was looking out of the open passenger-side

window, her face catching the full effect of the breeze as she watched the scenery speed by. When he glanced at her, Richard couldn't help but be reminded of a child seeing a new place for the first time, in wide-eyed wonder. This place had to be quite foreign to a woman like her, that was for sure.

"Little is certainly the word." She smiled as she turned to look at him. "Not that it's a bad thing but... Have you ever been to New York?"

"No." He laughed a little at the very idea. "I've never been to America at all, actually."

People called Richard a man of the world, but that wasn't true. His life had been spent in very close quarters, never many miles from one or two places that had been his home. Richard didn't mind, he wasn't exactly the adventurous type, but admitting as much to a woman like Annie, it was a little embarrassing to say the least.

"You'd probably hate it," she said of her home country then. "At least the big city anyway, if you're used to this place."

"Oh, I don't know," he replied, trying to sound smarter or perhaps more worldly wise than he really was. "I spent a lot of time in London before this, but it wasn't... Well, I must admit, I like Bennington better than I liked it there."

Anastasia wasn't sure what to make of the dark look that played across Richard's face when he spoke of London. She didn't know him well enough after barely a day to understand what that meant and she wasn't prepared to ask. Maybe she would find out eventually. She already had a feeling she had made a friend here, and that had to be a good thing.

"It's not hard to see why you love this place." She

sighed, eyes going back to the view as she breathed in a long breath of sweet air. "I swear, this is the most fresh air I've ever gotten my whole life, and I've only been here one day."

He smiled at her enthusiasm for the simple things in life. That was a comfort in someone who was now so rich. Richard had seen the paperwork, the large sum of money, the worth of the house and its contents, all of which Anastasia Addams had inherited. It meant she really was the richest heiress for miles. In spite of this, she seemed so unaffected, not at all arrogant or pompous. Despite the reputation of some Americans, Richard couldn't exactly say she was as loud and brash as he expected either. In fact, he was rather sorry to realise that he would have little in the way of excuses to keep on seeing her after today, a day he had enjoyed much more than he ever could've imagined.

For Anastasia, it had been an odd day, but a good one. She loved the idea of coming to England, finding this house that was now to be her own, and starting a new adventure. At the same time, she had been worried about it, being so far from the friends that she looked upon as family. It hadn't been half so bad as she expected in the end.

Richard had taken her all around the sights of Bennington today. Maybe 'sights' was the wrong word, but he showed her where all the important places were - the post office, the bank, his uncle's office - and he'd introduced her to some key people too. The mayor had smiled and shaken her hand, though he looked underwhelmed, whilst the lovely Eva who ran the cafe had treated Annie like one of the family within seconds of meeting her. It seemed odd that she hadn't actually met Richard's uncle yet, but apparently, he was out at meetings today. It didn't matter to Annie. She had all the food and supplies she would need for a while and Richard was transporting them and her back home. Home was such a strange word for a place she hardly knew, but Annie felt comfortable in the fact that she would feel she belonged here in no time at all.

They came to a bend in the road, the last turn before the path twisted uphill towards her house. Anastasia frowned.

"Hey, Richard, could we stop?" she asked him urgently.

He worried a little at the panicked edge to her voice and pulled over just as quickly and safely as he could. There was no real traffic to avoid on the road up to Bennington Hall, but he was wary of the incline and the cross-winds even on such a pretty late-spring day. Pulling on the hand-brake, he looked across at Annie who was still staring out the window.

"Are you okay?" he checked, watching her unhook her seat-belt and move as if to get out of the car.

"Yeah, I just..." she began, stopping with only one foot out in the road. "Is that where...? I mean, my grandma is probably..."

She was rambling as she glanced between Richard and a location somewhere just back along the road a short distance. He immediately realised what she meant.

"Ah, yes, she... she is there," he admitted awkwardly, feeling stupid for not having mentioned it sooner.

St Michael's Church stood at the northern end of town and Richard had pointed it out to Anastasia. She said it looked nice, but had no real interest in getting a closer look, so they hadn't paid a visit there, just drove on by. It hadn't occurred to him to mention that in the long rambling churchyard beyond, they would find Rachel's grave. He should have asked if she wanted to see that, he really should.

"I'm sorry, I never thought," he told her, watching her seem to have an internal debate as to whether she wanted to get out of the car or not.

"It's okay. I never thought either," she answered automatically, as if she only vaguely heard him and realised she needed to speak.

Richard sat stock still, reached to unhook his seat-belt and then changed his mind. He didn't want to hurry her on this. People handled death differently, he knew that much, not least from his work as a lawyer. Many a friend or family member sobbed over a dearly departed soul, whilst others seemed almost pleased to be rid of them.

After a long silence that was fast becoming uncomfortable, Annie hopped out of the car all of sudden.

"I just want to..." she said gesturing back the way they had come.

"Of course," he agreed, hurrying after her.

They walked back to the churchyard in silence, Richard getting a little ahead on purpose. Annie wrapped her arms around herself, falling into step behind her new friend as he led the way in through the gate and around to the spot where Rachel Wickfield had been laid to rest. There was no headstone yet, just a wooden marker that bore her name and the years she had lived. Annie's hand shot to her mouth at the sight and she bit back a sob. She hadn't expected to be so very affected by the grave of a woman she barely knew, but this was still her grandmother, a woman who had bestowed all she had to give on Annie.

"She got a good spot," she said after a moment, voice quivering with emotion that sat thick in her throat. "It's pretty here."

"It is," said Richard stiffly, feeling awkward as he watched her brave face crumble.

Comforting women was not something he was entirely used to. He reached out a tentative hand to Annie's shoulder, and got quite a shock when she turned into him, burying her face in his chest as she cried. Richard let his arms come up around her body and hugged her close, hoping to be of some help. He didn't say a word, just held on whilst she cried a while. It was barely five minutes before she backed up a step, sniffing hard and looking embarrassed.

"I'm sorry," she apologised. "I'm not usually like this, I just... I don't even know what I am right now," she admitted, pushing both hands back through the length of her hair.

"It's fine," Richard promised her. "I understand."

She found a brave smile at his words and thanked him again for being so sweet. Annie turned her attention back to the grave then, making sure to speak fast before she lost her voice to emotion all over again.

"Thank you, Grandma Rachel, for everything you've given to me," she said solemnly. "I'm gonna make you proud. I promise," she swore so faithfully, with a smile that was the bravest Richard thought he had ever seen in his life.

With that, Anastasia blew a kiss toward the wooden cross, glanced briefly towards the sky, perhaps the Heavens, and then began walking back to the car. Richard faltered a moment before going after her, stopping to follow Annie's example and speak in any direction by which he might be heard.

"She will do it," he said definitely. "I'm going to help her," he promised, before following Anastasia to the car to take her home.

Chapter 8

It was going to be one hell of an undertaking. Anastasia wasn't stupid, she knew how much hard work she was going to have to put into Bennington Hall if she wanted to make it decent and habitable again. There was no way she could live there forever, that would be insane, but if she could fix it up, make it useful to somebody so they would buy it, that money could set her up for life.

Plans began slowly. Before anything else, Annie had to be able to live in relative comfort in her temporary home. The obvious answer was to use the room Grandma Rachel had already fixed up, but somehow Annie just couldn't do it. It felt like an intrusion, even though she was sure her grandmother wouldn't really mind. Honestly, she wasn't sure what she was even basing these thoughts about Rachel on. Her memories of the old lady were so vague, but Annie went with her gut, because it was all she had.

The room across from Grandma Rachel's looked like it wouldn't take too much work and it was in a good stable part of the house. The upstairs was where the major state of disrepair began. It seemed the further up the stairs a person climbed, the worse the condition of everything got. Annie wandered up onto the first floor and added more items to an ever-growing list.

She had power, running water, and groceries, thanks to Richard Thomas, but that was just the basics to live by. There were so many repairs to make in this place, some more major than others. A structural report that Richard had given her proved she shouldn't even venture too far into the 'west wing' area of the house, and honestly, Annie wouldn't trust any of the banister rails with more than the gentlest of grips. It was going to cost a fortune and take a long time, so it was lucky that she had at least some funds and nothing at all filling her schedule, Annie thought, nearing the door that had caused her a near-panic attack two nights ago.

It had to be some kind of weird coincidence; just her imagination running away with her when her hand met the door knob and it wouldn't budge. It had been dark then and her head was full of the rumours of ghosts and hauntings. It was daylight now and she had her wits about her; Annie reached for the handle once again.

It didn't move. The door was definitely locked up tight, and there was no way of knowing where the key might be, if one even existed. Annie stepped back and looked seriously at the door. This room was the only one in the house she couldn't get into and it made her wonder why. Had Rachel locked this room up for a reason? Was it locked when she won the house and she never cared to force it open?

A shiver ran through Anastasia as she looked down and realised her fingers were still tightly gripping the doorknob. It wasn't a conscious decision, yet something made her keep a tight hold as she stepped in close to the door again and leant her weight against it. She forced the knob, pushed her shoulder to the wood, and then the pain came.

It was like a blinding headache, and right out of the blue. Annie staggered with the pressure, her vision blurring into flashes of red and black.

It was hard to tell if it was just seconds later or much longer when Anastasia opened her eyes to a clear view again. She was hunched on the carpet, perilously close to the top of the stairs, and at least ten feet from the door she had been leaning on before.

"What the hell is with that room?" she muttered, pulling herself up onto unsteady feet.

Unleashing the Spirit Within

A sharp knock on the front door made Annie jump almost out of her skin. Sucking in a deep breath and trying to be calm, she hurried down the stairs as quickly as she dare, calling out that she was coming just as soon as she was within a decent distance of the entranceway. Something made her falter with her hands at the lock, and then she realised how dumb she was being and flung open the door. Beyond it stood Richard, his hands in his pockets and a nervous kind of a smile on his face.

"Hey," she grinned at the sight of him. "I wasn't expecting you."

"I'm sorry, I don't want to intrude if you're busy or... Am I intruding? I am sorry if I am," he began to ramble, something Annie was fast learning he did a lot, especially when he was nervous.

In an acquaintance of all of three days, she was sure she had already heard him apologise fifty times, mostly for things that didn't matter. She had also caused him to blush at least twice without even trying, but he was a sweet guy and he seemed pretty gung ho about helping her out. Annie was not going to turn away any offer of assistance right about now.

"Honestly? I'm glad of the company, and the help if you're offering?" she said, ushering him inside.

"Well, I don't know how much help I'd be alone," Richard admitted, "but given the plans you mentioned about fixing up this place, I did have a thought."

"What kind of a thought?" Annie asked curiously, leading her newest friend through the house.

"Um, well, there are so many of us in town that would like to see something worthwhile done with the Hall," he explained, wondering where they were going but following on without question. "All those that have met you so far seem to like you and want to help, so we wondered if we might form a sort of group or committee, of volunteers, you understand? Several of the local tradesmen are willing to cut deals, and some of the women and younger people would like the opportunity to assist with cleaning, painting, that kind of thing..."

Richard stopped talking when he realised he had stepped into a kitchen towards the back of the house. As tumble-down as it looked in its way, it was remarkably clean when he looked more closely. Then he realised Annie was making tea and he smiled.

"Almost looks like a home in here, huh?" she said with a grin as she glanced at him over her shoulder. "Seriously? This room wasn't so bad. I think Grandma Rachel must've made a start on it, so I just deep cleaned most of it yesterday and now I have a place to cook... or at least to make drinks and microwave," she admitted, laughing at her own words. "So, back to what you were saying. People wanna help me? For free?"

"Some for free, others at discounted rates," Richard clarified as he came to lean on the opposite counter. "You're not obliged to accept, of course, it's just... Well, as you may have noticed, we're all quite neighbourly around here."

"I had noticed," she said, nodding as she handed him a cup of tea. "Hey, check it out, getting back to my English roots," she joked, taking a sip of her own drink.

"Indeed," he agreed, a little amused by her excitement. "But you were born in America, were you not?"

"Nope, right here in merry old England," she told him, trying for the accent and failing miserably - Richard almost choked on his tea. "See, Mom and Dad were both English, which means technically I am too, but they emigrated when I was still a baby, and he... well, he died before I was even old enough to know him," she said, taking a deep breath and focusing her eyes into her tea. "The only guy I remember being in the house was Ted. He was my Mom's boss and he helped out a lot after Dad died, at least that's what my Mom always said. I was five, maybe six, when she married him."

"And they're still in America?" asked Richard curiously, not sure what to make of the odd smile that came to Anastasia's lips then.

"I don't know. Maybe." She shrugged. "Truth is I was never close to my mom, and Ted was... well, he wasn't my Dad, and he never was interested in me, especially after Becky was born. My half-sister," she clarified. "I was almost nine when she came along, and she just needed all the attention, all of the time."

"You were pushed out," said Richard knowingly.

"Kind of, yeah." Annie smiled bravely anyway. "It's fine, I'm not looking for sympathy. Hey, I'm guessing it was my Mom's selfishness and my step-father's greed that made Grandma Rachel wanna leave me a freakin' mansion and all her cash!" She laughed in spite of herself. "Karma can be fun sometimes."

"Agreed." He smiled right back, lifting his cup towards hers. "Here's to everyone getting what they deserve in the end."

"I will definitely drink to that!" Annie agreed, clinking her tea cup against his own as they toasted, and then both dissolved into laughter.

* * * * *

It was late in the evening, and Anastasia was alone. Richard had stayed quite a while, helping Annie sort her lists of issues with the house and all. He had names and numbers for those that wanted to help her out with making the place habitable and ultimately sale-worthy, and Annie could hardly believe how friendly everybody was. She did consider that maybe they were a little nosy too, but told herself that was the cynic in her. So many years living in New York where you had to watch your back a not-small part of the time, she supposed. It was very different here. Everybody seemed so genuine and kind, and though she was alone now in her over-sized house, Annie felt safe in a strange way.

The clock in the corner of her laptop screen said that it was well past two in the morning, but Annie wasn't tired yet. She should be, but nothing could dampen her enthusiasm for her house renovations. It was still amazing to her that she could get the internet in such a remote spot. Apparently, there was a Wi-Fi tower not far from town and most of the time she could pick it up in the house, so long as she stuck to the ground floor.

Right now, she was sat cross-legged on an old rug in the centre of what was once a living room or a parlour maybe. Annie was typing like a crazy person, writing all kinds of things down that she needed to tell her friends back home, into what may yet be the world's longest email. She would send it off to Janine when she was done, and Annie knew her message would also get to Mike and Shanice, to be shared with their friends who worked at the supermarket in town. She thought of them all, going about their work, and felt stupidly tearful.

It was odd. Annie had been so happy to know she could leave the job she had never liked and struggled to be motivated for. Now she almost missed neatly stacking shelves and talking to the regular customers as she totalled up their purchases at the cash register. She and her friends couldn't exactly afford a lot of nights out or luxuries, but they had their fun, and it was strange to think that they were still doing all of that without her.

Unleashing the Spirit Within

Janine was half-way to being engaged when Anastasia left, Mike was trying to get up the nerve to get a tattoo, and Shanice was going on many an unsuccessful date trying to find Mr. Right. Annie hated the idea of things happening in their lives that she would know nothing of, or worse, get to hear all about but not be a part of.

Shaking her head free of maudlin thoughts, Annie continued with her email. She made sure to tell her old friends about the new ones she was making, about her house and the plans she had for it. She didn't say much about the whole haunted thing. It still didn't make sense to Anastasia, and the more time she spent here, the more she convinced herself it was all just a dumb coincidence. Wondering about the locked room wasn't helping anyone, and telling herself there might be a ghost or something equally as supernatural inside was just plain silly. What she needed to do was call the locksmith, get him to come break into the room for her so she could add any work it needed to her very long list.

Getting back to her email, Annie added a last paragraph, wishing all her friends well and begging them to keep in touch by replying soon. Calls at this distance were just too expensive and the internet spotty at best. She could get an email through if she was lucky, but for such wonders as video-chat, it would be a nightmare to keep a connection in this place, especially if the wind was bad or it was a cloudy day, or there was an R in the month, at least that's what Richard had said.

Finishing up her message, Anastasia saved it, just in case, and then pressed send. She stood up on shaky legs from sitting lotus style too long and waved the laptop around a little to make sure she got the best possible signal.

"Come on!" she grumbled when the connection looked fit to drop out on her any second. "Send already!"

she said urgently, only then getting the message that said it was done.

Anastasia was smiling as she sat a moment and shut down the computer. She reached for her cell phone abandoned across the rug, planning to turn that off too when she recalled she had received a text at some point. She assumed it had to be the phone company. After all, she had only had the thing two days, as she had the computer. Nobody but Richard knew she had even bought them. It occurred to her perhaps that the message was from him.

"What do you want, Mr. Lawyer Man?" she said with a smile as she pressed the button to open the message - the screen went black. "What the hell...?" she complained, smacking the cell phone against her other hand.

Anastasia couldn't understand it. She hit the power button but the phone would not come back on, and then the lights overhead flickered and flashed, in some kind of disco rhythm. Annie squinted in the strobe effect and scrambled to her feet. She would understand if there was a storm brewing outside, but the warm sunny weather had held ever since she arrived here.

Moving out of the room, Annie tried the lights in the hall. They flickered just the same, and all the way up the stairs. Quickly, she switched them off, suddenly worrying that something had gone askew with the electrics, which could be dangerous. Grabbing the flashlight from the table by the door, she headed up the stairs to check all the switches were off and nothing was amiss.

The familiar feeling of dread ran though Anastasia when she hit the first floor and saw the same locked room from before.

"This has nothing to do with you," she said to the

door, as if it were a living thing that was actively trying to scare her. "And I am talking to a freakin' door!"

Annie scolded herself for such ridiculous behaviour and continued to check the house for signs of trouble. Nothing was wrong anywhere, and within a half hour she was headed back to the living room where she had come from. No more flickering, she was happy to note, just stationary light pouring down from the old-fashioned looking chandelier.

Anastasia stopped still when she suddenly recalled turning the light out when she left the room. She tipped her head back, staring up at every lit bulb above her, and a cold sweat covered her body.

"There has to be a logical explanation. Haunted houses aren't real," she said with less conviction than she had hoped for. "Are they?"

Chapter 9

Bennington Town library had an awful lot of books about its own history, and quite a bit about the history of the Hall that sat above it. Anastasia hadn't made a big deal when she was here with Richard, though he had mentioned she might find some of the volumes interesting. Annie figured she could take a look sometime when she was bored or needed a break from the stress of figuring out all the issues with the house. She never did expect to be here in the library so soon, pouring over any book she could find that mentioned the lengthy history of Bennington Hall.

If asked exactly what she was looking for, Annie wasn't so sure she would be able to properly explain herself, at least, not without sounding like a fool. There was a room in her house that she had yet to get into. Not so very strange on the surface, but it had quickly become more than just a job for a locksmith.

Going anywhere near the door seemed to cause sensations within her that Annie couldn't explain. She had never in her life suffered from blackouts or spells of fainting, nothing of the kind, only when she was in that house, near that room. It was kind of scary in a way, and yet Anastasia refused to be afraid. The best way to extinguish fear was to find a reasonable explanation. After all, it was the unknown that was the scariest thing.

She came into town and talked to the locksmith, whose name she got from Richard. Danny Fletcher said he could come break into her mystery room tomorrow, which was fine with Annie. In the meantime, she wanted to look into any other strange happenings that might have occurred in her new home. Rumours were all well and good, but she knew how those things worked. Like Chinese whispers through the years, things got all out of context and hyped up. She needed facts, and when an internet search brought her surprisingly few results, Annie turned to books for help. So far, she had still found very little that was of use.

Sure, it was interesting enough to read about Dukes and Lords that had once owned the Hall. The history really did go way, way back, just as Eva had told her. Annie wasn't surprised, though some of the tales were a little more sordid than she expected. Affairs and intrigues, it made better reading than even some of the erotic novels she had often caught Shanice reading in the lunch room! So far though, no murder or even a suspicious disappearance. Everybody who ever owned the house or lived in it seemed to die of completely natural causes. In the early days, the usual issues that befell the rich and overfed, and later the regular heart attacks, accidents, unfortunate illnesses.

Annie wanted to be glad she found no evidence that she ought to have a restless spirit trapped in her house, and yet it was sort of disappointing not to have come across any real explanation for the strange happenings she had been experiencing.

"There has to be something," she muttered to herself, pulling a couple of previously abandoned books across the table again, double checking the notes she had been making.

The list of owners of the house she had compiled, alongside much of their family and any major events in their lives, had no gaps for there to be somebody she missed. She had every owner right up until the nineteen seventies when the house was boarded up and abandoned for good. Annie frowned as she had a sudden realisation.

"What about after that?" she asked herself aloud.

"After what, dear?" a voice replied, making Annie

jump a little. "Oh, I'm so sorry," said the softly spoken woman with the glasses balanced on the end of her nose.

Annie tried not to smile too much at the cliché stood before her. It was too quaint and perfect that the librarian was this little old lady with kindness practically radiating from her.

"I, er... I just inherited this house, Bennington Hall," she explained.

"Oh, you're Anastasia!" the little woman clapped her hands together with apparent excitement. "I've heard all about you."

"That's nice, but y'know, you should really call me Annie, everybody does," she explained awkwardly.

"Well, Annie, I'm Mrs. Franklin, and if you need anything at all, you just ask me," said the librarian, smiling widely and patting Annie on the shoulder. "I've worked here almost fifty years now, so there isn't much I can't find."

"Wow, okay," said Annie trying to wrap her head around the fact one woman had worked in this relatively small place for what had to be her whole working life, she would guess. "Um, I was just trying to figure out the history of the Hall. I got as far as when it was all boarded up in the seventies and I guess I was just wondering if anything happened after that? Y'know, between then and my grandma winning it?"

Mrs. Franklin looked awfully thoughtful and so still at the same time. Annie was about to ask her if she was okay when she suddenly pointed a finger to the sky and rushed off at a speed Annie never would have expected such a woman could reach. Caught between wondering whether she should follow or wait, Annie had got as far as standing up when suddenly Mrs. Franklin was back.

"Newspapers!" she declared, dumping a very large

book on the table near to Annie.

She pushed her other volumes aside to make more space and looked down at the new book before her. It was copies of newspapers going back years, she realised, though going through the entire thing would inevitably takes days, maybe even weeks.

"I'm not..." she began, but Mrs. Franklin was already moving again.

In less than a minute, she was back with a box of cards that she laid on the table and frantically began flicking through. Annie frowned and looked up towards the front desk then. It was only now she realised that there was no computer, not even a scanner for the books. This library was so old fashioned, she was just now realising they still literally stamped the books in and out, and kept all their records on cards and in files. "Amazing," she muttered, smiling straight at Mrs. Franklin then as the woman held out a couple of index cards to her.

"Here are the page numbers and date references for the Hall," she grinned proudly. "I'm sure you'll find something of interest."

"I don't doubt it. Thank you." Annie smiled back at her, trying not to laugh as she watched Mrs. Franklin hurry across the library towards a couple of other people who looked like they might be lost.

This sure was a friendly place, if not a strange one. Annie wasn't sorry she came here, not at all, though she would still like to know what in the heck was going on at her new home. Checking the index card, she flipped open the large book of newspaper copies and started searching out the relevant articles. She quickly realised that even with Mrs. Franklin's help, this was still going to take a while!

Valerie Sells

* * * * *

Richard couldn't help his eyes wandering to stare out of the window at the town life below him. He had always wanted to be a lawyer, at least, he had always supposed he wanted to. There were times when he wondered if he had made the choice himself or had just fallen into line with the wishes of his family. Certainly, being here in Bennington was more his speed than living in London. Everything so loud and busy, it didn't suit him at all. There were no big cases to be dealt with in a small place like this, but enough smaller work in and around the area to keep himself and Uncle George in business.

The trouble with Richard was he was easily distracted, and one person in particular seemed to be a permanent fixture in his mind of late.

Anastasia Addams was a singular sort of woman in his mind. She was the first American he had met, though that wasn't everything that made her so different to any other woman that had passed through Richard's life. There was a spirit to her, a drive, but it was nothing cocky or self-serving. She wanted to do what was right and proper in her grandmother's name, and she seemed perfectly willing to accept help with grace and smiles. Annie certainly got along with everyone she met, at least it seemed that way to Richard. No woman was perfect, he was not such a fool as to ever think so, but Annie was special, he had already quite decided on that.

"Richard!" his uncle barked then.

"Yes, sir," he replied, practically snapping to attention whilst still seated. "I apologise, I was-"

"Day dreaming the day away? Yes, I noticed that,"

Unleashing the Spirit Within

George completed for him. "Twenty-nine years old and still staring out of windows, as dreamy as a schoolboy," he muttered, dumping a couple of folders on the corner of his nephew's desk. "I have meetings to attend. See to it those documents are checked before you go for your lunch," he said sharply before turning to leave.

"Yes, sir." Richard nodded once, wincing as the door slammed shut in George's wake.

It was an awful habit he'd got into, calling his uncle 'sir' for the most part. It had started almost by accident. Of course, it was unprofessional to refer to their familial relationship in front of clients or business associates, and yet it felt wrong to call his uncle by his Christian name. The only other choice was 'Mr. Thomas' and that became a problem all of its own, given it was Richard's name too.

With a heavy sigh, he leant back in his seat and stared a moment at the ceiling. This was not how he planned to spend the rest of his life, and yet Richard couldn't really say what it was he would rather be doing. Something, anything, he supposed, but that was far too vague to be of use to anyone.

Right in this moment, all Richard really wanted to do was run down the street and catch up to Annie, offer her a ride back to the Hall, and spend the afternoon with her. It didn't matter that she hadn't replied to his last half a dozen texts or made any effort to come and see him in the last couple of days. He still wanted to chase after her like a pathetic sap. Richard couldn't find it in himself to care about that, even though he knew he should. Still, he wouldn't go running around town after Anastasia, mainly because the paperwork on his desk had to be done. Even if he were unruly enough to go and get his lunch before completing it, it would still have to be done by five. No doubt Uncle George would be back to double-check. He may even ring the office to ensure Richard hadn't wandered off. It was like being a child, and Richard hated it. Not as much as he'd hated London, but there were deeper reasons for wishing to be out of that place. Bennington had its advantages, quite a few actually. A smile curved his lips as he realised it had definitely gained a new one when Anastasia Addams arrived.

* * * * *

Annie had planned to walk back down from the library into the town centre to catch the bus that would take her most of the way up the hill. There was a stop almost two thirds of the way up before it took the other fork in the road and drove on to the next town. The distance left to walk was perfectly easy if Annie wasn't carrying much and the weather was fine. Still, when she came to exit the library, putting her shades on to keep the bright sun from her eyes, she instinctively seemed to look right instead of left.

The church was maybe half a mile in the opposite direction to the main bus stop, but Annie was pretty sure there was another along by the cemetery. It wouldn't make any real difference which stop she caught the bus from, and she sort of wanted to ask at the church if they could help her out with her research.

The newspaper archive books that Mrs. Franklin had shown to Annie were very interesting in their own way, but didn't seem to reveal anything astonishing about Bennington Hall. There were a few announcements about who had considered buying the house next, but nobody seemed to actually go through with the purchase. At least once or twice, someone in the town would start a fuss about the Hall going to rack and ruin, and how something should be done. Nothing exciting, nothing about crime, murder, ghosts. Annie felt silly for ever thinking there would be, but if there was no evidence in any books in the library, the only other place she could think to look was at the church. They always had old records, she was sure.

"Wow," she breathed as she stepped from the bright light of outside into the dark church, the stained-glass window shining beautifully from the far end.

"Quite impressive, isn't it?" said a voice behind her and she turned to see an older man in black and white robes. "I must admit, though I see it every day, and several times too, I am still somewhat astounded by its beauty," he commented, gesturing vaguely towards the window.

"It really is something else," she agreed. "Oh, I'm Annie Addams, by the way," she said then, remembering her rusty manners. "I inherited the Hall."

"Reverend Johns," he said with a smile, shaking her offered hand. "Very pleased to meet you, Annie. Mrs. Wickfield was your grandmother, I understand?"

"She was." Annie nodded sadly. "I, er... I'd've been here for the funeral, if I'd known. In fact, I would've been here before, I just... I'm sorry," she said, not really sure what she was apologising for if she were honest.

"Not to worry, my dear," Reverend Johns said kindly. "You are here now, where your grandmother wished you to be. Perhaps where God always intended you to end up?"

"I guess, maybe?" Annie shrugged. "I'm not... Well, no disrespect, Father, but I'm not exactly uber-religious," she admitted.

"Reverend, not Father," he corrected her gently. "This is a Protestant church; Father is a term for a

Catholic priest," he explained, moving on quickly so as to save her the need to apologise again. "In any case, I am not here to judge you. That is up to only one," he said, smiling as he pointed towards the ceiling.

Annie liked this guy already. Not that she went around making friends with men of the cloth as a general rule. Honestly, she couldn't actually name another that she had ever met, but that was okay. He had a sense of humour, which she hadn't really expected, and he didn't seem to care what her beliefs were.

"Reverend," she said carefully. "Can I ask you kind of a weird question?"

"Certainly." He nodded, offering her a seat in the nearest pew which she took, whilst he perched on the end of the one across the aisle.

"When I walked in here, I was going to ask a completely different question, about records you might have on who lived at the Hall years ago," Annie admitted. "But honestly, it doesn't really matter who it was if... Well, do you believe in ghosts?"

Reverend Johns didn't look stunned by the question. Maybe a little amused, but certainly not surprised.

"Ah, the rumour mill is in full swing, I see," he said, smiling kindly and folding his hands atop the ornate curves on the end of the pew.

"Yeah, rumours."

Annie wasn't sure she could explain herself well if she started telling the vicar about the weird happenings she had experienced in her house. She was a little concerned that he might throw her out for daring to come in here talking about spirits and ghosts on hallowed ground. Annie just wasn't sure where the church stood on such things. She had seen The Exorcist and such, but that was Catholic priests trying to suck demon possessions out of people. Besides, that was just a movie. This was real life.

"Every person has a spirit, a soul, the part of them that makes them who and what they are," he said eventually. "What we learn from God's teachings is that those who accept him, love him, and abide by his rules can get to Heaven. Those who choose a different path..."

"Go the other way," Annie filled in, not wishing to begin a deep discussion on fire and brimstone on top of everything else. "I know that much, good people go to Heaven, sinners go to hell."

"Ah, but we are all sinners." Reverend Johns smiled. "It really all depends on repentance and purity of heart... but that is not what you want to hear about in this moment," he realised, shaking his head before he went on. "I cannot tell you what might happen to those souls that may not be able to pass over. The Bible uses the word ghost in place of spirit, but never in the way the stories of supernatural dealings might use it. Souls go to Heaven or Hell immediately they leave the body. They are not supposed to stay in limbo. That ought to be impossible."

Annie nodded that she understood. She hadn't exactly expected a miracle from Reverend Johns, if she expected anything at all. Still, she had met a nice, friendly man here, another resident of Bennington who seemed willing to be a friend or mentor, and Annie was glad of that.

"I'm sorry to waste your time," she said then, getting up.

Reverend Johns assured her she had done no such thing as he followed her to the door.

"You know, Annie, perhaps if you really do believe something is trapped in your house, the best thing you could do is attempt to assist," he told her kindly, so much so she was certain he meant every word rather than being sarcastic like so many people might be.

"Something to think about," Annie considered, thanking the vicar again before she walked away.

Getting into ghost banishing rituals seemed a little scary, but honestly, she couldn't imagine it would do any harm to try. If she was haunted, the ghost would leave. If she wasn't, it wouldn't make any difference anyway. Annie started to laugh as she realised she was having very serious thoughts about her house actually being haunted! She had to be insane, and yet even the vicar didn't seem to think it was the craziest idea ever.

Annie shook her head as she reached the bus stop and sat herself down on the bench there. She wasn't going to do anything dumb until the locksmith had come over and got the door to the mystery room open. After that, there was every chance Annie wouldn't even feel like she had a problem in the Hall anymore. She was sure that one room was the reason why she felt so uneasy, and no doubt once it was open she would see it was just a normal space and everything would be fine. An involuntary shudder ran though her then as she glanced up the hill to where the very top of her new home was just barely visible. Then again, maybe not, she thought, just as the sound of the bus engine reached her ears. No time to worry about it now.

Chapter 10

"You think it'll be a tough job?" asked Anastasia as she watched Danny Fletcher, the locksmith, inspect the one door in her new home that she couldn't get past.

Before the guy could even open his mouth to reply, a flash like lightning lit up the hallway and a crack of thunder sounded overhead, making the both of them jump. Annie had her hand over her heart as she looked Heavenward, wondering where the noise had come from. She knew it was the weather, of course she did, but there had been no storm forecast for today, not even rain. It had been sunny when she got up this morning, a beautiful summer's day, but as time wore on, the clouds seemed to build as if from nowhere. It was just a little freaky.

"Shouldn't take long, Miss," the overly polite middle-aged man assured her. "These old locks can be tricky, get themselves stuck when no-one's tried the door too long, but nothing I can't get into eventually."

Annie nodded, waiting for more lightning and thunder, wondering when it didn't seem to come at all.

"If you have to bust the lock off completely and replace it, that's fine. I can pay for whatever."

"Very good, Miss." Danny nodded, in spite of the fact Annie had told him twice already that he should just call her by her name.

She offered him a cup of tea, glad when he accepted so she could go and make it. It was weird, but after all this time of wondering what lie behind her mystery door, Annie kind of didn't want to be here when it was opened. Maybe it was the storm, or her talk with Reverend Johns about ghosts and spirits. Whatever had her shaken, Annie knew it was dumb. In the end, the door would be opened and she would walk into that room and see it was just an ordinary space in an old dilapidated house. The storm today was pure coincidence, as were the headaches, blackouts, and electrical faults she had experienced in this house.

Maybe it would've been easier to convince herself she was making mountains out of molehills if the evidence of ghostly activity wasn't piling up so rapidly. Usually it was easy to explain things away, to say it was something and nothing, but there was just so much that didn't make sense in this place.

"Stop talking yourself into believing this," she muttered as she made two mugs of tea. "There is not a ghost in your house, you're being dumb."

Annie picked up the two teas and turned to leave the kitchen, just as lightning flashed at every window and the loud rumble of thunder sounded almost simultaneously. She yelped, completely thrown by the sudden brightness and noise. The mugs went flying to the ground, smashing to pieces and spilling boiling hot liquid over her hand.

"Damn it!" Annie exclaimed, rushing to the sink.

The burnt skin was under a heavy flow of cold water within seconds, and she remembered it was best to keep it there until her hand went numb. Again, she berated herself for her own stupidity. A storm meant nothing, it was just weather. She was the reason she thought there was a ghost here, her own over-active imagination and fantastically stupid ideas.

When no feeling existed in her hand anymore, Annie pulled it out from under the tap and inspected the damage. It was red, but she was sure it'd be fine. Carefully, she dried her hands and set about cleaning up the mess she had made. She was mindful now of any more thunder and lightning startling her, actively looking up and listening out for the slightest sign of any more overly exuberant weather. None came.

It was certainly the weirdest storm ever, since she could hear no rain falling, and the thunder and lightning seemed entirely intermittent. Somehow Annie couldn't help but worry about Danny. He was a locksmith breaking into a locked room, nothing dangerous about that, but she wasn't convinced she had properly warned him about the dodgy banister rails, and she just didn't trust that he was okay somehow. It was like an instinct she couldn't explain, and it had Annie rushing to the stairs before she had even finished picking up the broken china from the floor.

Thunder cracked one more time as her foot hit the bottom step. Annie blocked out her panic and just hurried along. When she reached the landing, she was surprised to find Danny wasn't there. His tools lie on the carpet there by the door, which was now open, but he was gone. Annie's breath caught in her throat, and her eyes fell shut on instinct as lightning flashed at all the window. The lock was broken, the door ajar, and the locksmith gone.

"This isn't cool," she muttered as she moved forward. She called for Danny but there was no answer. "Danny, if you're trying to screw with my head, it's not funny!" she yelled, throwing the door wide open but not yet going into the mystery room.

There was nobody there, and Annie hadn't really expected there would be. She didn't know Danny Fletcher that well, but off the back of their short acquaintance, she wouldn't have said he was the type to play a trick on her. Richard might, some of her friends back home, but not this guy. It was as if he just evaporated while she was in the kitchen, and yet, Anastasia wasn't focusing on that right now.

Valerie Sells

The room before her was looking decidedly less scary than she had expected. Annie wasn't sure what she thought she would find. A torture chamber? Maybe a body or two? Some scene of tragedy, in any case. In fact, it all looked quite empty and ordinary, and she couldn't help but feel the need to go into the mysteriously non-mysterious room for a closer look.

The storm outside was becoming so much background noise, failing to make Annie jump with every flash and crash now. She was so taken in by the room that had frightened her before. It was normal, fairly plain, almost boring. There was a very old rug on the floor, paintings on the wall that were thick with dust, and an electric-powered chandelier overhead, much like so many others in the house. Annie walked in with a curious expression and her arms folded across her chest against the cold.

This room definitely had more of a chill to it than any of the others, but that was easily explained away. It had been closed up all this time, no heating to speak of. Besides, there was a distinct whistle coming from what had to be a cracked or otherwise damaged window. The wind was strong, and the storm was still raging, though when Annie spared a glance out of the window, there really didn't seem to be any rain, and the sky was clear.

Frowning hard, Annie braced her hands against the window sill and leaned into the large bay window. Above her she could see the clear blue of the sky, and yet a storm was evident in its lightning cracks and deafening sound.

"Okay, weirdness factor five," she said to herself, still staring out.

A feeling, like a presence behind her, made Annie shudder then. The distinct touch of fingers at her shoulder made her spin around fast and lash out too. Any intruder would be pinned to the ground and it occurred to her too late she may have just grabbed her locksmith by the throat. Annie got a bigger shock than even that when her knees hit the wooden floor, her hands empty. There was nobody there in the room but her.

Her breath quickened in a second and Anastasia fought to keep her panic in check. This wasn't for real. She was just freaking herself out over something and nothing. Of course, the list of the unexplained was growing every second, and her own worries and fears couldn't explain a storm with no rain or clouds to be seen.

Scrambling to her feet, she bolted for the door, only to find it had closed again without her noticing. She grabbed at the handle and pushed, pulled, jiggled. In spite of the fact the lock had been completely broken, the door was stuck fast as if it were bolted tight.

The lightning crackled one more time, with electricity that made the air fizz, and Annie fought to breathe through it. The thunder sounded, rumbling so loudly it felt as if the floor shook beneath her feet. This was crazy and insane, but she had to calm down.

"Anastasia, get a grip," she told herself firmly.

There was no way any of this was real. No evidence to suggest ghosts were real. There were rumours, but a lot of those had reasonable explanations. Annie would freely admit, she wasn't sure she knew what they all were right now, but they had to exist. Richard didn't believe in ghosts, nobody with a brain ever could, right? Her mind spun as Annie continued to shake the handle, hoping in vain the door would give, but it didn't, and somehow, she knew it never would until she dealt with this thing. Taking a deep breath, she closed her eyes and forced herself to turn into the room again. Walking purposefully towards the centre, she tilted her chin, opened her eyes to the dim light, and yelled loud enough to be heard over anything the apparent storm could throw at her.

"I'm not leaving!" she yelled. "This is my house now, and I'm staying here until I choose to go! I don't know who or what you are, I might even be talking to myself right now, but anybody that can hear me needs to know this, I am going NOWHERE!"

The last word was the loudest of all, screamed against a rush of wind that seemed to come from everywhere at once, and a combination of thunder and lightning that was practically blinding and deafening all at once. Annie closed her eyes against the onslaught, but held her ground. After all she had said, she had nothing left to lose. She waited, braced against the craziness of it all, and after a few moments, it was over.

Anastasia felt everything go still so suddenly it made her gasp. Carefully, she opened one eye, and then the other. Nothing was amiss. No debris, no damage, not a scratch on her as she looked down at her body. The light was better, not so dim, and the storm was over. Bright sunshine was pouring in through the windows to her right, lighting up the paintings on the walls that had looked so sinister just few minutes ago. Annie saw her reflection in the mirror on the opposite wall, and though the glass was grimy and cracked, it showed just her, as she had always been, stood in the centre of a perfectly normal, if not kind of dusty room.

"Okay," she said to herself, realising now was probably a good time to try the door again.

Just as Anastasia started to turn, something almost made her jump out of a skin.

"Well, you're a determined little chit, I'll give you that much," said a laughing, lilting voice. "Gotta love a bird with balls, I s'pose, in a manner o' speaking."

Unleashing the Spirit Within

Annie was a little astounded by the way she was being spoken to, and by the sight of the man saying the words. Maybe he was a friend of Danny or just a guy from the town come to help her in some way. It was kind of weird that he appeared right now, and in this room, whilst the door was still closed.

"What the hell are you doing in my house?" she asked crossly, not caring if he meant no harm.

Annie was not having a good day all in all, and if this did happen to be a trick pulled on her, she was going to be so pissed. Strangers in her house was just one thing too many to deal with right now.

"Your house?" the mystery man echoed. "Yeah, I s'pose you would think that."

"Yeah, I suppose I would, since my grandmother left it to me and all," said Annie angrily, hands going to her hips as she stormed forward and got in the stranger's face. "So, how about you explain why you're here or get the hell out already?" she suggested, game face on, meaning business.

It was an unpleasant surprise when the man before her laughed at her anger.

"Come on, Anastasia," he said then, seeming to know how much it was freaking her out that he already knew her name. "That's no way to talk now, is it?"

His eyes danced with laughter, but they were so very dark at the same time. His whole being was black, top to toe, from the crazy styled jet-black hair to the leather jacket he wore, with jeans and boots to match.

A shiver ran through Annie as she looked him over, from the smirk to the clothes, and she got the weirdest feeling.

"Who are you?" she asked, wondering at the way her own voice came out then.

It wasn't strong or angry as it had been, it was oddly light and girlish, like a child wondering if Santa was truly who he claimed to be. If this guy was what he seemed, it would be just about as crazy as believing in the jolly old elf that supposedly came around at Christmas time.

"Name's Jack Green," he told her easily, hands still in his pockets. "S'pose it's only right you know, since we're gonna be living together and all."

Anastasia wanted to laugh at that ridiculous comment, but she was getting the distinct idea he was very serious. She didn't know him, but she already knew she couldn't throw him out. Reaching out a shaking hand she seemed to have no control over, Annie let her fingers go forward to Jack's shoulder... and pass right through.

"Damn!"

Chapter 11

Anastasia was officially in shock. All that time of wondering and worrying about what might be going on in this house of hers and now here was the truth. She really was being haunted, and yet this oddity of a punk-type guy stood before her now didn't seem at all scary. For all his attempts to drive her out of her new home, he was smiling at her, looking her over with some expression of apparent approval. None of it made any sense.

"This is crazy!" she declared, not really expecting a response and yet she got one anyway.

"You're not the first to think so," Jack told her, shrugging his shoulders that looked as real and solid as Annie's own, except she knew they weren't. "I've driven more than a couple of people outta this place on the strength they thought they'd gone past midnight on the crazy clock," he admitted, smirking wickedly. "'Course, no such luck with you, darlin'."

"No. No such luck with me," she echoed, as she looked him over. "Still, you're not what I expected, I'll give you that much. If I even knew what to expect in a ghost."

Jack's eyes sparkled as he stepped forward and began to circle her, sizing up his competition maybe, even though he had more or less admitted defeat already. He knew he couldn't drive Annie out, he had said as much. On the other hand, she doubted he would be easily removed either if he had been here a while. Annie had been expecting some person in old-fashioned attire, something akin to an Austen character or older. Jack had the potential to exist in the modern world as he looked now. He'd be called a freak by some, but people could be cruel that way. He wasn't so very out of style, if you were a goth or a biker anyway.

"You're really not afraid of me," he said as he came back into view, having walked a completely soundless circle around her.

"No," she confirmed easily. "Not now I know what you are. There's nothing to fear but fear itself, right? The unknown factor, that's what made you kinda scary, but your fake storm and music video wind? Not bothering me anymore." She shook her head and wore a winning smile. "So, you're a ghost, so what? Pretty sure you're not the first and you won't be the last."

Jack laughed heartily at that. Gone was the fearsome spook that wanted to hurt Anastasia or cast her out of what he saw as his home. Here was a man with a wicked sense of humour and an eye for a woman of substance.

"I like you," he said, moving in close. "You've definitely got balls."

"No, actually, I haven't," she reminded him, even though she knew it was merely an expression, "but thanks, I guess."

If she thought he could do anything to her, Annie might have been wary of the lack of space between her body and his right now, but as she'd already proven, one step forward wouldn't press flesh to flesh, she would just walk right through. She wouldn't do it, not right now. It might piss him off, and she still had questions.

"So, you and me, we're in this for the long haul then, are we, darlin'?" he asked when she was quiet too long.

"Well, like I said, I'm not going anywhere," she replied smoothly. "Not until I'm good and ready. You're certainly not going to force me out, no matter what tricks you pull, and I think you already pulled your fair share."

He smiled at that, almost proud of this woman he barely knew. She did have guts, and Jack always like that in a woman. He couldn't be doing with the prim princesses who wouldn't say boo to a goose. A bit of back bone, proper fighting spirit, every person ought to have that, male or female. He liked it, he admired it.

"You hang around as long as I have, love, you learn a few tricks," he told her. "Fake storms, that's child's play really."

"Flashing lights, blinding headaches, they child's play too?" she asked, her expression hardening further as she recalled the blackout she'd had trying to get through this door a few days ago, the one that nearly sent her reeling down a flight of stairs.

That wiped the smile of Jack's face. The truth of the matter was, he had been trying to scare her away. A few had run from his flashy parlour tricks, whilst others, as he said, thought they were driving themselves mad the longer they stayed at Bennington Hall. Anastasia was different. She wouldn't be afraid, or at the very last she refused to show that she was. As much as she might've considered she was going crazy before, she found a way to rise above it. She quite literally took him on, face to face, and didn't flinch. That took courage or stupidity, and Jack would like to think Anastasia Addams had much more of the former than the latter.

"Did what I had to." He shrugged, backing up a step then as he observed her. "This place, it's all I got. Couldn't have you swanning in thinking you owned the place."

"But I do own it," she told him firmly. "You only haunt it."

Jack didn't appreciate her tone or the words she was saying, but didn't get a chance to make a fuss. Annie started to frown as she realised he had completely distracted her from her original mission. She had come up to this room with more purpose than just to see what lie beyond the locked door.

"Where's Danny?" she asked urgently, rushing for the exit then.

In spite of the fact he didn't need to, Jack stepped out of the way as she flew by him, searching all around. She called for the locksmith several times, going down a few stairs and then back up, checking to see if she could spot him up the next flight.

"He's long gone," Jack told her, and she turned to see him seemingly leaning against the door frame. "You may not scare easy, Anastasia, but your man with the hammer? Terrified," he confirmed with a smile.

Annie wasn't sure that could be right. Danny Fletcher seemed perfectly manly enough to withstand a little haunting, but then she had to confess to herself that she didn't really know him that well, and this was a bizarre situation to find oneself in. Maybe Danny really had been scared and run away. That made him a coward, but she couldn't doubt his locksmith skills, since he had managed to break into her once locked room.

"Did he really break into this room?" she asked as she walked back down to the landing.

Jack looked back over his shoulder into the room that had been such a mystery to Annie for so long. His expression was that much darker when he turned to meet her eyes again.

"Not really," he told her simply, offering no further explanation, and the moment Annie tried to ask for one, Jack disappeared.

"Well..." she began, walking further into the room and then out again.

She turned full circle, looking all around, but there was no trace of the man she had just been talking to. He had genuinely evaporated before her very eyes, just as he had appeared a few minutes before. Annie shouldn't be all that shocked. After all, they had just now established he was a ghost, for lack of a better term, but it still seemed strange when it happened.

"Jack?" she called into the empty space, but no reply came.

Annie was annoyed. She had so much she wanted to know, like how Jack Green's ghost came to be trapped in her house, what he had been in life, why he couldn't seem to leave. She had no way of knowing if he could or would give her the information she was after, but the chance to ask might've been nice.

She yelled his name three more times, inside the room, out in the hall way and down the stairs, but he didn't answer, didn't reappear. There was a part of Annie that thoroughly expected to wake up at any moment, either in her bed or perhaps on the floor somewhere, realising she had passed out and dreamt this whole thing. The larger part of her brain over-ruled that, knowing it was nonsense. What had happened here was real. She had just met a ghost, however much she knew deep down that it ought not to be possible.

A knock on the front door made Anastasia physically jump. She continued on down the stairs and flung open the door without hesitation, smiling when she saw Richard on the other side of it.

"Hey, it's you," she greeted him happily. "Please, come in, bring sanity to the party for a while!"

Richard looked thoroughly bemused by her words.

"Am I missing something?"

Annie opened her mouth to answer but faltered. He was a nice, sensible, upstanding guy who she liked and considered a friend, even after knowing him just a couple of weeks. She was a stranger in a strange land,

and this was one person of a few she could really count on in this place. Annie considered carefully if she really wanted to risk Richard thinking she was a whack-job if she told him what had happened today, if she actually used the words 'I just met a ghost'.

"Er, it's been kind of a weird day so far," she said, deliberately skirting around the issues. "The locksmith got the mystery door open and then got spooked and ran for his life." She rolled her eyes. "And here was me thinking it was us girls that were supposed to scream and bolt at the first sign of trouble."

"What sort of trouble did he run from exactly?" asked Richard curiously, peering up the stairs as if he expected to see whatever was wrong from here.

Anastasia shook her head.

"Er, something and nothing," she said eventually, shrugging her shoulders. "Shadows on the wall? Something he thought he saw? Who's to say?"

Richard thought it was strange that a man like Danny would run out of a house like that over 'something and nothing'. It was particularly bad, in his opinion, to leave a defenceless woman alone in a house where danger might exist. He remembered a moment later that Annie was far from defenceless, recalling how she had him pinned to the ground in a second when she suspected he was an intruder. The memory made Richard smile in such a way that she questioned the look.

"Have I ever told you what a truly remarkable woman you really are, Anastasia Addams?"

Annie was a little taken aback. Since she obviously didn't know the thought process he had gone through, the comment did come decidedly out of left field. Seemed it was the day for that kind of thing.

"Thanks," she said, with a burst of almost nervous

laughter that even she couldn't really explain. "I, er... I'm sorry, did you just drop by for coffee or for something specific?" she asked then, realising he hadn't said and she hadn't asked up to now.

"Oh, yes, I brought you some information," Richard started to explain, showing her he had his briefcase with him.

Inside there was paperwork, lists of names and numbers of the tradesmen who were offering to help with fixing up the Hall, plus general volunteers for cleaning and mending.

Anastasia took Richard through to the kitchen and offered him tea, only remembering when they got there about the smashed cups on the floor. When he asked what happened, she waved it away, saying she was clumsy and that it was all part of the crazy day she was having. He accepted her excuses and didn't question anymore, just advised her on which offers she might want to accept and which to turn down from the local townsfolk that he clearly knew much better than she did.

Annie cleaned up the broken crockery and set about making a fresh pot of tea. She tried to listen to all that Richard was saying, but honestly, her mind was otherwise engaged. She thought of Jack, the apparent ghost, that had appeared as if from nowhere and vanished just as fast when he realised she had a real live visitor at the door. Annie thought that was strange in itself, though not half so strange as finding there really was a spirit trapped in her new home, assuming that was what he was.

Annie couldn't help but wonder when she might see Jack Green again, as well as why he was here, who he really was. She hoped it wasn't too long before she got to talk to him again, to meet those sparkling green eyes with her own gaze and ask all that she wished to know.

She smiled remembering the image of his face. He was good looking, that was for sure, and Annie almost laughed realising what she was thinking. He was a ghost and what he looked like was really neither here nor there. As she turned to give Richard his tea, he questioned her giddy expression. After all, he had been talking about plumbers and electricians for the last five minutes, nothing at all amusing or exciting.

"Can't a person just be happy?" she asked, shrugging easily. "So, give me the low down," she said, leaning over the papers he had laid out on the counter. "Who're the bad pennies and bad eggs?"

Richard laughed at her phrasing and exceptionally bad attempt at an English accent, but nevertheless gave her the information she wanted. He had no idea he was being watched by more than just Annie, by green eyes that were not at all thrilled to have him here.

Chapter 12

Anastasia was lost in a world of her own, sat lotus style on the rug in the main living room, papers spread out in front of her. This had fast become her comfy spot, the place she came to when she wanted to use her computer, write emails, organise or plan anything. She couldn't say why she liked the room so much, only that it interested her and she felt comfortable in it.

Sat there with her headphones on, loud punk hits resonating through her ears, she wasn't aware of anything but the music and the task at hand. Richard had left her with pages and pages of names, email addresses, and phone numbers. She was just now planning some sort of schedule, deciding who she might need and when would be the ideal time. She had to figure out the budget too, how much she could afford to spend and on what.

Rocking along to the rhythm of The New York Dolls, Annie was completely unaware she had company, until a shadow seemed to pass over her paperwork.

"Geez!" She jumped with shock, her hand going to her heart. "What are you trying to do to me, idiot?"

Jack smirked wickedly at the possible answers that ran through his mind, but that look quickly turned to a scowl.

"Not much I can do from here, is there?" he reminded her, passing his hand through the side table as a reminder of his ghostly status.

"You've done enough," she told him, pushing her headphones down around her neck and hitting pause on the music too. "What was with the disappearing act before? I mean, one minute we're having a conversation and the next 'poof', you're gone."

He raised an eyebrow at her choice of words. She

didn't seem to notice she had implied anything other than exactly what she meant, so Jack let it go. No use making an issue where there wasn't one, he supposed. Besides, she had asked a question of him, and it wasn't as if he didn't have an answer.

"Maybe I just don't like the company you keep, love," he told her, wandering aimlessly around a room he had no effect on or real presence in.

"Said the ghost that's haunting my house," she muttered, looking back at her computer screen. "If you're going to be cryptic and weird, could you just go do it someplace else? I've got work to do," she told him, getting back to her schedule, at least that was how it appeared.

In truth, Annie was still listening for any sound, trying to keep an eye on Jack as he moved in the edge of her peripheral vision. She couldn't understand why he had decided to pop up again now she was alone if it wasn't to talk. As he just said, there was little else he could do with her. That thought made Annie shiver a little as she thought of activities men and women who were both based in reality might share in the privacy of their own home. She had no worries of that kind with a man who she could pass right through if she had a mind to. Now she knew his tricks, Jack really wasn't scary at all, just an anomaly, and a possible pain in the butt, apparently.

"How long've you known the boy?"

Annie smirked when she heard the question.

"Richard or Danny?" she checked, sure she already knew but asking anyway. "Though neither of them are really boys exactly."

"Are to me," Jack told her as he came back into view. "S'pose the question applies to both anyway."

Unleashing the Spirit Within

"I met Richard the first day I was here, which you would know if you've been watching me like I think you have," explained Annie, giving him her full attention for now, detaching her headphones from the socket so she could stand without garrotting herself. "We're friends. As for Danny, he's just a locksmith I hired. Why'd you ask?"

"Just wonderin'," he said, cocking his head to the side as he observed her a moment. "And for your information, I haven't been watching you, not every minute anyway. What kind of man do you take me for, love?" he asked, tongue running along his teeth.

That same shiver ran through Anastasia's body again but she tried to ignore it. Technically speaking, Jack could probably have eyes on her at all times, whether she could see him or not. That meant when she washed or changed her clothes or anything. Maybe he could see through what she was wearing, she couldn't be sure, or maybe even read her thoughts clean out of her head. Ghosts didn't exist, not really. Jack was... Well, he was an anomaly, or so Annie believed. It was hard to know what so-called facts about ghosts applied to him and what didn't. He looked perfectly solid and real stood before her now, and yet she knew he wasn't, they'd both proved that. He could talk and she could hear him. He could interact with her as if he were present, but he could also evaporate from her sight at a moment's notice.

"What?" he asked when she stared at him too long, as if she were examining him under a magnifying glass.

"I was just wondering," she said, shaking her head slightly, "what's your deal, Jack Green?"

"My deal?" he echoed with a smile he couldn't help. "Honestly, you Yanks have no real respect for the English language, do you?" he said, just mildly condescending since he was still smiling when he said it

- Annie didn't flinch. "What exactly did you want to know, Anastasia?"

She was completely unfazed by the use of her real name. He probably knew it annoyed her, maybe heard her tell Richard or someone else inside the house. It was hard to recall exactly what she had said and to whom over the past couple of weeks. Whatever his reasons, Annie was not going to rise to the bait.

"I want to know who you are," she said definitely. "What's your story? Why are you here?"

"Not here by choice, that's for sure," he told her, standing in such a way to suggest he was leaning against the wall, arms folded across his chest.

Of course, Annie knew there was no pressure being applied to the brick and plaster. One false move and Jack would slip right through into the next room. She just hoped he didn't before they were done talking.

Dropping her headphones from her hand, they landed beside her laptop and papers. She stepped off the rug, her bare feet curling up against the cold floorboards as she walked over to stand right in front of him. He looked normal, like some sort of rebellious punk guy, but normal enough. Annie would've expected him to look paler, his whole form to be more white or glowing perhaps. She smiled to herself as she realised how dumb that would probably sound if she actually said it, so she didn't.

"Jack Green," she repeated the name he had given her. "That your whole name?"

"More or less. John Green as my mother gave it to me, but I was always Jack," he said, looking down a little as it was the only way to see her when she was this close.

There was maybe a three or four-inch height

difference, and were he in the same plane of reality as she was, Annie was certainly more than close enough to touch.

"When? When were you born?"

"Fifty-one," he told her, wondering how she was going to react to the news - still, she didn't flinch.

"Nineteen fifty-one." She nodded slowly, a smile creeping across her lips. "Wow, that's trippy. You're actually older than my mom," she realised. "Almost as old as Grandma Rachel."

She frowned then. Annie was genuinely surprised to see Jack's face fall when she mentioned her grandmother. He couldn't have known her, but then she supposed he must have done. It made Annie start to wonder how much her grandma had known about Jack. If they had become friends or if Rachel had been scared of him. Somehow, she doubted it.

"She knew about you."

"'Course she did." Jack smirked. "I'm sort of hard to ignore, as you might have noticed."

His thumbs were hooked in the belt loops of his black jeans, and with that look on his face, he was just so smug. Anastasia knew he was good looking and smart, but there was nothing attractive about a guy being pompous that way.

"I don't know." She shrugged, hands on her hips, almost mirroring his cocky stance. "When you give up on the parlour tricks, I don't think you're so special."

"Cheeky bint," he scoffed, almost a full-on laugh at her gall.

"Hey, you're gonna hand it out you gotta learn to take it," she said easily, not backing down for a second.

She had dealt with men like him before. Well, not

exactly like him, because they were real live human beings. This was actually less scary since he couldn't turn on her. His best and only defence was to disappear, or maybe fake a storm that wouldn't scare her anymore, not now she knew where it was coming from and why.

"Does nothing bother you?" asked Jack curiously.

She was so different to any other woman he ever met, and he was counting both his living days and after. There was no fear in her, not a hint. He liked that a lot.

"Not much," she told him easily. "Look, you're here, you are what you are, nothing I can do about it. You don't scare me, but... but you do confuse me," she admitted then. "Do you even know why you're here? I mean you're stuck, right? If you could leave, you would."

"Not going anywhere," said Jack firmly, his whole demeanour shifting in an instant at her words. "This is *my* house," he repeated what he said before, pointing an angry finger towards her.

When it came to how and why he was haunting this place, the guy just didn't want to talk about it. That made Annie all the more curious. Even as he glared at her with green eyes that practically glowed, she didn't shift her feet, didn't move her own gaze off his. There was no way Annie would give him the satisfaction of backing down for a second.

"We already established that it's *my* house," she corrected him. "Jack, nobody would choose this non-life that you seem to have, so... Jack?"

Somehow in the space of time it took for her to blink, he was gone. Anastasia turned a full circle around the room, but he was just nowhere.

"Damn it!" she cursed, making another final check in all possible areas of the space around her.

She could search the house, Annie knew she could, but it was just as likely that Jack was still here in the room and invisible as he was in any other place. It was just one more question she wished she could ask him, but apparently, talking wasn't his strong point. That had to suck for an incorporeal being, since conversation was one of the few activities left open to him, she supposed.

"Well, whenever you wanna talk, I'm gonna be here," she told the ceiling, figuring wherever Jack was now he ought to hear. "I told you, just like you, I'm not going anywhere."

Silence met her vow, and Annie wasn't entirely surprised by that. What really confused her was how disappointed she felt. With a sigh, she went back to her house plans in the peace and quiet.

Chapter 13

Anastasia was yelling The Ramones iconic phrase and literally jumping in time with the rhythm of 'Blitzkrieg Bop'. The music blared as loud as she could get it from the speakers attached to her phone in the corner. She wasn't a massive fan of cleaning, she didn't suppose for a moment that anybody was, but dusting down cobwebs and airing out rooms became less of a chore when she danced her way through it.

In her tattiest clothes with a scarf tied on her head to keep her hair up and out of the way, she did her best with cloths and dusters and worked her way around the rooms that might be the easiest to salvage. She wasn't doing a thorough job exactly, just making a start. As of Monday, Annie would have a house full of eager volunteers to help her get all this work done, including a whole load of kids fresh out of school for the summer, who were curious to see inside the mysterious house on the hill. For now, it was a bright sunny Saturday which Annie intended to spend alone, rocking out, and getting things at least partially in order.

Of course, alone wasn't entirely accurate. Jack was around somewhere, she was sure on that. Spirits that had haunted houses all these years didn't suddenly just up and disappear, not completely. He was hanging around, but Annie wouldn't give him the satisfaction of trying to tempt him out again. She didn't need to call his name or perform any kind of search, Annie was sure he would be back before long, and he proved her right.

"You got better taste in music than your grandma, at least."

Annie smiled as she heard the familiar English tones but forced the expression down before she turned to look at him. He appeared to be perched on the cabinet on the opposite side of the bedroom, even though she knew technically he wasn't putting any weight on the furniture. He looked altogether too cool and smug about his 'entrance'. Annie wouldn't give him the satisfaction of reacting. She just walked right by him to turn the music down a notch, so they didn't have to yell over the top of Joey Ramone as he went into 'Beat on the Brat'.

"You probably wouldn't appreciate everything I have on there," she shrugged, gesturing to the music player even as she walked away from it again. "Call me eclectic."

"I thought I called you Anastasia?"

He smirked, and she faked a hearty laugh.

"Wow, so not a comedian in life then, huh?" she quipped. "Did they have DJs back then? Because you seem to show up mostly when I'm rocking out."

"Back then?" he echoed. "You make me sound ancient, love."

"You make me think you're very touchy about your age," she countered, hands on her hips. "How old are you anyway? I mean, how old were you when...?"

For one so confident, she faltered when it came to asking the big questions. Jack Green was dead. He was here, present in the room, but not in a real sense, not solid and alive like she was. He couldn't have been much older than she was now when whatever happened to him happened. The thought of it made Annie suddenly very sad.

"Forever twenty-seven," he told her, his expression unreadable.

"There's a club for that," she answered like a reflex, not quite surprised when he didn't react even then.

It was quite possible he had no idea what she was talking about, or maybe he did and he just wanted to pretend otherwise. 27 Club, a list of famous people who all died at that young age, some of them suicides, quite a lot in accidents, and many involving drugs somehow. It made Anastasia wonder what Jack's fate had been. His own fault or at someone else's hand? He didn't seem to want to tell her, which made her all the more suspicious. Her eyes narrowed as she stared at him. He didn't seem to appreciate the intensity of her gaze.

"Oi, what's up with you today?" he asked, shifting away from her as if uncomfortable with how close she was getting.

"Nothing," she replied, already knowing it was no good starting another conversation about how Jack came to die or to be trapped here.

"Coulda fooled me."

Anastasia heard him muttering but she already had her back to him, walking over to put the music back on. This guy just didn't want to talk, not about anything real that mattered, anything she really wanted to know. Now he was giving her obscure clues that just made her more annoyed, and so she quite decided to let him alone until he wanted to tell her something worth hearing.

For the most part, he was just being a nuisance, getting in the way of work she was trying to do. She went back to her cleaning as if he wasn't there. Somehow it wasn't easy ignoring him, even though she couldn't see or hear him. Anastasia couldn't explain it but she knew Jack was still there for a good five minutes after she chose to ignore him, and she was quite aware of the moment when he finally disappeared again.

Turning around, she would've sworn she saw a vague outline of his body before he was gone, but it could easily have been her imagination.

Unleashing the Spirit Within

* * * * *

"No, that's great," said Annie, smiling and shaking hands on the deal she just made. "Honestly, everybody has been so kind."

"Nice to see something bein' done with that old mess of a house," said Bob, a builder who was probably twice her age with whom she had just made friends apparently. "No offence to your gran and all that, but in her position I'd've got something done sooner. Wasn't like we didn't offer, but I s'pose it was a lot to take on at her time of life."

"Well, at least it's being done now, in her memory."

With that Annie said her goodbyes and turned to go. After a morning of cleaning, she had felt she just couldn't do any more right now, better to come into town whilst people were likely to be around and finalise arrangements, then get back to her cleaning mission tomorrow. Sunday was likely to be quiet, she was sure. Bennington was nothing like New York, not least because it seemed to be a town that definitely did sleep, especially on a Sunday. For today, Annie had lots of other people to see and make arrangements with, but so far, they were as friendly and helpful as Richard had said they would be.

Anastasia found herself making friends wherever she went, being invited into houses for tea and cakes, introduced to children and pets. It was overwhelming in the best way to feel so welcome in a place that had no obligation to her, and actually barely knew her. All in all, it was just nice to have company, Annie supposed. She didn't mind spending time alone, in fact, sometimes she craved it, but her only contact these past few days had been Richard and Jack. One visited rarely, and the other, well, Annie wasn't sure what to think about the form of a man that haunted her home. She wondered if she ever would figure him out.

"Oh, I'm sorry!" she said as she suddenly realised her focus had been anywhere but the direction in which she was headed.

Annie went ploughing straight into a man coming the other way, almost dropping her folder full of papers. Only one or two got away and it was Richard who dived to save them before they blew into the road on the summer breeze. Annie was grateful to him, but more occupied for a moment by the older man that was glaring severely at her.

"Do you often walk the streets with your eyes closed?" he asked her abruptly, looking entirely old-fashioned in his tweed suit and hat.

There would be nothing wrong with his appearance, Annie decided, if he would just smile and be a gentleman, instead of scowling and yelling at her.

"It was an accident," she said snippily. "I did say I was sorry."

"As you should be, ridiculous young woman," he muttered as he strode away, all airs and graces that Annie cared nothing for.

"Well, I'm..." she began to yell after him, but Richard grabbing her arm, distracted her.

"Please, Annie," he urged her. "I know he's... well, unpleasant sometimes, but he is my uncle and I could really use him not being in a worse mood than he already is."

Anastasia opened her mouth to protest - a lot - but changed her mind when she met Richard's pleading eyes. He was almost as much of an anomaly to her as Jack Green in a lot of ways. On occasion, he could be so confident and then he was back to meek and mild in a moment. Annie didn't know what to make of it. He certainly seemed afraid of his tyrant of an uncle, but that could easily be because he worried about losing his job. She relented with a heavy sigh.

"Fine. For you, I'll let it go."

"You're wonderful, Anastasia Addams! Never let anyone tell you any different," he told her then, grabbing her by the shoulders before she could stop him and planting a kiss on her cheek.

Annie was laughing out of surprise as much as amusement, watching Richard jog to catch up to his uncle and no doubt apologise for her 'coarse American ways' or however George Thomas might describe her attitude. She had a few choice ways of describing his too, only Annie had promised not to voice them right now, for Richard's sake. Maybe one day.

Annie looked up and realised she was outside of the cafe where Eva worked. She didn't really need another cup of coffee, but a sandwich might be good. It was almost lunchtime. Besides, she had something on her mind that the kindly older lady might be able to help her with.

"Hello there, lovely," said Eva, smiling the moment Annie walked in. "Now, how are you on this beautiful sunny day?"

"I'm good, thank you," she said, smiling right on back as she came over to the counter and propped her folder there. "Could I get a decaff latte and a sandwich... tuna mayo, please?" she chose from the chalk board.

"Indeed you can, my dear," said Eva getting straight on to her order.

Annie watched her a moment, wondering how best to start a conversation she wasn't sure about even beginning. She was saved the trouble from speaking first when Eva did so herself.

"How're you settling in to that big house of yours then, Annie?" she called over the noise of the coffee machine.

"It's great. I'm loving the challenge of organising getting it fixed up and all," she explained. "Plus the atmosphere and the history. It's kind of exciting."

"Ah, so you're not haunted like they say then?" Eva chuckled, turning to place Annie's coffee on the counter and then moving on to make her sandwich.

Annie bit her lip, considering what to say next.

"You don't believe in that stuff, do you?"

Eva continued to laugh into her response as she finished off Annie's tuna mayo and turned to hand it to her.

"Not really, love," she told her. "Do you?"

"I don't know what I believe right now." Annie shrugged, digging into her pocket for some money to pay, but Eva waved the cash away. "Everyone is making me feel so welcome." Annie grinned and thanked her. "Well, almost everyone. You know Richard's uncle?"

"Oh, don't you worry about old George Thomas." Eva rolled her eyes. "He's a funny sort and no mistake."

Annie felt a little better for knowing that it wasn't just her that Mr. Thomas didn't like for whatever reason. Still, it didn't make a massive amount of sense. It wasn't as if she thought he ought to be nice because Richard was. It was the fact that he had apparently gotten along with her Grandma Rachel.

Pulling herself up onto the nearest stool, Annie stirred her coffee around and around in deep thought whilst Eva served other customers. She had a reason for coming in here, a conversation she wanted to have and yet she felt odd about it. It wasn't as if she was lying to Eva or doing anything wrong by not telling her exactly why she was questioning her about the history of Bennington Hall. Bringing up Jack seemed silly and pointless, especially when Eva had already said she didn't believe in ghosts. Annie would've said she didn't either, not really, at least not until the last few days, but that didn't matter right now.

"So, has Mr. Thomas lived here the longest of anybody?" she asked as Eva came back over, wiping her hands on a tea towel.

"Oh, no, dear. My family goes back furthest," she told her proudly. "Did you want to know something about the town or your house perhaps?"

"Actually, yes." Annie smiled at her friend's intuition. "Who lived in the house before my grandmother?"

"Well, no-one actually lived there," said Eva thoughtfully. "Squatters sometimes," she said softly, leaning on the counter so only Annie would hear. "But it stood empty a long time, as far back as when I was a little girl, I shouldn't wonder," she considered.

"So, the eighties?" Annie checked, not entirely serious but knowing it was better to guess way too late in the calendar than too early and cause offence.

"Oh, get away with you!" Eva chuckled, swatting her arm. "I'll be sixty-two next month!"

She was forced to walk away then, to deal with customers who wanted to pay for their food. Annie gave some attention to her sandwich, but she was still thinking about the house and Jack. Nobody lived in the house as far back as the fifties, and that was when Jack had been born too. Eva had to be living here in town when Jack died, and yet she said nothing of a scandal at the hall. Nobody had even been living there then, at least not officially.

"The plot thickens," she muttered to herself, taking another bite of her sandwich.

Chapter 14

The light was disappearing fast as a bright Sunday fell into dusk. Anastasia was tired, and yet she couldn't stand the idea of going to bed right now. She was so ready for the work that started tomorrow. Mostly it was volunteers coming in to help with clearing out rubbish, cleaning and dusting, that kind of thing. The specialist workers and tradesmen, most of which were not free labour but on reduced rates, would help out at weekends when they didn't have any regular jobs to take on. Still, the house would have people in it from tomorrow, a whole lot of new friends and strangers besides. It made Annie wary too. She didn't worry for her safety or the state of the house. To save on confusion, she planned on locking the rooms she was actually living in, as well as making sure nobody wandered into the unsafe parts of the house. Her main concern was something entirely different.

Jack hadn't shown himself since quite early the day before. Annie didn't know what to think about that, but she did know she couldn't risk him playing any tricks on her helpers or making a nuisance of himself when they were here. They needed to have a serious conversation, but Anastasia was determined not to call out his name as if she were Juliet on the balcony wondering where her Romeo had got to. She had wondered if the music would draw him out, since it had so many times before. Hours of her eclectic taste in rock, punk, country, and pop had done nothing to entice him. Now she was running out of time and options.

Annie smiled as a thought suddenly came to mind. Pulling out her cell phone, she flipped to the folder of received texts. Richard had sent more than one today and she re-read them with an over-sized grin on her face.

"Oh, Richard. You're such a good guy," she said with a sigh, trying to stifle a smirk when she felt a presence behind her.

"He's not that great."

'That worked better than I thought,' she considered, turning to face Jack.

He had the appearance of leaning on the end of the mantelpiece, all cool and nonchalant. Annie resisted the urge to roll her eyes.

"Good timing. I need to talk to you," she said, shoving her phone into the back pocket of her jeans where it had come from. "You and me, we gotta have some ground rules about all this popping up and disappearing that you like to do," she told him, complete with hand gestures to match her words. "I have people coming here tomorrow, people who want to help me get this place looking like a house again, somewhere people could actually live or work or whatever. I need you to behave for me, please. No fake storms, no weirdly locked doors, nada," she said, making a cutting motion with her hands as if to draw a line right through every trick he might decide he wanted to play.

There was a long moment when he just stared at her without reacting at all. Annie wondered if she had surprised him or amused him, maybe even offended him. Just when she was about to ask if he even heard a word, that smirk she was becoming accustomed to returned to Jack's lips.

"What's it worth?" he asked her with a quirk of his pierced eyebrow.

Now it was Annie's turn to smirk.

"What exactly could you want from me?" she asked, hands on her hips, defiance in her eyes.

She knew very well the kinds of favours men asked

of women when making deals, sometimes serious, sometimes joking. The difference was, Jack wasn't a man. He had the form of one and used to exist as a human male, but as he was now, he couldn't touch her, couldn't really threaten her. She had nothing to fear of him, and very little she could offer in trade for his co-operation.

"You have no idea, love," he said with a look she didn't entirely care for. "Anyway, all I'm asking is that if I'm gonna be a good boy for your visitors and all, we have a deal that you owe me a favour."

Annie would never consent to owing a guy an undisclosed favour in any normal situation, but this was far from normal. She couldn't see what harm it would do, so she nodded her head.

"Okay. I mean, I'd offer to shake on it, but..."

She returned the smirk he was wearing, letting him know there was no malice in her words. His lack of physical presence was just a fact of life, or perhaps death, to be more accurate. She wasn't trying to insult him, and he seemed to know that. Right now, they were getting along like the oddest pair of friends. It made Annie feel like she could say anything to him, and yet she knew that wasn't true.

"So, while I have your attention, you wanna tell me now why you like to disappear on me so much?"

Immediately, his body language changed. He shifted as if trying to physically get away without evaporating as he usually liked to do. His eyes were everywhere but on her and seemed steelier in a second. Any trace of a smile was gone.

"Maybe I don't like being given the third degree."

Annie was about to argue that, until she realised exactly what he meant. He disappeared on her every time she asked any kind of probing question. He didn't seem to want to tell her anything real about himself, and most especially nothing at all about how he came to be here.

"Fair enough," she said, nodding once and turning away.

Annie walked over to the rug in the centre of the room and sat herself down. She crossed her legs and set her hands on her knees, looking up at Jack who was still standing.

"I can't ask you questions, fine. Maybe you'd feel better if you asked me something? C'mon, anything you want," she said, making a gesture of encouragement with both hands. "Lay it on me, all the things you've been dying to know about Anastasia Addams, lady of the house. I have nothing to hide." She smiled.

Jack looked amused by her attitude. He often did, and Annie didn't mind. He wasn't the first and he wouldn't be the last, she supposed. Of course, when his expression turned somewhat more intense, she started to wonder how exactly he had taken her words.

"No, you've got nothing to hide, have you, darlin'?"

He smirked a little, and Annie felt sick.

"You haven't...? I mean, when I'm changing or...?"

"No!" he told her sharply, apparently terribly offended by the implication that had come off his innocent words. "Like I said before, what do you take me for? My mum raised me to be a gent."

"Really?" She giggled at that, her previous panic immediately gone as he straightened up and pulled at his leather jacket, trying to look smart and proper. "Y'know that's the first real thing you've told me about yourself so far."

Jack shrugged his shoulders. "What business is my

life, or my death, to you?"

"People who live together usually know a little more about each other," said Annie immediately.

"People who live together are usually family," he replied. "Or married. Or at least shagging." He smiled wickedly. "That means-"

"Yeah, I think I can guess, thanks," she said, waving a hand to halt his explanation.

British slang was a minefield to her still, but the look on Jack's face and the general subject matter of the sentence gave away his full meaning. Annie didn't mean to squirm, but somehow, she just couldn't help it. When she looked up again, she realised Jack was right in front of her, only his legs visible, unless she tipped her head right back and looked up. Even then, the bright light from the chandelier on the ceiling nearly took away her vision entirely.

The next thing she knew, Jack was sitting down in front of her, mimicking her position with his legs crossed lotus-style. He looked a little silly, but then Annie figured she probably didn't look all that 'cool' herself. They were alone here, it didn't matter.

"You really so eager to get to know me, Anastasia?" he asked, seemingly astonished that she would.

"Yeah. Well, no," she amended, not wishing to make his head any bigger than it already was. "I just... You're here in my house, twenty-four seven, and all I know for sure is that you were born before my parents, you're not a pervert, and you dig The Ramones."

Jack considered what she was saying and realised she was right. She knew next to nothing about him, and as much as he could hang around watching her, listening in on her conversations like the spook that he was, it wasn't like knowing her. There were things he wouldn't mind asking, and perhaps it wouldn't matter so much if he let her in on just a few facts about himself.

"Okay, three questions," he said then, with a single nod, seeming to lean his weight back on his hands. "I ask you, then you ask me. Both of us answer with the truth. That sound fair?"

Annie smiled, trying not to feel too triumphant at getting her own way.

"Go for it," she agreed, waiting to see what this anomaly of a person might want to know about little old her.

Jack's first question came as a surprise, but she had no problem with it.

"How the bloody hell did you land up with a name like Anastasia?"

"Hmm. Well, my Mom is kind of a romantic and she likes her legends and fairy tales," Annie explained. "That whole story about the Russian princess that got away when her entire family was captured and killed, I think she liked that idea, so she gave me the name. Simple as that." She shrugged. "So, my turn. Were you born in Bennington or at least around here?"

"Nah." Jack shook his head. "I'm from Watford, that's north London to you, love," he explained, knowing she was unlikely to know where he meant without further help. "You got any other family about since your grandma...?"

Annie was more surprised by how awkward he seemed when it came to saying the word 'died' than she was by his interest in her family situation. He had to know she was single and without children, so all he could mean was parents or siblings. Clearly, he hadn't been listening in when she explained things to Richard. It wasn't something she wanted to repeat right now.

"Not really," she told him. "Nobody that I care about or that really cares about me. Did you?"

Jack took a moment to look at her, to consider the sadness that crept into her voice when she spoke of having no-one to care. She put a brave face on it, but it hurt. Oh, Jack knew how much it hurt.

"Same as you really," he admitted. "Nobody that meant that much."

They shared an odd smile and a feeling of the strangest solidarity in their joint confession. They had both come here alone, it seemed, and were both staying. For very different reasons and in very different ways, of course, but here they were.

"So, when you're done doin' up this place, what happens to it?" he asked after a moment more of silence.

Annie looked from his face to the room around them.

"Honestly? I don't know yet." She sighed. "I have lots of ideas but... I don't know for sure."

Silence reigned for a minute or more. Jack was waiting for Annie to ask her next question, having no idea that she was just trying to get up the nerve to do so. Just when he was about to ask her what was up, her eyes returned to his, blue meeting green with a strange intensity that he was sure would've made him shiver if he had the ability.

"How did you die?"

Anastasia jumped as the cell phone rang in her back pocket. Knocked completely out of the moment, she grabbed it and looked at the screen. 'Richard calling,' she read on the display, about to hit 'cancel' when suddenly she looked up and realised Jack was gone again.

"Damn it!" she cursed, knowing it was probably as much this call as her question that made him evaporate that way.

Annie figured she may as well see what Richard thought was so important now. She answered his call, perhaps a little more snippily that was necessary, and he immediately asked if something was wrong. Since Annie wasn't prepared to explain that he had just interrupted an interesting conversation with her friend the ghost, she was forced to say everything was fine, and moderate her tone accordingly.

"I know it's late to be calling you," Richard apologised for the intrusion, "but I got a bit tied up with other things, and I really wanted the chance to wish you luck for tomorrow with everything, and let you know that should you need me for anything... well, I'm here for you, Annie."

She could almost see the genuine smile on his face when he spoke those words, and immediately felt bad for snapping at him before. Poor Richard, he wasn't to know he was making a nuisance of himself. The men in her life just seemed to be good at that lately, if she could really count the ghost of Jack Green as a man in her life.

"Thanks, Richard," she said genuinely. "I appreciate that, but I should really go. Like you said, gettin' kinda late."

They ended their call and Annie shoved the phone back into her pocket. She may as well give up and go to bed, she knew that, but somehow, she just had a feeling Jack was still around, still considering that last question she asked him. Just when she was about to tell herself what a dumb idea that really was, she heard a voice near her ear.

"You ever been stabbed?"

Anastasia shuddered at the sudden and shocking words, spoken in a low tone that was probably designed to scare her. She wouldn't give Jack the satisfaction of seeming affected by the question, even if it had genuinely freaked her out. She pretended like she hadn't heard exactly what he said just to buy a little time as she turned to face him.

"You ever been stabbed? Blade through your flesh?" he asked, eyes a darker shade of green somehow, face very solemn and serious. "Not just a minor slash, but something passing right through you," he said slowly, pushing his hand forward towards Annie's abdomen.

She didn't mean to flinch. After all, he couldn't touch her, and yet when she looked down and realised his arm was spearing her body, she could've sworn she felt something.

Swallowing hard Anastasia took two deliberate steps back to get out of his reach.

"That's what happened?" she checked. "And you don't know who did it? That's why you're here?"

"I already answered three questions," Jack told her, smiling slightly as he too backed up one step then another. "You hit your limit, love."

By the time he reached the wall, he was fading out and then gone. Annie knew even if she rushed to the next room, she wouldn't find him. Jack hadn't gone through the wall, he had vanished on her again.

He was right, he had answered as many questions as he promised to, and didn't have to feel obliged to answer any more. Still, he had said enough. Someone had killed Jack, murdered him in cold blood by the seem of things. A blade right through his body, it was like something out of a horror movie or a medieval tale of torture. Annie shook all over, unable to stop. She didn't want to be scared or in any way bothered by what she had discovered, but she couldn't help it. As irrational as her fear was, it was also very real and intense.

Grabbing for her phone again, she never really thought of calling Richard, not this time. Her fingers fumbled with the keys, her mind racing with overseas codes and the like. It seemed to take too long to hear the ringing on the line, and then finally he answered.

"Annie?"

"Hey, Mike!" she said, smiling widely. "You have no idea how much I just needed to hear a friendly voice right now." She sighed, sinking down to sit on the rug where she was usually so comfortable.

"Annie, honey, not that it isn't great to hear from you, but this must be costing you a fortune!"

"I can afford it," she told him, literally waving away his concern, even though he couldn't see her. "I just... I needed to hear you. I need to know how everybody is doing. How're you? How's Shanice and Janine? I miss you guys so much!"

Mike had no problem telling her everybody was just fine, going on to explain in detail, with anecdotes about work at the supermarket, nights out on the tiles, and all. Annie barely spoke, just listened with rapt attention, laughing at the funny parts, sympathising with any problems.

She could picture her friends in the world she had left behind, and she missed them. Not the scraping around for cash all the time or almost freezing to death come winter, but the people, the feeling like home that was tough to hang onto when she was so far away in a strange place, mostly with a ghost for company. For now, Annie put Jack out of her head, along with the distance between her and New York. She concentrated on Mike's voice and all that he was telling her. It felt good to disappear into her past, just for a little while.

Chapter 15

The house was full of activity. Anastasia felt a little overwhelmed at first when wave upon wave of helpers arrived on a bright Monday morning, determined to assist in getting Bennington Hall back to its former glory. It was going to take much time and effort if they were to achieve their goal. Rome wasn't built in a day, and a house this size was not returned to greatness in such a space of time either. There were months of work ahead, but Annie didn't mind. She had money, she had help, and above all, she had determination to see the project through.

A yawn overtook her, making that determination seem less than true. It wasn't that the work was so very hard or even boring. Annie had been up late last night, into the early hours in fact, talking to Mike. There was so much to say and even more to hear. It thrilled her to know that her friends were doing okay, that everyone was so happy and well. At the same time, it broke her heart a little. Annie missed them all so much when she let herself reminisce. Mike, Shanice, and Janine had been her very best friends for so long, and they were just so far away. When she was busy, she could let herself forget how alone she was, but when Annie allowed herself to consider it, she could get quite upset over the absence of her friends.

Right now wasn't the time, and she knew it. There was so much to do and she threw herself into the activities with gusto. Much of the time she was being called upon to make decisions or just to see some new treasure that had been uncovered. Behind dusty curtains and layers of grime, some beautiful paintings and stunning wallpaper had been revealed already, and this was only Day One. It made Annie happy enough, but underneath it all she couldn't help but be a little sad.

When her mind wandered, it wasn't just her old friends that Anastasia thought of, it was a new one too. Perhaps calling the ghost that haunted her house a friend was a little twisted, but nevertheless, he sure was on her mind a lot. Jack was hard enough to ignore before, but now, after what he had told her about how he came to die, Annie couldn't help thinking of him.

All that research she had done, history books and newspapers, asking around town. Everyone knew the rumours that the Hall was haunted, but that was practically a joke amongst most sensible people she had met. There was no real substance attached to it, no story of grizzly murder, and yet Jack had died here at the hand of another. That was what he told her, at least, and Annie had no real reason not to believe him. He could be lying, trying to scare her, but she genuinely believed they had moved past all that by now.

There had been no more fake storms, flashing lights, or locked doors, not since Jack revealed himself to her. Anastasia knew she was probably being a fool, but she trusted him. She believed that when he told her something it was the truth, however idiotic it might seem. If he said he was killed, then he was. What she needed to know now was who perpetrated the crime, if Jack even knew himself. If he didn't, that would mean Anastasia solving the crime, and at this point, she had no idea where she would even start with such a task.

"Miss. Addams?" said a voice.

"Annie," she replied like an instinct, turning around and forcing a smile to cover her previous frown. "Please, call me Annie," she told the young volunteer whose name she really couldn't recall.

"Sorry, Annie." The teenager smiled. "Er, we've done almost everything we can with the stairs and first floor landing," she explained. "Do you want us to keep going up or start on the rooms up there?"

Anastasia took a moment to think. The room next to the stairs on the first floor. The one that had taken so long to access. The one where she first met Jack. A horrible feeling ran through her when she realised why the door had been locked so long, why it was the first place he appeared.

"No," she said, shaking her head. "I mean, yes, keep heading up the stairs, but be careful of the rails," she reminded her helper. "The guy isn't coming to check them until Saturday?"

The girl agreed and walked away again.

Annie wished she could remember her name. It seemed rude not to know somehow, but there were so many people here and she never had them all listed, especially some of the younger ones that just tagged along with their parents or friends. She should really make an effort to get to know them all before long, if only so she could give them proper thanks for all their hard work.

Blowing loose strands of hair off her forehead, Annie turned back to her work. There was so much to do, and no time to stand around being overly thoughtful. Unfortunately, it was hard to stop her mind from wandering right now, and even harder to push through the pain barrier when she was so tired. Still, she did her best, and hoped no-one would notice or mind at all if she seemed distracted. They would probably assume she was just concentrated on the overall plans for the Hall. Nobody would ever suspect the truth - it was entirely too crazy to contemplate!

* * * * *

Valerie Sells

He never should have told her what happened. Jack knew he was a fool. He had vowed never to have that conversation with anyone, the one where he revealed how he came to haunt this place. She didn't know details, but the moment he appeared before her again, Anastasia would ask. He just knew she was the type to want all the facts, not of how he came to die exactly, but the events leading up to it, at least.

A part of him actually wanted her to know. The other part knew it was stupid to say a word. If she weren't so beautiful, so clever, so bloody persuasive! Anastasia Addams was all those things and more. Jack was starting to wonder if he was haunting her or if it was the other way around now.

Moving through the Hall, invisible and silent, nobody ever knew he was there, but just about everywhere he went, Anastasia would appear. Called by a volunteer to assist or make a decision, or just because she seemed to like to wander. It was almost as if she knew exactly which room he was hiding in and headed there on purpose. Jack knew that was dumb and impossible, but it didn't stop him wondering.

Much of what he was remained a mystery, even to him. He was pretty sure he didn't have the power to control a person's will. He certainly never tried. Anastasia was different to any other person he had ever known to be in the house, and there had been plenty, more than most realised.

The conversations around the place today were largely mundane. The ones about hauntings and potential ghosts made him itch to play tricks, but Jack had promised Anastasia he wouldn't. It made him wonder how much of a fool he really was. Jack Green had no physical presence, very little to entertain himself in this non-life he possessed, and he had allowed this woman to take away what little fun he might've made for himself.

'Bloody stupid bugger, you are,' he thought to himself, watching Anastasia as she scrubbed at a much-neglected solid wood floor with all her strength and best effort.

She was so alive in everything she did, the complete opposite to the being that Jack was now. Somehow, when he was watching her, more so when he was talking to her, he forgot that he wasn't really there. Jack felt alive by proxy, so much a part of Anastasia's world because she let him be. She seemed to want him around, to find out about him, to be his friend in a strange way. Jack never felt like this before, not even in his living years. Nobody ever cared so much, not a person that he could recall.

It didn't matter, she wouldn't be here long. When the house was done, well, she said she didn't know what would happen to it next, but Jack could imagine. A single girl like her, beautiful and intelligent, she wouldn't want to rattle around in a massive house all on her own in the middle of nowhere. She'd sell it off, he was sure, and then she would be gone. No more Anastasia Addams, just Jack on his own again, with strangers he would have to scare away. That or learn to live in the shadows again, as he had for decades up to now.

Anastasia sung to herself as she wrung out her cloth and then scrubbed at the floor some more. Words he recognised, a song by The Clash. Jack smirked. She was amazing. If he'd known her in life, then maybe... But it was no use even considering it. Jack was well aware how futile his situation really was. The two of them barely existed on the same plane of reality. One day she would be gone, and here he would stay, tied down whilst she flew off into the great unknown of the world, places he could only imagine.

With a bitter laugh at his own idiocy, Jack drifted away. Anastasia never even knew he had been there.

* * * * *

"I'm sorry, what?" asked Annie when she realised a woman was standing over her, talking animatedly.

Pulling her headphones down to hang around her neck, she made herself listen as Mrs. Bevin started over, asking Annie what she knew about the paintings on the walls.

Getting up off her knees that ached from being pressed against the wooden blocks too long, Annie wandered over behind the much older woman to see the pictures she spoke of. It almost seemed like a family tree of portraits, she had thought so when she visited this room before. Various older couples, suave looking sons, and beautiful daughters. Originally, Annie supposed it was the Bennington family that lived at the Hall, and maybe these people were members of that clan, but she couldn't be sure, as she told Mrs. Bevin with apologies.

"I suppose so," she said, nodding her agreement. "Did you leave all of your family in New York, dear?"

Annie bit back a smile. She wondered at Mrs. Bevin ever thinking she would know a thing about these paintings. Now it was clear that she didn't really believe that for a second, she just wanted an easy in, a leading question so she could be nosey. Annie could be mad about that, but it didn't really matter if she told a little about herself to a kindly old woman.

"No, no family, only some very good friends," she explained. "My Dad died a long time ago, my Mom remarried and had another daughter. Last I heard, they were somewhere in the West Indies for Ted's work, but now? Could be anywhere," she said, shrugging her shoulders. "Honestly, my friends were the only family I needed for so long. They seem so far away now."

Annie swallowed hard, feeling stupid as tears came to her eyes. Just last night, she had spent hours talking with Mike, catching up with the news and gossip on all her friends. That ought to make her feel better. In truth, it made her miss them all the more.

"Well, you'll make new friends here, my dear," Mrs. Bevin told her kindly. "I dare say you already have. I've seen you about town with young Richard Thomas, and we're all friendly people in Bennington, you know."

"Oh, yeah. I know." Annie smiled genuinely. "Everybody is so nice, and I am making new friends, every day."

There was a sadness in her eyes still and she knew it, ever more so when Mrs. Bevin looked so sympathetic. She rubbed Annie's arm reassuringly.

"It's not quite the same, is it?" she said with a sigh. "Well, maybe your American friends can come and visit you sometime? We'll have rooms enough ready for them to sleep in the rate we're going anyway!"

When Mrs. Bevin walked away a few moments later, Annie still didn't move and go back to her cleaning. Maybe she could invite her friends over. She had asked them to come visit when she left them behind at JFK, and yet they all knew that affording the plane ticket would be impossible for any of them to manage. That didn't mean Annie couldn't pay for their trip. Three plane rides from New York and back again would be pricey, but she had plenty of cash thanks to Grandma Rachel, and she was saving so much with all the volunteers here, and labour on what the locals called 'mate's rates'. She chuckled to herself, going back to her bucket of soapy water and getting on her knees to continue cleaning. Just imagining Mike, Shanice, and Janine in this house seemed crazy, and yet picturing herself in such a place had seemed equally as nuts once upon a time. Maybe she would have them come over. The more Annie considered it, the more she wanted to make it happen, and sooner rather than later. She scrubbed at the floor with renewed vigour, with no idea that she was being watched, again.

Chapter 16

"It's looking really good in here, Annie," said Richard, eyes all around the room. "I know you had a lot of help, but the organisation alone must have been hard work, and I know you wanted to do as much as possible yourself..."

He went on to praise her efforts and ask her plans. The truth was, Anastasia wasn't really hearing most of what was said. It wasn't fair and she knew it. She tried her best to pay attention, but her mind kept on wandering. There was more than one topic fit to distract her and she had always had the problem of losing focus when her brain was so busy.

Jack hadn't shown himself in almost a week. She understood it during the day when the volunteers and workmen were around. After all, it had been Annie herself that asked him to keep a low profile whilst she had company of any kind. He was as good as his word and better, but Annie hadn't even encountered Jack at night or at times when she was completely alone in a room. He would've been welcome company then.

It was strange to miss a person you only just met, and stranger still when said person wasn't even alive. Annie told herself over and over what a fool she was to miss the company of the spirit who haunted her house, but it was hard to convince herself. He was a personality, that much was for certain, and kind of hot if she let herself think about it. Mostly she tried not to. In reality, this person was older than her parents, and physically dead before she was even born. Yet he was here. In some form, he existed within her world. At least he did when he let himself appear to her. Six days and counting since that last happened.

The final conversation they had was about how he

had come to die. The memory of that, the odd sensation when his ethereal hand passed through her body, the whisper of his words that explained the blade that sliced through his body. Annie shuddered every time she allowed herself to recall it, to imagine what Jack must have gone through, the pain of such a wound, the darkness of death.

When she was trying her best to put it out of her head, Annie's brain headed home instead. She thought of Mike and Shanice at the supermarket, and of Janine at her office, working hard. Annie pictured them at the bar in the evening, laughing, flirting with the bartenders, having fun. As much as she loved it here and believed in what she was doing at Bennington Hall, a part of Annie wished she had stayed in New York. She missed her friends and the world she knew, even if survival hadn't been easy there.

"Annie?" said Richard, his hand on top of hers startling her from her deep thought. "Are you okay? You look... Well, I'm not really sure how you look, just not quite right."

She smiled at his concern, but shook her head in the negative.

"I'm fine," she assured him, knowing she could never fully explain her zoning out. "I'm sorry, I should've been listening. I just... I was thinking about New York, about the friends I left there."

"Of course, you must miss them," he sympathised, his hand still on hers, and Annie didn't mind at all. "As much as we can all try to make you welcome here, and I hope we have, you would still miss them."

"Yeah." She nodded her agreement. "Honestly, Richard, you've been great. You are great," she amended with a genuine smile, "but it is weird being so far away, not seeing those same people every day. They mean so much to me. Like family."

Her expression shifted back to something more distant and sad.

Richard felt for her terribly.

"You think it would be crazy if I invited them over here?" she asked then. "I mean, they could never afford the plane tickets, but I can. I have enough money, and I have the space now that so many rooms have been cleaned out and fixed up."

"Why would it be crazy? They're your friends, Annie, and I'm sure they're missing you too. Ordinarily, I know some people can be a little awkward about accepting expensive gifts from friends, but if they are like family, as you say, and they would be doing you as big a favour as you're doing for them by saving you from all us Brits for a while," he said, smiling at his own joke.

Annie did the same.

"Like I need saving from a nice guy like you." She rolled her eyes, unaware of quite the effect her compliment had on him, or how he felt when she gripped his hand in both of hers. "It would be so good to have them here though, just for a while. Kind of a culture clash, but still." She laughed and it made Richard smile all the wider.

"Well, you fit in just fine, for a New Yorker," he told her, wondering how much different her friends could really be.

"Yeah, I guess, but Mike is... Well, first off he's gay," she explained. "I'm pretty sure I haven't met anybody in Bennington that bats for his team, if you know what I mean."

"Ah, in that you may be surprised," said Richard with a look.

Annie's eye widened a fraction, and she watched his expression change entirely to panic.

"Oh, no! Not me!" he said definitely. "Not that I have a problem with men that... I mean, that's their choice, or their business at least, I'm just not... I've never... I like women."

"I know that," she told him, giggling like a kid. "I was just teasing."

His panic had been too much fun to resist. Of course, she knew Richard was straight, she never thought anything else. The way he looked at her sometimes, that proved it if nothing else. He never really asked her out or spoke of them being anything but friends, and Annie was just fine with that. He was probably just looking because he was a guy and they did that sometimes. She looked at guys too, no harm, no foul.

"Anyway, Mike isn't in any way subtle about who or what he is," she went on to explain. "Over the top is practically his middle name, but that's kind of why we love him. Then there's Shanice. She's... she comes off pretty open and frank, but honestly? Deep down she's really shy. She hasn't had the best luck with guys, but even though she's got almost ten years on me, somehow she still believes one day Prince Charming will come sweep her off her feet."

"You think that's naive?" asked Richard curiously. "Because she might be right."

"Maybe she is." Annie shrugged. "I'm not saying it couldn't happen. Well, maybe not with a literal prince, but a nice guy? Yeah, I suppose." She smiled. "I want Shanice to have whatever she wants, because honestly, she's the nicest person. And that just leaves Janine," she explained. "She was my best friend in high school and then my community college buddy. We took the same classes, had just about everything in common, movies, music, you know? The only difference is our families. Hers is awesome and mine is... well, pretty non-existent until my friends became a new one for me."

Richard listened intently to the explanation of Annie's closest friends. She was this amazing person and there was no better way to realise it than to hear her speak about those that meant most to her. She waxed lyrical on all the best things about each of them, about their strength to overcome troubles they had been through, and problems they had faced. These three had been her support network when she most needed help. Janine worked with her on her college courses, helped her get one of two jobs she held down from then until she inherited her grandmother's estate. Shanice and Mike she had met at her second job and they had become like siblings in no time at all, looking out for each other against a sleazy boss and helping one another navigate the social scene in New York City. Annie had quite a life over there. Richard was enthralled by every word.

"I'm sorry. I have to be boring you to death by now," she said guiltily when she realised how long she had been talking.

"Not at all," he assured her. "It's all fascinating to me. My life has been filled with long stretches of grey offices and paperwork for so many years. Anything and everything you tell me of your life before this place, it's a positively thrilling adventure by comparison."

"But you have friends, right? I mean, from college or other jobs?" she checked.

"Um, well, those I knew at University, we sort of lost touch when we all moved back home," he explained awkwardly. "Work has always involved family, a cousin of mine on my mother's side for a while, and now Uncle George, who is my father's brother."

"Oh, okay," said Annie, not really sure how else to

react.

For reasons she couldn't begin to figure, Richard seemed to have this odd little sheltered life, without friends, certainly without a girlfriend or anyone special. He was such a nice guy, it really didn't make any sense. Sure, he could be kind of shy, that much she had experienced herself, but everyone in town liked him. He seemed to make friends easily enough in that way, but there was no-one specific, no one friend, be they male or female, apart from Annie herself, and she had only been here such a short time really.

"So, when do you think your friends might be coming over?" Richard asked then, making a big deal of pouring himself another glass of water from the jug on the table, mostly so he didn't have to look at her.

Annie so wanted to press him on why he had so few friends, why his life was so boring when clearly he never wanted it to be so. She knew he had lost his parents a long time ago, and she guessed that was why he was close to his uncle, in spite of George being so mean. Asking any more when he was clearly avoiding the subject seemed wrong. Pushing questions at Jack was probably why he had disappeared on her. Annie didn't want that to happen with Richard too, she couldn't let it. If he wanted the topic dropped, then she would, at least for now.

"I don't know," she answered his question honestly. "I didn't even ask them if it's something they would wanna do yet, or if they can all get time off from their jobs, but I'm hoping soon." She smiled. "The sooner the better."

* * * * *

Unleashing the Spirit Within

Jack tilted his head as he peered down on Anastasia and her little friend. He had learnt a lot by listening in, more than he wanted to know about dopey Richard Thomas, and a lot about Anastasia that made him smile. She really was an incredible woman, and she came from a place he had always intended to visit during his life. New York City, home of CBGBs, birthplace of the legend that was Joey Ramone. He had always wanted to see the places he only ever heard about in songs, read about in books, and saw in movies. He was saving up when he came here, hoping to use some of that cash and maybe double or triple what he already had in the poker game his cousin was laying on. He wasn't the world's best player, but the rest of those invited weren't so bright and tended to like their booze and more hypnotic substances than even Jack enjoyed. If he could moderate his intake while they didn't bother to try, he was sure he could make plenty of cash that weekend. In fact, he had made quite a tidy sum. Never got to spend it though.

It was good to know that Anastasia had friends back home, and that she might get to see them again soon. Jack wanted happiness for her, a full life, the like of which he never really got for himself. His twenty-seven years were not entirely lacking in fun and adventure, but there was so much he never got, never had, never knew. Now he never would, not really and truly.

As he listened in, watching the two friends at the table sharing stories, laughing, holding hands, something clenched in Jack's heart. He wasn't sure how that worked, how he could still feel so much in a body that was not truly there. Things still hurt. Not physically, but feelings, emotions. He had supposed he didn't have them for so long. He spent his time scaring people out of the house he had come to call home because it was the place he had stayed longest in his existence. It was only when the old lady came that things started to change.

Annie was a lot like her grandma. She had a similar spirit that Jack admired. At the same time, she was young, beautiful, and determined to be all that she could in the life that lay before her. Jack liked her a lot, more than was right in the circumstances.

In spite of the type of person he had been in life, what he looked like and how he behaved, Jack knew right from wrong. A man that had lived as long as he had been around, with an interest in a woman like Annie, it would be more than questionable. The difference was, as many years as he had existed, he wasn't old, he wasn't anything anymore. Even Jack Green himself didn't know what he truly was, or why he had taken on this strange form.

Talking to Annie made him feel alive, like the real human male he had been once upon a time. It didn't mean he became one by being in her company, but the feeling was nice. When she pressed him to explain how he came to die, he thought he may as well tell her. It was as close to scared as he had ever seen her, and yet she still didn't break, didn't give any indication that she wanted to cower or cry. It was a true strength that Jack respected and loved about Anastasia Addams above all else.

That word jarred in his head the first time he thought it. Jack had never been in love, not really. He never expected such a thing to happen to him, not in his whole life. Well, this wasn't really his life anymore, so maybe that was why he felt this way. He was a complete and utter fool for even considering such a thing, but there was little to do as a ghost-like figure than to think, and altogether too much, Jack had found.

"Just so you know," he heard Annie say, catching his attention because he knew for certain she had just seen

Richard out and nobody else was in the house, "I am going to invite my friends here. It's only going to get harder for us to be alone for you to put in an appearance," she told Jack, looking to the ceiling and then around the walls, as if she were hoping he might be there. "You want to talk or anything, now would be a good time."

He thought about it. For the full five minutes that she seemed to be waiting, the twice that she literally called his name in that time, Jack gave it serious consideration. In the end, he knew they couldn't talk about anything right now. Her only topic of conversation would be his death and that was something he didn't want to dwell on, at least, not now. She knew enough truth to be going on with. The details, those he had at least, they would wait, for now and possibly forever.

Chapter 17

"Honey, I know what Mikey told us, but you cannot be serious, girl!"

Shanice was loud enough to disturb the entire room, Annie was sure, but all she could do was smile and laugh her way through a positive response to her friend's confusion. She had made arrangements for the three of them - Shanice, Mike, and Janine - to go to the coffee shop after work and video-call her so they could discuss her offer to bring them over for a visit. Annie had called Mike to tell him and had him pass on the message, but either something got lost in translation, or they simply thought Annie had lost her mind.

"Seriously, guys," she said, smiling widely at their faces all smooshed together before the camera lens, "I have the money, I have the room, and I miss you like crazy! Please, don't tell me you're going to let me down. I so want you to come over!"

"Annie, you know we'd love to," said Janine. "But there's so much to figure out. I mean, I'd have to get the time off work and run it by my cousin. Y'know, I've been baby-sitting for her every weekend for months now, I couldn't just-"

"I know there is stuff to figure," Annie insisted. "I know you all have lives and jobs and everything, and I don't want to come off like the queen summoning you all here," she assured each of them. "It's just that I miss you, and if you could all co-ordinate a week or two of freedom to come visit, just know that I have the money covered, okay?"

"We can figure it out, sweetie, I know we can," said Mike with the same confidence he put on everything. "I'll get these two organised and it will happen, I promise!"

Unleashing the Spirit Within

Anastasia wanted to laugh and cry at the same time when she realised this could actually be happening. Mike would be as good as his word, she knew, especially since he was completely desperate to come see Annie himself. This was kind of an all or nothing deal in the circumstances, since leaving one of their friends behind seemed wrong and cruel. Mike would have Shanice and Janine organised as fast as possible, and Annie already had several last-minute flight websites bookmarked on her computer ready to go. The second she knew which week they could come, she would get those tickets booked and set up three rooms near to her own. This was going to work out, and she couldn't be happier.

"I come over there, you better find me that Prince Charming you promised me, honey," said Shanice with a wink.

Annie laughed.

"Hmm, a real prince might be pushing it, but I'll do what I can."

"How about you, Annie?" asked Janine. "Any mysterious strangers we should know about?"

Annie bit her lip at the sound of that question. Her first thought was Jack, which was simply ridiculous. Sure, he was mysterious and a stranger in a lot of ways. At the same time, she knew she couldn't mention the man that haunted her house, because being labelled insane by her three best friends really didn't appeal at all.

Wracking her brains, Richard's face came to mind next, and yet, he really was as far as anyone possibly could be from the tall, dark and handsome type her friends would be thinking of. He was cute, kind of built, Annie supposed, and with a sense of humour when he allowed himself to own it. Maybe it would be wrong to dismiss him as just another random guy she knew.

"I have friends here, and yeah, some are male, but nothing like that," she said eventually, shaking her head. "I've been too busy for dates!"

"Sweetie, there is no such thing as too busy for dates!" insisted Mike. "All those English hotties I keep seeing on the TV, you gotta have met at least one eligible bachelor?"

"Mike, I live nowhere near Prince Harry or Tom Hiddleston!" she laughed long and loud, knowing his taste a little too well. "And even if I did, I really don't think I'd have much of a shot."

The conversation continued in a similar vein for a few more minutes before a check of her watch alerted Janine to the fact she had to go. Mike and Shanice knew they couldn't afford to be too far behind and the call was soon ended.

Annie sat there for a while after the screen went blank, just staring at the spot where her friend's faces had been displayed. She missed them, and somehow talking to them, getting closer to having them here, it made her miss them even more.

"Not long now," she told herself quietly, before checking the clock.

It was past midnight and she was due another house full of workmen and volunteers tomorrow. Now seemed like a good time to go to bed and get some sleep. Heading out of the living room, she flipped off the lights and walked towards her room. She stopped at the bottom of the stairs a moment, looking up.

Annie wasn't sure why she felt compelled to head up there right now. A part of her expected that when she stepped into the familiarity of the first room on the next level she would find Jack waiting for her, but he wasn't there. The cold and draughty room, just as dirty and uninviting as the first day she saw it, stood empty as ever. Nobody had been in there but her. Somehow, she couldn't allow it, and Annie wasn't even exactly sure why.

After a moment, she let out a sigh, closed the door again and locked it up tight. Danny had come back and put a new lock on there for her, the day after he ran out on her. he apologised for having to leave abruptly but never did say why he had. Annie thought it best not to ask. Now the key to that new lock went with her everywhere and always, on a silver chain around her neck where she couldn't lose it.

Someday, when Annie finally saw Jack again, maybe he would help her unravel the mystery of that room, tell her if it really was what she thought, the room in which he died. Maybe he could explain why she felt so strongly about it, though she doubted it somehow.

Annie let out a yawn and headed to her bedroom at last. She really needed to sleep.

* * * * *

Richard stifled a yawn behind his hand as his uncle looked his way. It was six thirty in the morning, far too early to be up and in the office working, as far as Richard was concerned, but George thought differently. He had meetings to get to, a client in London who he had to visit early. Though Richard had suggested his uncle travel down the night before and stay over, George insisted that was a waste of time and money. If he set off early enough in the morning it would be just fine. Of course, that meant the two of them meeting at this ridiculous hour of the morning at the office to run through case files before he left. Richard was sure that his uncle did these things in no small part to make his life a living hell. He would wonder at why he put up with it, if he didn't already know clearly enough.

"Do you think you might actually complete all the tasks I've given you for a change before you go running off after that floozy up the hill?" said George nastily.

"Annie is not a floozy!" his nephew protested more loudly than he meant to. "Honestly, I really don't know what your problem is with her," he said more quietly.

"Where to begin!" His uncle rolled his eyes. "She is a brash, upstart American who thinks she can come here and make Bennington Hall her own. She has no right to it!" he said gruffly.

"Pardon me, sir, but her grandmother left it to her in her will. As long as she was of sound mind at the time of making said will, Anastasia has every right in the world."

"At least Mrs. Wickfield had some manners and decorum. She was a proper English lady, and a good, kind soul," he said, speaking highly of Annie's grandmother, as always.

Richard just couldn't understand how his uncle could have liked old Mrs. Wickfield so much and yet absolutely despise her granddaughter. Somehow, he didn't even seem to blame Annie's Grandma Rachel for leaving her home and money to the 'brash American'. A couple of times now Richard had tried to get to the bottom of exactly what George's problem was with the situation, but he never seemed willing to properly explain. Richard gave up, lest he cause a permanent rift. Sometimes it just wasn't worth it.

"You know I think if you just gave Annie a chance, you'd find she's a perfectly nice young woman," he said, smiling perhaps a little more than he really meant to.

Unleashing the Spirit Within

"What you mean to say is that you are smitten with the girl, just because she bats her eyelashes and shows off her legs," his uncle muttered. "I don't have time for your childish chatter, boy, and neither do you!" he said then, pressing his finger into the pile of folders and documents piled on the corner of Richard's desk to hammer his point home.

A minute later, George Thomas was sweeping out of the office, assuring his nephew he would be back by six o'clock this evening to ensure all the work had been done.

"Yes, sir," Richard dutifully replied, smiling until the door closed behind his uncle. "Miserable old goat," he added then.

There really was a lot of work to do. Sometimes he wondered where it all came from. Richard saw little of any profit the business was making, and yet he stayed. He had his reasons, which primarily lay in his dear departed parents' wishes. They so wanted him to make something of himself, to be a great doctor or lawyer. Given that the sight of blood never failed to make him queasy, Richard went into the law, following in the footsteps of his uncle and grandfather. He so wanted to make his parents proud, and yet he struggled. Just when he was getting back on the right track, the car accident had happened, taking both of them away.

The only close relation Richard really had was his uncle and he owed that man so much. He had paid off debts his own brother had been hiding, seen to it that Richard had a job and a home in the nice quiet village of Bennington, saved him in so many ways. It didn't change the fact that George was not a nice man to work with, or even to know, as a general rule.

With a heavy sigh, Richard started on the first task in his great pile of paperwork, wondering at the way his life was going. He wanted to change it, he just didn't know how. For now, he continued to work as hard as he could, and looked forward to happier moments in his quiet, unchanging life. Chief among the bright spots within his days was seeing Anastasia Addams.

Of course, his uncle had a point about her being beautiful. Richard would have to be blind not to notice how well Annie was put together, her bright eyes, her slim figure, but it was so much more than that. She had a spark in her, an attitude, a spirit that he so admired. She could make him laugh so easily, and yet she had a serious side too. She was determined to make Bennington Hall all that it should be, and was gracious in accepting the help others offered, without being willing to take advantage. If Richard was going to love a woman, it would be someone like Annie.

He thought in these vague terms because anything more explicit gave him cause for concern. Allowing himself to feel too deeply for Annie, to care too much about her, it could only lead to no good. Women like her didn't date men like him. He was a friend. She had said so many times that he was 'the best', but never in a way that made him suspect she had any real romantic intentions where he was concerned. The thought occurred to Richard, more than once, to ask her out to dinner or something, but he always changed his mind. Having Annie for a friend was just fine. It was much better than not having her in his life at all.

The phone in his pocket vibrated, catching Richard's attention, and he pulled it out to see a new message had arrived from none other than the very woman that was on his mind. He smiled as he read her text.

How busy are you today?
Wanna come out and play? ;)

He thought about it. Richard seriously considered just

dumping all the folders from his desk into his uncle's in tray and leaving the office for the day, maybe forever. It was a momentary thought, a passing folly. He would never do it, not in a million years.

Sorry, Annie. Can't today. Hope you have fun anyway.

She replied once more with a sad emoji and that was that. Richard threw his phone across the desk and concentrated his mind on the paperwork in front of him, at least for a while.

* * * * *

"Hello, my love!"

Annie responded to Eva's greeting with a smile when she realised her friend was there. She had been so concentrated on her phone, she really hadn't noticed where she was or who was speaking for a moment. It was a shame that Richard was busy today and couldn't spend any time with her. Annie was fine by herself, she was used to it by now, but these last few days in particular, she was just craving company. Richard was so much fun to talk to when she got him loosened up. Still, she could run her errands by herself, and maybe have lunch in the cafe later.

"You're certainly up and about early!" said Eva then.

"Yeah, I couldn't sleep," explained Annie, watching as her friend wiped down the front window panes and put out the advertising board on the pavement. "I started walking towards town, taking in the sights and all, saw the sun come up. It was beautiful." Annie smiled widely. "Now I'm here and I'm not really sure what to do. Not so many places open yet or people around this early, and I was thinking maybe Richard would be free but he's not."

"Oh dear," Eva sympathised. "Well, how about you come inside? I'll make you some breakfast, and we can have a good old girly chat until the other shops and such open, then you can see what's to do. How's that sound?"

"Sounds great," said Annie with a grin as she followed Eva inside.

Her friend asked what sort of tasks she had in mind for the day. Annie didn't lie when she told her she needed to order a few things for the Hall and organise some of the voluntary labour and tradesmen due to visit later in the week. She spoke honestly about needing supplies for when her friends came to visit, and was giddy at the prospect of being able to introduce Shanice, Mike, and Janine to Eva someday soon. The only partial lie was really just an omission from the whole story. Annie planned on stopping by the library again at some point today. No matter how much she tried to concentrate on other things, her mind just kept creeping back to Jack and what he had told her.

If he truly was killed in the Hall, there had to be a record of it somewhere. Maybe she hadn't looked thoroughly enough, maybe there was a book of newspaper records she had missed altogether. She was going to try again, one more time, to uncover the whole truth. She was never going to rest easy until she found out exactly what happened, and shared that truth with the man it concerned most.

* * * * *

Annie was tired when she got home from town. Maybe she should have caught the bus back up the hill, but the weather was so nice, and after hours shut in the library this afternoon, she thought the fresh air would make her feel better. It turned out a mile of uphill walking only made a person's legs want to fall off, especially after such a long day.

Nearly twelve hours since she left her home, Annie arrived back and was quite ready to give in and go to bed already, even though it was barely seven o'clock. Unfortunately, as tired as her body was, Annie's brain was buzzing. She wasn't going to get any rest, not for a while anyway. She had spent so long making plans and arrangements for the Hall, and then when she got to the library for deep research, she couldn't stop herself from diving into every source of information.

The original plan had been to find out what was happening with her house around the time of Jack's death. The more she researched, the more history she found, and so Annie eventually decided to put together an entire timeline, see if she couldn't better track events that way. No matter what she tried, from old books to newspaper clippings and the internet too, there was always a hole in the data.

During the Second World War, the Hall had been turned into a hospital and a base, anything useful for the war effort. Then came the nineteen fifties and the house seemed to have been quite given up by its owners. There were a few vague references to what would be done with the Hall, complaints about squatters and such for the years that followed.

An eccentric old man seemed to have been the owner right before Annie's Grandma Rachel, and presumably he was the one who she won it from in the first place. After her came Annie, and that completed the timeline, but the gaps remained between the fifties and now. It was frustrating.

All that Annie could think was that Jack, and

whoever he had come to Bennington with, were one particular group of squatters here in the seventies, or maybe they just came for a party or something. It was almost impossible to tell for sure, and Annie knew the only person who could really give her any more information was Jack himself. He didn't seem overly willing. In fact, he had a habit of disappearing just about every time she asked a serious question about his life, and moreover his death. It was almost two weeks now and she had seen not a glimpse of him.

Sometimes she spoke to him, just hoping he was listening in. A part of Anastasia was starting to wonder if he had disappeared altogether, if he was unable to show himself any more, but she didn't really believe that. After all these years, she couldn't imagine a ghost-like figure would suddenly vanish entirely just because someone asked how they came to die and they deigned to explain themselves. Besides, Annie knew, deep down inside, that he was still there somewhere.

"Do you know how frustrating you are?" she asked in the general direction of the stairs and the ceiling. "I mean, I have enough to do here. This Hall isn't going to get itself into a decent state of repair. I'm budgeting, I'm organising people and deliveries. I'm working my ass off to get this done, as well as trying to get my friends over for a visit, which by the way is a logistical nightmare, and I'm not saying I don't want any of this, because I do. All of it, actually. It's exactly what I want, but it'd be a whole lot easier to achieve without you in my head!"

Jack didn't appear, didn't speak, seemed for all intents and purposes not to exist. Annie sighed and wandered through to the living room as if defeated, and yet she wasn't done.

"Why can't you just tell me what happened?" she started up again, yelling frustratedly into corners where she had seen Jack appear before. "I know how you died, at least the violent, gross part that you told me, but why can't you say more? What does it matter to you if I know?"

Still nothing, and honestly, Annie hadn't really expected it either. It was so frustrating, especially since the information Jack was holding onto was nothing she could ever find anywhere else. She had tried to uncover the truth. Annie had spent all those hours at the library searching and searching. Every time she got a lead it turned into a dead end, and yes, Annie was well aware of the pun she never intended to make.

There just seemed to be no record at all of anything that happened in Bennington Hall between the last of the traditional line of owners and the guy who lived there before Grandma Rachel. He was nobody with any connections, as far as Annie could tell. A Mr. Whitelaw, with more money than sense, by the seem of things. Rich enough that he could afford to lose an entire house the size of a mansion in a poker game.

From what Anastasia had read, nobody knew much about Timothy Whitelaw. Every search she did on the name brought up details of a lonely older gentleman, with no family connections, no wife or children, and an obituary that said the booze had done for him in the end, not long after Annie's Grandma Rachel won the house.

"He had to have bought the house from the government or debt collectors. Whoever the house went to after the last of the original line left?" Annie mumbled to herself, checking over the print outs and copies she had brought home from the library. "And he bought it long after Jack died, so he can't be connected."

Annie pieced together the time line across the living room floor. Pages of her own handwriting mingled with print outs from the internet and photocopies of book pages. She had a complete run from the year the Hall was built way back when, through to the present day, with one noticeable void. Short of a single newspaper article telling how the local residents complained of squatters in the Hall causing noise and trouble in town, there was nothing from the late fifties through to Mr. Whitelaw and then Rachel owning the property.

"So, what happened in '78?" she asked herself, sitting back on her haunches and looking over the timeline again.

Out of nowhere, a gust of wind seemed to blow, disturbing all her pages at once and tossing them out of order. Annie cursed and hurried to gather everything up before it got too far away. She looked around, already knowing she would not find an open window or similar. She was pretty sure what had made all her hard work blow away.

"Very mature," she said sarcastically into the empty room. "I'm not going to stop looking, Jack, so you may as well get used to the idea!"

Annie gathered up the papers and stuffed them into a folder for safe keeping, before taking herself off to the kitchen to make a cup of coffee. She missed Jack's appearance right after she was gone, but then she was supposed to. It was true enough that he had blown her research right across the room. Perhaps it was childish, but he didn't like her poking around in his life, or moreover his death. It shouldn't matter to her, and he had no desire to talk to her about it.

At the same time, Jack couldn't help but be flattered, even touched, by her persistence. Sure, Anastasia could be passed off as simply nosy, but Jack had a feeling it ran a lot deeper than just curiosity. It was almost as if she wanted to know what happened for his sake. There were stories of ghosts and spirits being set free from the places they haunted if only they knew the truth of their own deaths, or if some other unfinished business could be put to rest. Maybe Annie was just trying to help him. For now, he couldn't face finding out for sure.

Jack disappeared as easily as always, and this time, Annie never knew he had been there at all.

Chapter 18

The plane would land in a little under two hours. Anastasia could hardly believe it and her hands shook as she tied back her hair and checked herself in the mirror. It was getting late, around the time Annie would usually go to bed, but tonight she was still up and getting ready for when Richard arrived to take her to the airport. He was such a nice guy and a real sweetheart to offer to do this. Annie never had learnt to drive, and suspected that even if she had an American licence, the English roads would be confusing at best and dangerous at worst. Safer to get taxis and busses most of the time, or be chauffeured by her good friend when he was so kind as to volunteer. She offered him money for gas. After all, it was a long way to the airport and back. Honestly, she told him three times he really didn't have to drive around all night just to help her out, but he had been insistent. Tomorrow - which would be today before they even got home again - was Sunday anyhow, so it wasn't really a problem for him to catch up on his sleep before work came around on Monday.

Smiling at her reflection a moment, Annie thought of Richard in terms of a knight in shining armour. He was so helpful and kind. She couldn't imagine how she would have achieved all she had so far without him. She would've got there eventually, she supposed, but perhaps not as quickly or easily. Richard was without question her best friend in Bennington, and very soon he would meet the rest of her closest friends, those she looked upon as family.

It would be as strange having them here as it was wonderful, Annie thought. Michael, Shanice, and Janine were not at all like the people she knew from town. They were New Yorkers, loud and brash as Annie herself could be, far removed from the quiet sleepy place called Bennington Town and all its residents. At the same time, they were the nicest people, and she loved them so much. That alone should mean they would fit in somehow into her new home and life, if only for a short while.

Two weeks felt like a life time and no time at all as she thought about it. Annie had so many plans when it came to spending time with her three best friends, though she was determined not to leave Richard out in the cold while they were there. That would be grossly unfair after he had been so good to her, and besides, she knew she would miss him if she went completely without his company for two weeks. That particular thought process made her think about another who had been absent from her life too long already. Turning to look up the stairs, Annie suddenly found her feet carrying her to the next floor. She hesitated outside the door of the first room, and then carefully unlocked it, and stepped inside.

It was one room in the house amongst many that had little to no work carried out in it so far. Some had asked why the door was always locked and Annie had made various excuses. None of them were the absolute truth, though a few bore a passing resemblance to it. The real reason was that this was Jack's room. Not one he lived in or even exclusively existed in, but quite possibly the one in which he died, the one in which they had first met. Days had turned into weeks and still he had not shown himself. Her research into why he was ever here, who might have taken him out of the world in all but the ghostly form that remained, it was put aside that day he blew Annie's paperwork across the living room and refused to answer her calls. She certainly shouldn't be thinking about it now, not with her friends visit as imminent as it was, but she couldn't help it.

"This is your last chance," she said softly in the centre of the room, turning a full circle so her eyes skimmed every wall, every corner. "I'm leaving for the airport in ten minutes to pick up my friends. For as long as they're here, I won't have time for you and your games. I'm asking you not to appear in front of them, or even in front of me while they're around. Jack, if you can hear me-"

"You know I bloody can," he said suddenly and in completely the opposite direction to which Anastasia was facing.

She swallowed hard, startled by his sudden appearance, oddly grateful too, but determined to show neither emotion as she slowly turned to face him. There he was, Jack Green in all his punk-styled glory. Annie had told herself she exaggerated how good looking he was when she pictured him in her mind - she had lied to herself.

"Nice game of hide and go seek we had going for a while there, huh?" she said, folding her arms across her chest. "Y'know for a guy that lived twenty-seven years, and has been hanging around for a damn long time since then, you're a real kid sometimes."

"I'm sorry," he told her honestly, which was perhaps more surprising than his appearing all of a sudden. "I was... You're right, I was being a kid. S'pose it comes from never really getting the chance to fully grow up before it was too late?"

He quirked an eyebrow, offering up his explanation as a question, a suggestion that he wanted her to consider and give her own opinion on maybe. Twenty-seven ought to be grown up enough, Annie thought, and yet she was twenty-six herself and couldn't say she felt anywhere near mature and adult enough for much of what life threw at her.

"I don't know." She shrugged. "Sometimes I wonder if any of us are ever grown up enough to know better, to be exactly what we should be. Nobody can know everything or be perfect, so I guess there's always more growing to do."

"Very philosophical."

He smirked when he said it, though it was not meant as sarcasm, Annie was sure. It was almost like he was trying to pay her a genuine compliment, and she didn't know how to take that, not from him, not now. She hadn't a chance to ask about it or challenge him at all before Jack spoke again.

"So, given up on the grand search into what happened with this little old house of ours then?"

"No." Annie shook her head, determined not to be affected by the way he was staring her down, thumbs in his belt loops, like a cowboy preparing to draw. "I told you, I have my friends coming to stay a while. Call me crazy, but I kinda don't think I want my opening line to be 'Welcome to Bennington Hall, come meet my new buddy, the ghost'," she said with a smile. "White jackets with sleeves that fasten in back aren't a good look for me."

"Possibly not," Jack agreed as he moved in closer, so close that Annie knew she would've felt his body heat if he had a body at all.

Still, she could fool herself that his presence was real. Standing there with sparkling green eyes staring down into her own, she could quite believe she could feel his breath in her face when he spoke, even though it was impossible.

"I doubt there's much you don't look good in." He smiled then, not a smirk but a genuine smile that completely bowled her over. "You're an amazing woman, Anastasia Addams. You should be told that more often."

"How do you know I'm not?" she challenged, tipping her head back a little to better meet his gaze, even as she wondered when her voice had got so low, so quiet.

Jack shook his head, almost imperceptibly. In any other circumstances, stood like this with a real human male looking at her this way, saying these words, Annie would have anticipated a kiss. As it was, she knew it was impossible, and still she was stuck to the spot by the very thought, breathing shallow breaths at the ideas her imagination was conjuring.

"I know you think you're helping, looking into this house, who lived here and all. None of it's worth anything to anyone, love."

"It's worth something to me," she insisted. "You matter, Jack. What happened to you, what could happen next, it... it matters, to me," she admitted shakily.

He didn't know how to take it, words that were two parts fact and one part compliment. She cared about him, as stupid as that was when she barely knew him, when there wasn't really a person here to know. He was a ghost, a spirit, whatever the true word was, if one even existed, and Annie wasn't sure it did. Jack was an unprecedented anomaly so far as she could tell, and he was a hell of a man for a person that didn't exist in any real form at all.

"Oh, sweetheart," he said with a sigh. A sad sort of a chuckle escaped his lips as his right hand came up as if to cup her cheek. "Shame really, that you're so many years too late."

The longing in his eyes and tone gave Anastasia the shakes. Her brain was barely processing what he was telling her. It could easily be that he thought she might have saved his life if she had been around on the day he met his demise, but she doubted that was his true meaning. He wished he could have met her when he was still alive. Jack actually seemed to be telling her that in another life, another world, they might've had so much more than the quasi-friendship they had found here.

"Jack," she said, then swallowed hard, unable to say more for a moment. "If it were possible, you know, I... I mean, I feel like..."

"Ssh," he hushed her words before they were ever spoken, a heart-breakingly amiable smile on his lips that made Annie want to cry. "What's done is done, sweetheart," he told her, hand still hovering near her cheek.

The shock came when a sense of cold came to Anastasia's face, like cool fingers against her skin. Her eyes widened as she realised what she was experiencing, that Jack's hand wasn't passing through her as it had once before, but was actually touching her. He looked as stunned as she was in that perfect moment, even as one lone tear streaked down Annie's cheek.

"Jack..."

A loud rapping on the front door made Anastasia physically jump, and suddenly she was alone. It took two or three deep breaths before she got her bearings back and felt able to move. Even then, she lingered at the door a moment before locking it up and heading down to where Richard would be waiting. He had begun calling her name by the time got there, concerned perhaps that she had not heard his knocking from too far into the house. He seemed to sigh with a real sense of relief when she finally opened the door.

"There you are." He smiled. "Ready for the off?"

"Er, yeah. I... I think so," she said vaguely, still feeling overwhelmed by what had gone before.

Richard's hand at her elbow and the look of concern on his face startled her a little.

"Are you alright, Annie? You look very pale. Almost as if you've just seen a ghost."

A strange gurgle of laughter escaped her throat at that remark, but she forced it down as fast as she could and found as convincing a smile as she could muster.

"I'm fine," she told him. "Really, I am."

Whether he knew it was a lie or not, she couldn't be sure. Annie just hoped he would let it go for now, and was glad when he started to talk on other topics, such as her friends' arrival in the country and all. She tried to keep the conversation going and push Jack out of her head, but just the merest thought of him and Annie could see his eyes boring into her own, feel his cool hand at her cheek. It was going to be a long two weeks until she saw him again. A part of her worried that maybe she never would again.

Chapter 19

Anastasia Addams could not stop smiling.

Missing her friends was something she always expected when she decided to up and leave not just New York but America entirely. Still, Annie hadn't realised quite how much she was feeling the loss of Michael, Shanice, and Janine until they arrived at the airport this morning. Never had she been so tightly hugged, and it felt great. Her friends were quick to tell her she looked good and how the English country air must be akin to good therapy or something. They seemed to like Richard when she introduced them, and though he was perhaps a little overwhelmed by two large personalities out of three, he was polite and lovely as always.

He didn't stay after dropping them back at the Hall, knowing as he did that Annie would want to catch up with her friends. He was right, of course, and now they were all sat around in a second living room, complete with comfy sofas and chairs only bought last week. It was perhaps a little odd that Annie didn't want to bring her friends into the room she usually used and that she hadn't decided to put furniture into there at all. She still found herself perfectly comfortable laid out on the rug or sat cross-legged on the floor. She decided just to let her friends think this was normal for her, to be in this room. It really didn't matter anyway.

"All I know is if he a specimen of what this town has to offer, count me in, girl!" Shanice was saying when Annie tuned back into the conversation.

"I don't know," said Michael thoughtfully. "He's a little plain for me."

"Who, Richard?" Annie chuckled. "Honey, he doesn't play for your team, so it really doesn't matter. And Shanice? I think you might be a little more personality than he could handle," she said with a smile. "Richard is..."

"Already taken?" suggested Janine with a knowing look the moment Annie's voice trailed away.

"Not that I know of, and definitely not by me. I like the guy, don't get me wrong, but we're just friends, that's all."

"Uh-huh," said Shanice, stretching out the phrase in a way only she could.

They didn't believe her. Annie looked around her assembled friends and realised in a second they simply did not believe she and Richard were no more than friends. It was amusing at first because they were so far off the mark, but then she started wondering why they would think that in the first place. Maybe it was just because she mentioned him a lot and he helped out by picking them up from the airport today. That might make it seem like they were closer than they were, but he was just a friend, her best friend in England, she supposed. That was all. Annie frowned and shook her head. They were all being ridiculous. She wasn't going to get sucked into their teasing and that was that.

"You okay, Annie?" asked Janine with genuine concern. "Seriously, we're just kidding about Richard. We didn't mean to upset you."

"I'm not upset," she promised with a genuine smile. "I know, it's fine. I'm honestly thrilled you guys are here. I guess I'm just kinda tired and... overwhelmed? I don't know. It's so crazy having you all here, like worlds colliding!"

"Well, then, here's to world's colliding, honey," said Shanice with a grin, toasting with the bottle in her hand.

"Here's to it," Mike agreed, clinking his own drink against hers.

Unleashing the Spirit Within

Annie laughed as she and Janine completed a full set for the toast.

It was true what she said, it was great to have them here, but also crazy to have her friends from NYC in a place like Bennington. She wondered how they would fit, even for two weeks, but then she had found her own place easily enough.

As little as she really had in common with the friendly townsfolk, Annie liked it here. As much as she missed her friends before they came to visit, and doubtless would in a fortnight's time when they left again, she really couldn't imagine going back to her old life now, her old job, her apartment in New York. It felt like a whole other world.

"So, when do we get the grand tour?" asked Mike curiously. "This place has to have a hundred rooms!"

"More like twenty or so," Annie corrected. "But it's still a pretty big place, which is why I figured you'd prefer the tour after you get some sleep. Seriously, you'll probably be tired just climbing one flight of stairs to your rooms. The hallways are long and the steps are steep in this place."

"Honey-child, you ain't wrong about needing to sleep," said Shanice definitely. "I'm okay for an hour maybe, but after that and this?" she said, gesturing to her drink. "Girl, I gonna be dead to the world."

"As much as I love you, sweetie, I'm not carrying you up any stairs," said Michael definitely. "Save that kind of thing for when you find Prince Charming."

Annie smiled at that remark.

"I'd love to say this place was crawling with hotties, but that wouldn't be entirely true," she considered, sipping her own drink. "Not that I've been paying all that much attention. This house is awesome, but it's as much work as it is pleasure."

She sighed, leaning her head back against the sofa cushions and staring at another ornate moulded ceiling. Her friends continued talking without realising they had lost her concentration. Annie's eyes stayed fixed on the ceiling, sure as she was that she saw something up there move. It couldn't be the bottled cocktail in her hand, she had drunk them before and been fine, and she was barely half way done yet. It occurred to her that the only thing that moved of its own accord in this house was her friend, the ghost. Had she been alone, she would have called Jack's name, asking if it was him making her think she was going crazy. With the gang here, she just couldn't.

"Honey, you're doing it again," said Janine, tapping her hand where it sat on the arm on the couch. "Are you that tired? Should we all call it a night for now?"

"No, I... Um, well, yeah. I guess maybe we should all get some sleep," she considered, making herself look at Janine. "I'm sorry."

"Don't be sorry," her friend told her easily. "Geez, you paid for all three of us to come here. That was so generous and so amazing. If you wanna sleep, you can. It's no big deal."

"I'm not generous." Annie shook her head, feeling stupidly emotional all of a sudden. "I'm selfish. I just wanted you all to be here so badly."

"Oh, sweetie," Mike reacted with a sniffle of his own as tears filled his eyes, his hand flapping wildly in front of his face, as if that would really help.

"You're such a baby, Addams," said Janine, leaning over to give her a one-armed hug. "But we love you, Annie. We wanted to come here. If we could've afforded it ourselves, you know we would've paid."

Unleashing the Spirit Within

"I know," her friend replied, hugging her back. "I honestly love that you're here. Tomorrow, I wanna show you everything; the house, the town, everything."

Annie meant every word. She wanted her friends to see the wonders of the place she now called home. At the same time, she had another reason for throwing herself into these plans. She needed to not think about Jack, at least for now. Knowing him, caring about him, it was an emotional rollercoaster that she feared not getting out of alive, or at least not without her heart shredded. She had meant what she said about needing to get some sleep, and yet she knew as she showed each of her friends to their rooms, she was unlikely to get any real rest tonight with Jack on her mind.

* * * * *

True to her prediction, Annie checked the clock for the eighth time and realised it was five a.m. She had literally looked at the time every half an hour since she got into bed, and sleep just refused to come to her. She wasn't surprised, even if it was just the excitement of her friends being here that was keeping her awake. As it was, she knew there was another reason, a much bigger reason, if she dared to think of him as such.

Jack Green had been dead since before Anastasia was born, and yet he was here in the house. If she called his name, he would appear, at least sometimes. Other times he hid from her like a naughty child afraid of facing his mother. Annie had assumed that his avoiding her was when he was mad about something or just wanted to be a pain. She hadn't thought for a moment he was trying to avoid getting too close.

Ghosts couldn't fall in love, that was crazy. Of

course, Annie reminded herself that the very concept of such a spirit even existing was pretty nutty. She hadn't believed in this kind of thing before, she wasn't sure she really believed in it even now, but she couldn't deny Jack was very real in his own way.

Annie's hand came up to her cheek and touched the spot where Jack's own fingers had been just a few hours before. He had touched her. It ought to be impossible, but she knew it had happened. The shock on his face in that moment proved for certain that she hadn't imagined the sensation, and that it was something Jack never knew was possible either. It was one more mystery to solve, though Annie was pretty sure it would be even more impossible to unravel than the truth of Jack's death.

"Your timing sucks, Green!" she whispered harshly towards the ceiling. "You wait until the night my friends come to visit to... to pull the magic trick to end all magic tricks!" she told him crossly, feeling stupid when tears came to her eyes all over again.

It was wrong to mock him or be mad at him. For all that she could tell, Jack hadn't known he could touch her and was as surprised as she was when it happened. If he did feel something for her, if he were capable of it, Annie didn't suppose he could do much about that either. She wished he could. She wished she could unravel her own mixed-up feelings for him and extinguish them too. Falling for a ghost, it was ludicrous. Still, the more Annie thought about it, the harder it became to deny.

If Jack were a man, as real as Richard, then he probably would've kissed her tonight, and she probably would've let him. Scratch that, she definitely would've let him. Actually, Annie was sure there was every chance she would have run out of patience by now and taken the initiative to make the first move herself.

Unleashing the Spirit Within

As it was, the what ifs did no good, they never did. Jack wasn't an option, not as a boyfriend or a future. He was a ghost, or similar, already dead and gone in all but this mystical form that showed itself to her once in a while.

"Just put him out of your head!" Annie told herself crossly and yet as quietly as she could, given that Michael was in the next room. "Your life is more than the pursuit of Jack Green!"

Annie did her best to think of other things, listing off itineraries and plans for herself and her friends to enjoy, even getting into the upcoming work to be done on the house when they had gone home again. It sent her off to sleep eventually, and Annie was glad, but her dreams were haunted by the same figure that haunted her house. She wondered if that would ever change. Annie doubted it, until she saw Jack again and figured out what the hell was going on between them.

* * * * *

Jack always appreciated the part of his existence that meant he could walk through walls. It saved an awful lot of time and effort. Not that he really got tired or had anything better to do with the long hours in Bennington Hall, but he still thought it was pretty cool.

This particular night, he waited until Annie's guests were asleep in their temporary beds and then took a wander through each of their bedrooms for a closer look at them. He had been there in the living room when they first arrived, drinking their weird beverages and chatting away, but it was easier to get a good look at people when they were still and quiet. Probably was a bit creepy, Jack considered, but in his current form, he supposed that was just exactly what he ought to be.

They were quite the selection of people, a phrase that could have been used to describe the motley crew Jack hung around with in life too, though in a very different way. Annie liked these people, so there had to be good in each of them. He hoped so, for her sake. She deserved the best of everything, and since Jack had no chance to give that to her, he wanted to know that at least her friends were trying.

He hesitated at the wall of the third room, the one that would take him into Annie's room if he kept on walking. Jack told her once he never spied on her when she changed clothes or was in the bathroom, and that was true. To his knowledge, he never said he hadn't watched her sleep, though in truth he hadn't done so. It seemed like going too far, being too intimate, but after what happened between them today, he couldn't help himself.

Two more steps took him through the brick and plaster so he was standing on the far side of Annie's bedroom. He had seen it in daylight and thought nothing of the decor or furniture then, and less so in the dark of night.

Walking silently over to the bed, a smile came to his lips unbidden as he looked down at her sleeping form. She was so peaceful, so beautiful. It was strange to have her so still and quiet. Awake she was a constant force to be reckoned with, like a restless wind or an incoming storm. Her eyes always sparkling, head held high when she was refusing to take crap from anyone, least of all him. There weren't words for what she could make Jack feel, or maybe there were, but he couldn't bear to think of them. Things he never felt in life now took a hold of a heart he didn't truly possess anymore. It made no sense, but as much as Jack knew that, he also knew he did feel these emotions, this magnetic pull towards Anastasia

Addams.

"What have you done to me, love?" he whispered, hand hovering over the smoothness of her cheek, the very place he had touched her before and still wondered how he could.

It all had to mean something, and yet Jack couldn't explain it, any more than Annie would be able to. All he knew for sure was that strange things were happening ever since she came to Bennington Hall, and as much as it bothered him in one way, it thrilled him beyond measure in another.

He made her a promise not to show himself whilst her friends were here, and that promise he would keep. Because it was her. Because as insane as he knew it was, Jack was in love with this woman.

Because of her, he disappeared, for now.

Chapter 20

Anastasia stood in front of the bathroom mirror and painted on a smile. It looked genuine enough, and if she thought about her friends being here and the fun they were going to have these next two weeks, it felt genuine too. The trouble was, she had reasons enough to be sad and confused, and even angry too. She wanted desperately to put Jack Green out of her head but he was there all the time, all the more so when he wasn't actually showing himself for real. Perhaps that was the wrong word, Annie considered. Jack was real enough when he stood before her, spoke to her, even managed to touch her that one time, but she knew better. His body was dead and long gone from the world, only his spirit remained, taking the form of the man he once was. Annie longed to talk to someone about all this, if only so she felt a little less crazy, but her friends, as great as they were, could never understand, not when she barely understood herself. Shaking her head, she put that smile right back on her face and headed out.

It was late morning. Michael, Shanice, and Janine had needed to sleep in as much as Annie had, but now they were all ready for breakfast and their hostess had said they were going to get the best meal in town. She was taking them down to Eva's cafe for what the Brits called a 'full English' and everyone was intrigued and happy to go. The cab arrived promptly. Annie would usually walk or take the bus down into town, but this was a special occasion.

"Did anybody else get a weird vibe last night?" asked Mike as they headed on into town.

"Weird vibe, how?" asked Shanice. "'Cause me? I was dead to the world the second my head hit that fluffy white pillow!"

Unleashing the Spirit Within

"I don't know." Her friend squirmed in his seat. "It was like something was there, or somebody was watching me."

Annie's head snapped around from the view out of the window, her eyes wide as they landed on Michael. Thankfully, nobody seemed to notice her almost giving herself whiplash.

"Y'know a lot of these big old houses are rumoured to be haunted," Janine considered. "But ninety-nine times out of a hundred there's a perfectly logical explanation for the noises and feelings people get. Draughty doors, creaky floorboards, that kind of thing."

"There are rumours," Annie agreed. "When I moved in, all kinds of people were trying to scare me with spooky tales," she said, laughing and rolling her eyes, as if the whole thing were ridiculous. "I mean, I've never seen anybody rattlin' chains or whatever."

"You pro'ly imagined the whole damn thing, Mikey," said Shanice easily, not at all fazed by his talk of ghosts apparently.

Annie kept on smiling, and yet Janine couldn't help but think there was another look hiding behind the grin. They had been such close friends for so long, practically like sisters. If there was something to know about each other, they knew it, and Janine knew that smile on Annie's face wasn't genuine. She wouldn't say anything now, not in front of the others, it wasn't fair, but something was wrong here, very wrong indeed.

* * * * *

There was much laughter in Eva's cafe and the source of it all was the table of four in the centre of the room. Actually, the number of people around said table was five more often than not. Though Eva had other customers to attend to, she was very easily getting dragged into conversation with Anastasia and all her friends

It was strange to think that Annie had worried her New York family might not mix well with the friends she had since made in Bennington. To look at them now, she couldn't imagine why she ever thought it would be a problem. Though Eva had thirty years on her, Annie thought of her as one of her greatest friends already. They had a similar sense of humour, something she also seemed to share with Shanice and Michael. Janine looked somewhat embarrassed every time the laughter reached a new level of unseemly decibels and Annie could've used a few less people staring at them like they were strange, but mostly it was fine.

"Our little Annie did that?" Eva gasped when the story had been told about how she came to leave the supermarket, and how she had embarrassed her boss in the process.

"Yes, our little Annie sure did." Michael giggled into his coffee. "I don't think I've ever been more proud of her."

"Thank you, kind sir," Annie teased, mock-bowing in her seat.

The laughter started up again and it felt good. Annie could almost forget any problems she had been having, any worries or concerns. For once Jack Green was not forefront in her mind. She was reliving the good old days and some of the newer adventures all at once, with friends from both sides of the pond. There was no bad here.

"Man, he just ain't been the same since," said Shanice, wiping her eyes that ran with hysterically happy tears. "Every time he tries gettin' it on with a new girl, somebody done tells her what happened with Annie here, and Darryl loses another date!" she cried, laughing heartily.

"It's nothing less than he deserves," said Annie herself. "That guy is a creep."

"Oh, yes!" they all raised their various cups and glasses in agreement of that and then went back to their breakfast.

Eva moved away a little to speak to one of her waitresses that had a problem. Janine smiled as she watched her go.

"She's cool," she told Annie. "I mean if you saw her picture you'd think she was this quaint frumpy English lady type, but seriously? She's a riot."

"Eva's great," her friend agreed. "She's been a real help to me. Somebody to talk to, y'know? This town is full of great people, they're all so friendly and nice."

"Well, I'm glad you figured that out," said a voice behind her.

Annie nearly jumped clean out of her seat from the shock, her hand over her fast-beating heart as she turned and looked daggers at Richard.

"What are you trying to do? Kill me?" she checked, though she was smirking through the panic because she supposed it was kind of funny.

"I did think you might be trying to kill me the first day we met. You weren't exactly friendly," he noted, with a look that caused her to blush.

Richard was a nice guy but he did like to tease her sometimes. Annie knew her friends would jump on that fact and get the whole story out of her, especially when Janine insisted Richard come sit down and join them for breakfast.

"I really can't stay long," he told them, taking the offered seat anyway. "I was just on my way to work and I saw you all in here, so... Well, thought I'd say hello."

"Well, hello, honey." Shanice winked at him as he sat down beside her.

Richard squirmed under her gaze. He had just about learnt to be around Annie when she was feeling flirty, in fact he quite liked it, even if she did put him all at odds with himself. Shanice was a whole other ball game, and Richard wasn't sure he knew how to play.

"So, what happened when you two first met?" asked Michael, intrigued by the looks being sent across the table.

"Nothing major." Annie rolled her eyes. "I just... He startled me, and I... reacted."

"Oh, no!" Janine gasped, clearly trying not to laugh. "Annie, you didn't?! Those killer moves we learned at the Y?"

"Oh, she used the killer moves alright," said Richard with a look. "On my back in three seconds flat. It was the last thing I was expecting."

"So that's what it's like, huh?" said Shanice grinning. "Flat on his back in three seconds?"

"Oh, for God's sake! Could you all just stop doing that?" said Annie sharply as all her friends seemed to be wearing significant looks. "Me and Richard are not dating. We don't want to be dating. It is not going to happen!"

An uneasy silence fell over the table, and nobody looked more shocked than Richard himself. Annie wasn't sure what to make of it when she glanced up and saw him shifting awkwardly. She hadn't meant to insult him, she only spoke the truth. She shouldn't have snapped at her friends anyway, she knew that, but all the ribbing she was getting about guys and dating, especially when it came to Richard, it was all making her very uneasy. Annie knew it was only because the guy she was closest to and most attracted to was one she could never mention in conversation, because he wasn't a guy at all, just the ghost of one. Unfortunately, that was not really something she could explain right now, if ever.

"I'm sorry," she muttered into her iced coffee.

"No, we're sorry," Mike replied, putting his hand over hers on the table and squeezing. "We didn't mean any harm, honey. We're sorry."

"Yeah. Sorry," said Shanice, before looking to Richard. "We weren't tryin' to embarrass y'all."

"It's fine," Richard told her, clearing his throat. "Um, I should really be going anyway."

He was up from his seat and gone in a second. Annie opened her mouth to call his name but changed her mind last-minute. She didn't really know what to say other than sorry, and in a greater sense, she wouldn't mean it. She had told the truth, as far as she knew anyway. She hadn't a mind to date Richard, especially not with Jack in her head all the time. She couldn't imagine Richard really had any genuine interest in her that way either, or surely, he would've said something by now.

Annie frowned when she realised maybe he wouldn't actually. He was skittish about women, and about people in general. For the most part, she blamed the fact he was an orphan and his uncle was so domineering. He had never had a chance to be anything but shy and awkward, she supposed. Annie internally cursed herself for being so thoughtless, and with such a good friend too. She would have to talk to Richard later and figure things out.

"Um, so, there's not exactly a whole lot to see around this place," she said, taking a breath, forcing a smile.

"But what sights there are, I'll show you, and the countryside is pretty spectacular all by itself."

Annie didn't want things to be awkward. Her two weeks with her friends was already dwindling down to a mere thirteen days and she had planned so many fun things for them to do. There was no time for being petty and ridiculous. Each of her friends seemed to agree and they were back to happy chatter in a moment.

Eva came over again to see if they wanted anything else to eat or drink. They ordered sandwiches and such to take with them, planning to spend time in and around town and probably have a picnic somewhere.

"Can we head that way first?" asked Mike, gesturing down the High Street as soon as they stepped out of the cafe.

"For a reason?" asked Shanice, pulling her sunglasses down over her eyes and adjusting her hair.

"Oh, there'll be a reason." Annie smirked a little at her friend. "Somebody wants to see what's hanging out on the scaffold around the Town Hall, huh?"

"Busted!" said Janine with a grin, sure that Annie was right when they all watched Mike turn puce.

* * * * *

The weather held until the last moment. The sun shone with barely a cloud to get in its way the whole time Annie was showing her friends Bennington Town and introducing her old friends to her new ones. They were in the cab on the way back to the Hall when the sky turned darker, and then were forced to run from the car to the door as fast as they could, shielding their heads as best they could with plastic bags and their hands.

Unleashing the Spirit Within

Annie couldn't help but think of Jack as she glanced over her shoulder and saw that the sun was shining not more than a mile away, whilst rain poured down on her home. This wasn't his doing, it was just the way weather worked sometimes, and no doubt a rainbow would show itself before long. She smiled almost sadly at her own thoughts and put her attention back on her friends.

Shanice was still talking about a guy she met in town, smiling widely as she waxed lyrical about his sparkling eyes and cute ass. Annie bit her lip and tried not to laugh. It turned out Tommy Barrow from the builder's yard was just about as brazen as Shanice could be. They got on so well it was almost scary.

Mike was more concerned with having got wet in the rain. Of course, he was used to cold, wet weather in New York, he just hadn't really expected it today in Bennington, and his knock-off designer clothes were bound to show water marks.

Janine was the quiet one, as usual. She had been very attentive where Annie was concerned, and not just because of her outburst in Eva's cafe this morning, she was sure. It had begun last night with her zoning out on her friends. Annie knew that Janine was too smart to be fobbed off for long. Eventually, she would ask what was up, in such a way that Anastasia would have to give some kind of real answer, though how she was ever going to explain herself without sounding like a mental patient, she still had no idea!

"Why don't you go get changed, Mikey?" said Annie, shaking too many serious thoughts from her head. "Actually, all of you should. I'll make coffee and then I'll give you the grand tour of the whole house... or at least the parts worth seeing," she said with a smile.

Shanice and Michael immediately headed for their rooms, but Janine hung back. Annie had half expected her to. She had been the last out of the cab and so the front door was unlocked in time for her to run directly in, no hanging around getting wet on the doorstep. She wore nothing that showed signs of the rain and therefore didn't feel the need to change. She ran her hands back through her hair, shaking out rogue droplets, and then re-tying it into a ponytail.

"I'm fine. I'll help with the coffee."

Annie smiled and led the way through to the kitchen. Janine followed on in silence, but she was watching her friend closely the whole time. Something was wrong. She couldn't quite put her finger on what it was but there was something, and she suspected it had to do with Richard more than anyone. Of course, she had to broach the subject carefully after this morning's outburst, but broach it she must.

"So, you're happy here, right?" she checked, looking in the cupboards for mugs whilst Annie fired up the recently-purchased coffee machine she was so glad to have purchased.

"Of course," she replied easily. "I mean, sure, I miss you guys, and this is a very different place to New York, but... I don't know, it feels weirdly like home. I never really had that before."

Janine nodded along, knowing that to be true. Anastasia came from a broken home, a mother who wasn't fit to earn the title, and a father who had passed away long ago. She had struck out on her own at a young age and though she had earned her qualifications from community college, she didn't really aspire to anything big. She worked her hours to keep her apartment, spent time with her closest friends, kept herself fit, and dated when the mood took her. It wasn't a very exciting life, but Janine liked to think Annie had been happy up to now. In her own home, though it was miles away from all that she knew, she really seemed to have finally found her place. Via email and video-chat, she was convincingly happy and content. In person, Janine couldn't help but feel something just wasn't right.

"Annie, I don't want to start another fight here but... Well, the whole situation with you and this Richard," she said carefully. "I mean, you said you're not dating, that you don't want to date him, but something is making you quiet and thoughtful. The last time you were this moody, it was a guy."

Anastasia might have argued if she had any argument to give. The truth was, Janine was right. The last man in her life that had meant anything at all was Ray Turner. She had pined for him, knowing they couldn't date because, of all unholy things, he was a teacher at the college. He wasn't actually teaching her, and he was only four years older than she was, but he refused to get close to anyone who was attending classes.

By the time they graduated, Annie was too late. Ray was engaged to another woman and her ship had sailed. Still, the point wasn't the loss of him, or even how long it had taken to get over the guy, it was the confusion in her heart and mind, the way she had felt when she knew she couldn't have him, the way she was feeling now. Janine thought Richard was the guy Annie pined for and yet felt she couldn't have. That wasn't it at all, but the truth was too ridiculous for words.

"J, do you ever...?" she began, watching her friend's expression, wondering just for a second if she dared to tell her what was really on her mind - she didn't. "Do you ever wonder what your life might've been like?" she asked eventually. "I mean, every decision has a consequence, every move you make could end in so many ways. Do you ever think about where else you could've ended up? The people you might've known or not known?"

"Sometimes." Janine shrugged. "Everybody gets a little philosophical now and then, I guess."

There was a long lull in conversation until suddenly another thought occurred to her.

"I'm such an idiot," she said, rolling her eyes. "Annie, I'm sorry. Of course, this isn't about a guy." She literally face-palmed before suddenly reaching to hug her friend. "Sweetheart, you must feel terrible about your grandma, and I get it, I do, but she obviously loved you. She wanted you to have this house, so it's not like she could've been mad at you for not visiting more or whatever."

Annie let out a sigh of a breath as she hugged Janine back and thanked her for being so sweet. She did feel bad about Grandma Rachel sometimes, but that wasn't why her mood was off-kilter lately. Still, it was easier to let Janine believe it for now. A lie by omission was still a lie, but Annie didn't see she had any choice in the matter. The alternative was just too much of a risk.

Chapter 21

Annie had spent four glorious days in the company of her best friends in the world, and so far, it had been wonderful. When she was with Michael, Shanice, and Janine, they just talked about everything, and laughed about most things too. They got completely caught up with each other's lives, sharing tales that were too long or not worth putting into emails before.

Some of the time they spent in the Hall, other times they were in Bennington Town itself. Eva loved to see them and feed them at any given opportunity, and Annie loved that everybody was getting along. Shanice had the widest smile on her face, most especially when she was mentioning Tommy Barrow, and Mike waxed poetic on the wonderful effect the British air and sunshine were having on his complexion and his hair. Janine was her usual quiet self, but she was evidently happy to be there too.

Annie was sure she must be putting a braver face on her worries than before, because Janine hadn't asked again what might be bothering her. The truth was, amongst her friends and having fun, Annie had started to find it easier to forget her troubles. Out of the Hall and having a laugh with people she had known long before Bennington was a blip on her radar, Annie could put Jack right out of her mind, but at night he returned.

Lying in bed and trying to sleep, she stared at the ceiling half-expecting him to appear there. Whenever she was alone, Annie considered calling to him, making him face her, but she never did it. She had secured his promise to remain hidden for as long as her friends were in the house and Jack was only keeping to his word. Annie knew it would be unfair if she asked him to break it, and so she kept her silence.

Valerie Sells

So often she thought about him, wondered how much he had seen and heard since her friends came to visit. Some would be freaked out at the thought of being watched, even Annie herself at one time, but now she almost liked it. Jack had her back, he was watching out for her, maybe even gazing at her with some kind affection. She hoped so.

One who had not looked at her with any kind of nice feeling these past four days was Richard Thomas. It had occurred to Annie that maybe she should call him or go see him at his office, but somehow, she just couldn't bring herself to. Apologising for what she said would be wrong, or so she thought. She had meant what she said, at least, she supposed she must have. She hadn't considered dating Richard, and yet she couldn't really come up with a reason why not. He was a nice guy - good looking, dependable and sweet. They had enough in common and would talk and laugh for hours when they had a mind to. Perhaps she was as foolish as her friends must think for shoving away a perfectly reasonable, decent man. They would think she was stranger still for pining over a ghost.

Even this morning, as the cab went by the office where Richard worked, Annie couldn't help but sigh. She had to fix things with him, she just had to, but today wouldn't be the day, and any more thoughts of either man in her life was just going to spoil the adventure. As much entertainment as she could find for her friends in Bennington and the Hall itself, they were never going to have a fun-packed two weeks in the place, it was just too small. Annie was taking her friends to Dalton, the nearest big city, so they could shop, see the sights, and so forth. They could get there, spend a good number of hours, and be home before dark given the length of the mid-summer days. It ought to make it easier for Annie to

Unleashing the Spirit Within

forget Jack and Richard both for now, and so she tried her best to do so.

* * * * *

Dalton turned out to be a great idea for a place to visit. Annie had never ventured this far but she came armed with an appropriate app on her phone and physical maps as well, just in case the internet failed, so she knew exactly where she was going. That wasn't entirely true because there was a mix up with which bus to get on that resulted in Annie and her friends being carried in entirely the opposite direction to which they intended, but they soon got it sorted out and ended up in all the right places. They laughed about the mistake that didn't really matter and carried on their day's adventuring and shopping.

The exchange rate had been shockingly kind to them, and Shanice was overjoyed by how much she could afford to spend. Annie did advise not overdoing it, given that all this stuff did have to find room in her suitcase to go home, but Shanice was hard to influence when there was shopping to be had.

"You seem happier," said Janine, as she and Annie walked arm in arm behind Shanice and Mike, who were way more into the shopping scene than their friends.

"I am happy," she promised, with a genuine smile, though just being forced to think of why she hadn't been made the expression want to give way.

The moment Jack and Richard both started infiltrating her mind, Annie forced them right back out again. She was having way too much fun to let anything at all bother her today. She could quite happily let the fun go on forever.

"Guys? You want a pit stop for coffee?" asked Mike as he turned around to look at them, gesturing to the well-branded shop on the corner with a grin. "I didn't even know they had these in England!"

"Not exactly a third world country, Mike." Annie rolled her eyes. "I don't know about coffee, but sitting sounds good, and maybe something with ice in it to drink would be good."

Janine and Shanice grabbed a table whilst Michael accompanied Annie to the counter to place their order. She said she would treat everybody today and there was to be no arguments.

The barista turned around with a wide smile and flashing onyx eyes.

"Okay, wow!" Annie gasped, before clearing her throat and giving her order. "One medium skinny latte, one large caramel macchiato, a small flat white, and a medium strawberry and cream frappuccino please."

The guy, whose name badge said 'Chris', grabbed the necessary cups and noted down the details with a nod of his head, then set to work on making each beverage.

"It's just like back home." Mike sighed. "'Cept the help is hotter."

Annie giggled but swatted his shoulder at the same time. She was sure Chris could hear what had been said because he seemed to be smirking when he turned to grab a glass and fill it with ice.

"I thought you wanted a bathroom break while we were here," said Annie pointedly, knowing her friend had been complaining about the lack of decent rest stops on the journey around town so far.

Michael wondered if she was really being one hundred percent considerate or just wanted a little alone time with the barista. Either way, he wasn't really concerned.

"May as well," he said, sighing dramatically. "My finally tuned senses tell me he plays for your side anyway."

Annie felt like literally face-palming as Chris faced her once again, clearly trying not to laugh.

"I am so sorry about him," she apologised. "There's just no filter between the brain and the mouth, y'know?"

"It's fine," he assured her, pouring the last of the drinks out. "So, are you tourists? We don't get that many Americans in Dalton."

"They're tourists." Annie gestured to her friends at the table. "I actually live here now. Little place called Bennington?"

"About ten miles south of here? Yeah, I know it." Chris smiled. "Well, I've driven through it. There's a big house on the hill as you go out of town, isn't there?"

Annie smiled a little too much and bit her lip to stop the laughter that rose in her throat.

"That there is," she said eventually, clearing her throat to cover the humour she was feeling.

Chris finished the drinks and put them carefully onto a tray, wiping his hands off on his apron.

"So, how long have you lived in Bennington?"

Annie wasn't oblivious to how interested he seemed to be in her, and honestly, she didn't mind that much.

"Couple of months now," she told him. "Actually, as much as I call myself an American, I was born in this fine country of yours, to English parents yet."

"Ah, so not really a foreigner after all," he said with a smirk, expression fading as he seemed to replay that sentence in his head. "Sorry, that didn't sound flattering. I didn't mean..."

"It's okay, I know what you meant," she assured him, meeting his eyes.

Chris looked transfixed for a moment and Annie was hardly less so. There was no denying this guy was what Shanice and Mike would term a 'Grade A hottie'. It wasn't that she wasn't interested exactly, he was probably a really nice guy, but it came as a surprise lately for a regular guy to be interested in her.

"I know you've probably heard this a hundred times before, it sounds like such a line," Chris said then, "but you've got amazing eyes."

She felt herself blushing and wasn't even sure why. Anastasia was not the easily embarrassed type, not usually. Still, he was being very intense in the way he was looking at her.

"Actually, not often been said, but thank you," she told him, digging in her purse for the cash to pay. "As pick-up lines go, I've heard worse."

"Really?"

"Oh yeah. Usually guys find out my name is Anastasia and all I get are princess nicknames and 'run away with me' jokes. Gets a little old."

"Still, that's a beautiful name. It suits you," he said smoothly, before realising she was waiting patiently to pay for her drinks order. He swiftly punched the numbers into the till and told her the total.

Annie handed over the cash with a smile. "Keep the change."

"I would but... Well, that would make me feel awkward if I took out," he said as he pushed the till drawer closed with a snap, putting his hand out to give her the two coins she was owed.

Annie picked up the tray and shook her head.

"Not that I'm not flattered, but seriously, keep the change."

As much as she felt bad for shutting him down that way, Annie couldn't help the grin on her face as she headed for the table where her friends were waiting on their drinks. It still felt kind of nice to know she was worth the attention of a hottie like Chris, and she couldn't resist telling her friends about it.

"So, the barista just hit on me."

"Really?" asked Janine, craning her next to see the guy in question. "Wow, he's really cute."

"Yeah," Annie chuckled, "and probably barely out of high school."

"Like anybody cares about that anymore," Shanice waved away such a suggestion with a flick of her wrist. "And honey, you could pass for twenty, no problem."

Annie smiled and thanked her friend for being so kind.

"Seriously though, he's not my type."

"Who's not?" Mike wanted to know as he joined them. "The barista? Since when is hot not your type?"

Anastasia listened as her friends discussed Chris, how cute he was, and how crazy she must be if she didn't like him. The fact was, Annie wasn't trying to deny the guy was good looking, and he might be a really nice person too, she just didn't want to date him. She kind of didn't feel the need to be dating anybody right now. She figured it was because she had so much other stuff going on, everything with the Hall and such. Her head was always full of schedules, task lists and the like, up until her friends arrived anyway. She didn't have the time or the inclination for a man in her life. There was Richard, of course, but he had been more like a best friend than a boyfriend, at least until she upset him. Annie knew she really had to fix that. Then there was Jack.

"Annie?" prompted Janine when her friend zoned out again.

"C'mon, sweetie, make the guy's day," Mike literally nudged her towards the counter.

Annie glanced back and realised Chris was still looking over at every spare moment, and with a winning smile on his face too.

"God, why is everybody so worried about my lack of dating lately!" she said, laughing into her words and proving she wasn't angry, just amused. "I'm just... I'm not in a dating mood lately. I have so much to think about, I'm not interested, y'know?"

"I cannot even pretend to understand that," said Shanice, stirring her drink vigorously.

"Aaw, poor guy has it bad." Mike sighed. "He's making goo-goo eyes at the back of your head."

Annie glanced over her shoulder one more time, and Chris winked at her before serving the next patron in the queue.

"Oh, God!" she groaned, turning back and covering her face with her hands.

The rest of the table laughed with her. It was too silly, and all very childish, but Annie was having fun today and she figured that was all that mattered. She could use a few days of carefree silliness whilst she had the chance. Everything would become lists and schedules, and mysterious men in the dark again before long. It was nice just to laugh and flirt and be crazy for now. She intended to enjoy it for just as long as it lasted.

Chapter 22

One whole week of having her friends here at Bennington Hall with her, and Annie was sure she had never had so much fun. It was going too quickly and she was acutely aware of that, but she couldn't bear to complain. They talked and laughed like they always had, no weirdness or issues borne out of her supposedly being rich now or living so far away. Nothing had really changed in her relationships with these people that she looked upon like family, and she was so enjoying having them in her life for just as long as they were here.

There was one black spot in the bright, shiny time Anastasia was having, and for a change it wasn't the creature of supposed darkness that haunted her house. Though in the first few days, Annie had missed having Jack around and wanted to talk to him about what happened before he disappeared, she had kind of compartmentalised him in her mind now and was okay with leaving him be until her friends went home. He was still there, she knew he was, and it wasn't as if he was likely to disappear permanently whilst her back was turned. She cared about him still and longed to know what he was thinking and feeling, what it had meant that he could touch her the way he had, but what bothered her more just lately was Richard.

Here was a real live human man who had been nothing but kind to her, and the more Annie thought on it, the more she knew she had insulted him. She really ought to apologise for that. She still meant what she said about not really being interested in dating him, at least not right now, but she should have been more thoughtful in how she said it. Seeing Richard walk past her on the other side of the street without so much as a glance made her stomach lurch. She needed to talk to him and it needed to be now.

"Annie, are you coming?" asked Janine, the last of her friends to go into Eva's cafe for lunch.

"Er, you guys go, I'll catch up in a minute," she replied, barely turning to glance back before bolting across the quiet road to the lawyer's office.

It occurred to her only as she reached the stairs that Richard's uncle was likely to be up there as well. That wouldn't be any good if she was planning a private conversation and an apology, but then she hadn't seen his car out front, now that she thought on it. George Thomas drove a big silver Beamer and it was hard not to notice it when it was present. She shook her head, knocked on the door and stepped inside. A sigh of relief escaped Annie's lips when she realised Richard actually was alone.

"Hey," she greeted him before he had quite got around to looking up to see who was there.

"Good morning," he replied stiffly when he saw it was her. "What can I do for you?"

"Well, for starters you can stop with the cold shoulder treatment, please. Richard, I'm sorry about the other day."

"Really?" he said with a look. "Taken you long enough to come and tell me."

He knew very well he was being childish and cutting off his nose to spite his face, as the saying went. Annie had come to say she was sorry and she certainly looked as if she meant it. Richard knew damn well she had been busy entertaining her friends the last few days, so it was hardly surprising she hadn't come to see him sooner. He was just making things more difficult than he needed to because his pride had been hurt. He knew all this, and yet Richard couldn't help his snippy attitude somehow.

Unleashing the Spirit Within

"Look, at first I was just mad that you were mad and... it was stupid," said Annie, throwing her hands in the air. "I admit, I did not handle the whole thing very well, but my friends... They just kept going on and on and on, and sometimes I lose my patience with them. I guess I forgot how they could be or something," she admitted helplessly, coming further into the room and closer to Richard's desk that he seemed determined to stay at, focused on paperwork he couldn't really be this deep into so quickly. "I never meant to hurt your feelings or anything. I just needed Shanice and Mike to stop making assumptions, going on and on at me about how you and I were dating when they knew we weren't. It's ridiculous!"

"Is it?" he asked, looking more at the pen he was moving between his hands than at her. "Is it so ridiculous that you and I might be more than friends?" he asked, eyes darting up to meet hers then.

Annie didn't really know how to answer that. She didn't want to make this situation worse, but she really couldn't lie to Richard either. If she cared less it would actually be easier to just cut him out of her life, but she didn't want that. She had missed him so much these past few days. Annie hadn't expected to feel his absence as much as she had, and dreaded to think how much worse it might've been without her visiting friends to distract her. She had to get this right.

"Richard, it's not that I don't... I mean, you're a great guy, the best I've met in a very long time," she told him honestly. "I love that we're friends, and I don't want that to change, I just..."

"You just?" he prompted, unwilling to let her off the hook it seemed.

He got up from his chair at last as he waited for her answer, standing before her and staring down into her eyes with such an intensity, Annie couldn't bear to keep his gaze, and yet couldn't look away either. He was such a nice guy and it would make life that much easier if she could just be with him, but something stopped her, something she couldn't really explain without slipping back into way too many crazy thoughts about a man that didn't even really exist.

"Richard," she said, sighing. "Can't we just be friends?" she practically begged him.

He shook his head almost imperceptibly. A part of him really wanted to tell her no, that it was all or nothing because it was killing him by degrees being so close to her and knowing he didn't stand a chance, even if he could summon the nerve to make a move. At the same time, Richard knew he had been particularly miserable and lonely these past few days since his spat with Anastasia. Having her in his life as a much-needed friend had to be better than nothing, however much it hurt.

"Just tell me one thing, please. Is there someone else that you... that you're seeing, or want to be seeing?"

Annie opened her mouth to answer and then closed it again fast. If only she could explain it to him, it might actually help both sides of this conversation, but she didn't know where to begin. There was no way to tell a guy that cared about her this much that the reason they couldn't date was because she was kind of seeing the ghost that haunted her house!

"It's complicated," she opted for eventually, which was a version of the truth at least. "All I know for sure right now is that I had the four best friends in the world last week, and now I'm back down to three. I wanna fix that."

Richard looked away a moment, shaking his head, but the smile that crept onto his lips was irrepressible.

She was too sweet, too beautiful, just too much of everything good to be denied.

"You've got four," he promised her. "And I'm sorry too. I probably over-reacted, it's just, well, fragile male ego, you know?"

"I know. Thank you," she said then, pushing herself forward to wrap her arms around him in a tight hug,

Richard hugged back for as long as he could, breathing her in, enjoying her body against his own. This was perhaps as close as he would ever get to Anastasia Addams, so he was going to make the most of it. He said he would be her friend again and meant it, but that wasn't going to be easy, not at all.

* * * * *

A cab came by Bennington Hall in the evening to pick up the lady of the house and her three guests and take them over to the other side of town where a party was taking place. It was Shanice's new 'friend' Tommy that had invited them to his birthday celebrations, and all were eager to go at the time of the invitation. Unfortunately, when the time rolled around to leave, Annie wasn't really in the mood. She claimed a headache that was very real, but insisted the others go ahead without her. They protested at first, but gave in eventually. After all, Shanice so wanted to see Tommy, and Mike never could refuse a party invite. Janine might have been more insistent about staying behind. In fact, she was the most willing to drop out, if needed, but in the end, she decided to go, if only to keep an eye on the others.

They left in a flurry of goodbyes and a cloud of mixed cologne and body spray. Anastasia was glad enough to breathe the fresh air beyond the front door a while before taking herself back inside. She stood alone in the foyer and looked round at the silent hall and stairs. Immediately, a voice in her head told her to call for Jack, but she resisted the urge. She really didn't feel good. This would not be a good time to try and figure out whatever was going on with them. Besides, he was keeping his promise about staying invisible for as long as her friends were here and enticing him to do otherwise wasn't fair on anybody.

Annie held her aching head a moment, deciding she definitely needed to take a couple of aspirin before it got any worse. After that, she thought a nice relaxing bath might be in order, with some bubbles and candles maybe. It would be good just to relax for an evening. She hadn't done much of that since she moved here. The house was in such a state when she arrived, there really wasn't anywhere in it a person could feel genuinely at ease, and then she was always so busy working, arranging work for others, researching into Jack's untimely death, or organising things for her friends' visit. Tonight was perhaps the first and only night so far that Annie would get to genuinely relax.

With the drugs put to work on the pain in her head, Annie took herself off to the bathroom and filled the tub. She threw in a generous amount of bubble bath and swooshed her hand in the water.

Within minutes, she was sinking into the warmth and bubbles, eyes closed and all her worries drifting away. The radio played softly in the background, not her usual station which would be screaming some raucous rock or punk song, but a nice relaxing classical piece to help her fully relax.

The bath worked so well, that Annie didn't even realise she was falling asleep until she was gone. She woke very suddenly, a good half an hour later, to find the water mostly cold but her headache almost completely gone too. She wondered what had woken her at first, until suddenly she heard a noise.

Sitting up fast, Annie reached for her towel and practically leapt out of her bath. She listened carefully for any further sounds, thinking it unlikely her friends were back from the party yet. A quick glance at the time proved it was way too early for their return, but they had her keys, so they ought to be the only people who could get in. Nobody else ought to be trying to visit, since most people would assume she had left for the party when her friends did.

Anastasia felt vulnerable. Usually she was okay, she knew her self-defence moves and all, she was confident she could handle most situations. This was different. There was somebody she couldn't see out there in her house, in the dark, since most of the curtains were drawn and hardly any lights left on. There could be more than one person, strangers come to burgle her home, or maybe attack her, possibly both.

Grabbing her robe from the rail, she pulled it on, letting the towel fall to the floor. She had no actual clothes with her, so this would have to do. She looked around for something to arm herself with, smiling slightly when she spotted the socks abandoned in the corner. She never tried it before but she had seen in a film once where someone put a bar of soap into the end of sock and made a passable weapon. Constructing something similar for herself, she opened the bathroom door and crept out. Moving carefully down the hall, she listened for any further sounds, looked in all directions for the slightest movement.

For a moment, Annie started to wonder if she had imagined this whole thing, or if maybe whoever had been there was now gone. She knew her first instinct had been right when there was another clattering sound, seemingly coming from the living room she alone used. The door wasn't locked, but she hadn't let her friends in there and it was not the first place they would wander to if they had come home early, which was something she couldn't imagine them doing anyway.

Moving down to the door, Annie swallowed hard and braced herself for whatever came next. Through the gap where the door had been left ajar she could see a shadow moving by the light of the only lamp. Just one person, which was preferable to a gang, but still she was wary. Annie considered running back to her room and calling the cops, but it might be too late by the time they came. Still, disturbing a burglar that could be armed with a knife or a gun, that wasn't smart. She had learnt from the streets of New York, and just because Bennington was a much quieter, less crime-ridden place, she was still cautious.

Whilst she was trying to make up her mind on how to proceed, an almighty crash of thunder sounded overheard, startling both Annie and the intruder. There shouldn't be a storm, not today. The weather was mild and pleasant, and forecast to be so for days yet.

"Jack?" she whispered towards the ceiling.

Another rumble came, louder than the first. The supposed burglar turned around, and that was when Annie stopped being afraid and started being angry.

"What the hell do you think you're doing?!" she yelled, flinging open the door and brandishing her unlikely weapon.

George Thomas seemed to shoot three feet in the air with surprise, and yet got his composure back remarkably quickly, even managing to smile at Annie. It was a false nasty smile that she didn't care for one bit.

Unleashing the Spirit Within

"Good evening, Miss. Addams," he said, nodding politely. "I do apologise, I assumed you were out. I did knock but there was no answer and the door was unlocked."

Annie scoffed at that. There was no way her front door had been left unlocked, and even if it had been, he should not have been letting himself into her home unannounced.

"I repeat, what the hell do you think you're doing?!" she asked again, another crack of thunder sounding swiftly behind a lightning flash beyond the curtained windows.

"I came to retrieve some paperwork of mine," said George, seemingly as cross as she was, despite the fact he was the guilty party. "Documents belonging to myself and your grandmother, dear Mrs. Wickfield. When you didn't answer and I found the door unlocked, it seemed to make sense to just come in and help myself. She never did mind."

"Grandma Rachel may not have minded, but I do!" she said forcefully. "You want papers from my house? You ask me and I will find them for you, if I think you need them, but don't you ever come busting into my home unannounced ever again!"

"I'm not going to stand here and be spoken to like that," George grumbled.

"No, you're right, you're not," Annie replied angrily. "You're going to get out of my house before I call the cops and have you arrested for breaking and entering, trespassing, and anything else I can stick you for. You're the lawyer, you know I have the right!"

George looked furious, but then so did Annie. She was right in what she said and he knew it, so he had no choice but to leave. He did so in a flurry of grumbles and complaints, which Annie duly ignored.

She followed him to the front door and bolted it behind George just as soon as he was gone. She would go on to check all the other doors were secure after that, before something strange occurred to her. Outside the sky was clear still, even as the moon took the sun's place in the sky for the night. Thunder and lightning so out of place like that had to be Jack, but she figured it also had to be significant.

"What are you trying to tell me?" she asked.

There was no reply from Jack, but that didn't mean Annie was giving up. She was now more determined than ever to find out the truth about this house and all that went on in its past, and she would do it too.

Chapter 23

Annie had deliberately been in bed when her friends got home from the party. She couldn't face explaining what happened with George or how it had made her feel. Bad enough that he had dared to break into her home, and on top of that been so rude to her. He had been searching for something, not her jewellery or money, but papers of some kind. His claim was that Grandma Rachel had paperwork he needed hidden away, but Annie wasn't buying. If that was the case, he could have retrieved it before Annie ever moved in. It all made her very suspicious if she thought about it too much, but it was the sounds of thunder and flashes of lightning echoing around the house that really had her attention. When outside her window the sky was dark but clear, not a cloud to be seen, she knew the anomaly in the weather had to be Jack trying to tell her something.

Though they had made a pact about him not putting in an appearance for as long as her friends were around, Annie had still called to Jack and begged him to be there, just for a few minutes. She knew the others wouldn't be back for a long time yet, and given his ability to disappear and reappear quicker than a blink, Annie couldn't see a risk. Either Jack was very serious about keeping his word, or he just wasn't ready to talk yet. She wondered then at the big deal he seemed willing to make over George being in the house. It had to mean something. When she added together all the evidence - the way Richard's uncle disliked her so much on top of the break in and Jack's other-worldly reaction - Annie knew it just had to be important.

She had quite decided that George had to have more to do with Bennington Hall than just being Rachel's lawyer back in the day. Maybe he had been in and around Bennington as far back as when Jack was around, though Annie had asked Eva about the family history and she insisted it didn't go as far back as all that. Something was strange though, something didn't add up, and Anastasia was determined to find out what it was. She told Jack as much that very night, making sure he understood that eventually she would solve the mystery of both him and the house, whether he wanted to tell her the full story or not. Clearly, he didn't right now.

It was two days later when she got up early and decided to head into town before her friends were even out of bed. She left a note telling them she had gone for a walk to fetch groceries from Bennington, but she would back in a couple of hours and they could plan what they wanted to do with the day that was a blank canvas so far.

The truth was, whilst they did need bread and milk, plus a few other things, Annie's chief reason for heading into town was to talk to Richard. Things just weren't the same with them since she snapped about not wanting to date him and seemingly caused a rift. They had sort of made up, and yet when she tried to talk to him in the street he all but blanked her, and every text she sent had been ignored but one. The only one he answered was a direct invitation which received a very brief response - 'Can't, sorry.'

Things were not right and Annie knew it. She needed to talk to him face to face and the only way to do that was to go to the office alone and just have it out with him again. It bugged her that he would accept her apology and then be so off with her, but at the same time Annie felt bad for causing the problem in the first place. She really hadn't meant to, and hadn't realised how much she might miss Richard if he wasn't around. Even with her friends staying at the Hall, there was something missing, and that something was Richard.

When she got into town, she headed straight to Eva's cafe. Being just a little way down the street from the Thomas & Thomas office, and with Eva being as observant as she was, there was no doubt in Annie's mind that she would be able to tell her if George was in work today, without the need to get close enough to check for his car.

"Well, no, my dear," Eva told her with a shake of the head. "Old George won't be in there, but then neither is our Richard," she explained. "From what I hear they had some serious business to attend to in that London."

"Oh." Annie must've looked as crestfallen as she felt.

"Not to worry, love. They'll be back in a few days, I'm sure of it." Eva smiled encouragingly. "You two still not right since that falling out you had?"

"Not really," Annie confessed. "I mean, I meant what I said about not wanting to date Richard, but then it comes to the why and I don't even know exactly."

The only reason Annie really had not to want to get closer to Richard was a man that barely existed in this plane of reality. She couldn't say for sure if things would be different with her and Richard if Jack wasn't in the picture. She certainly couldn't find fault with her good friend the lawyer, except for maybe his profession itself, and Annie would never be so shallow as to judge on that alone. Richard was good looking, sweet and kind, helpful and a good laugh. He seemed to have had this tragically lonely, sad little life, but any time Annie managed to get him out of his shell a little bit, he was so very much alive and just a great person to spend time with.

"Oh, Annie." Eva sighed. "Honestly, sometimes I'm glad I'm past all the bother of young men and courting and such."

Anastasia wasn't really listening for the moment. Dating hadn't been a huge factor in her life even before now. She had dates in high school, just like most average teenage girls, but nothing serious. When she was older, there was Ray at community college, but that was a mess from the beginning and nothing ever actually happened as such. Since then, she had seen a couple of guys in a casual, going out to dinner, kind of a way. Nothing serious there either. Now here she was, though she was loath to admit it, pining for a ghost and feeling awfully confused over a guy that seemed to like her more than she ever expected he might.

"Eva, how long have you known Richard?" she asked curiously.

"Ooh, must be going on five or six years now," she considered. "Always such a sweet lad. Quiet though, but then I s'pose that's to be expected. He lost his parents so sudden, and they were very close from what I heard."

Annie had to agree that would probably affect a person profoundly. Her own experience of family was very diffcrent, a father she barely knew and a mother who didn't care. To have people you loved and adored torn away, those that not just created you but raised you and loved you for twenty years, Annie couldn't even begin to imagine how much that would hurt, what damage it would do to a young man's confidence and such. Poor Richard, and yet somehow, she didn't think he would want her to feel sorry for him.

"C'mon, love," said Eva when she caught Annie in another daze. "Keep thinking that hard you'll hurt yourself," she teased, at which her friend laughed.

"You're probably not wrong," she agreed, even as her mind spun on to a new topic that had been bothering her.

Unleashing the Spirit Within

Richard was one issue to be dealt with, but George was a whole other ballgame. There was a voice in Annie's head suggesting quite strongly that the reason the elder Mr. Thomas suddenly had business in London was so he wasn't around to be accused of anything. Annie hadn't told a soul about the night he broke into her home, mostly because she didn't see the point. Telling her friends would scare them and make them want to call the cops. The same applied to anyone in town. Annie had hoped she could pick Richard's brain on the topic of his uncle's odd behaviour but that certainly wasn't going to happen now.

Annie couldn't find anything missing after George left, and no matter how she tried, she couldn't summon up a real appearance from Jack. The thunder and lightning had been enough though. She was sure there had to be some real reason why Jack disliked not just George but Richard too. At first Annie had selfishly assumed she was the only reason, that Jack just didn't want her being friends with any other guys. Now she was suspicious of George in particular. She just had a niggling feeling that wouldn't quit when it came to that man and what happened to Jack. Richard had to be in the clear. At twenty-eight, he simply wasn't old enough to know what happened to Jack Green, but George was a different story.

"How long did you say George Thomas had been in Bennington?" she checked with Eva then.

"Oh, well, longer than the lad certainly, but not half so long as me," Eva considered. "Ten years or fifteen perhaps?"

Annie continued to frown as she realised that wasn't long enough either, not for him to have been around when the Hall was abandoned and a murder had to have taken place. It still puzzled her that the local library had no newspapers that talked of a fatal stabbing at the old house. Somebody had to have reported it, found a body, something. It made no sense otherwise.

"Are you alright, Annie?" Eva checked after another long moment of too thoughtful silence.

"Not really," she admitted, hopping down from her stool. "But I will be," she promised, finding a smile. "Thanks for your help, Eva."

"Well, you're welcome, love. Though I'm not quite sure what I did."

Annie didn't have a reply for that, she just hurried to go fetch her groceries and then head back to the Hall. Suddenly she had a plan for what she wanted to do today, and her friends would be equally as happy about it as she was, of that Annie was certain.

* * * * *

Michael and Shanice were in their element when they were shopping, and they had so enjoyed Dalton the last time, Annie knew they would be happy to return for Round Two. They didn't have much money left to spend, but that didn't stop them from trying on the clothes they liked and testing the free samples from the make-up counter. They barely looked up when Annie said she was just popping across the street to the library for a little while. Janine took more notice, asking why on earth Annie would want to go there. It wasn't that she was exactly illiterate, but Anastasia had never been a great reader and only ever had a library card back home for the books she needed to study on her college courses.

"There's just a couple of things I need to check about the Hall, that's all," she said, smiling easily, because it really wasn't a lie.

Unleashing the Spirit Within

Before any arguments could be made, Annie hurried out of the mall and straight across the street to the Dalton Public Library. It was easily five times the size of its counterpart in Bennington Town, maybe bigger actually, spread over three floors of an old stone-crafted building. Annie hurried up the steps and in, quickly checking the floor plan for which section she needed. There would be more information here, potential records about her home that had been archived at the larger library.

Inside half an hour, Annie had located some large books full of newspaper articles and was flipping through the pages for 1978. There were several volumes for that year alone and she had no idea which month to focus on. She found a lot of references to Bennington by using the indexes but it didn't narrow the search by much. She was so focused on what she was doing she didn't realise somebody was approaching her until they suddenly sat down in the next seat over and spoke.

"This is important to your house?" asked Janine with a look.

"What are you doing here, J?" Annie replied, startled by her presence. "How'd you even...?"

"Find you? I asked the nice guy at the front desk where the American went to." She rolled her eyes. "There's not exactly a lot of us in this place. So, something is going on with you," she said then, a statement not a question because she already knew it was true. "Annie, you're just... Something is off with you, and the longer we're here, the more I think it has to do with the Hall. I just can't tell what exactly. Before, you let me think it was because of your grandma, but now I'm not buying. What is going on?" she asked desperately, hand going over Annie's own on the table.

She was genuinely worried. Unfortunately, all Annie could think was that if she told her the whole truth she might be even more freaked out. Still, there seemed to be no other way forward and it would be a huge weight off, this whole burden lifted, if she shared it with someone else.

Janine was pretty open-minded about most things, she might understand. If anybody was going to, Annie thought it would probably be her.

"J, I... I know that something happened in my house, way before I owned it. Before my grandma even had it," she explained in a low voice so nobody else would hear, not that anyone was particularly close to them or listening anyway. "A guy was murdered."

"Woah!" Janine reacted with surprise. "Uh, okay. Who told you this?"

Annie took a deep breath, practically wincing at the sound of her own words as she replied; "The guy that was killed."

She had her eyes half closed as she anticipated a myriad of over-the-top reactions from Janine. Maybe she ought to have known better. When she forced herself to look properly at her friend, she realised Janine looked perfectly calm, if not surprised.

"Okay," she said, shaking her head a little as if to clear a fog that had landed in it. "Um, like a voice told you, or...?"

"A guy, or at least he looks like a guy. A really hot guy," Annie admitted awkwardly. "I don't know what he is, even he doesn't know for sure. He's just... Well, he's dead, but he's there, and he can talk to me and I can see him, but only if he wants me to."

"So, he's a... ghost?" her friend checked, feeling strange just asking the question.

"Kind of, I guess?" Annie shrugged. "I don't know, J, I just... I like him, and I know that's probably the craziest part of all of this, which is really saying something given the subject matter, but he's... he's different to any other person I ever met."

"Well, yeah," said Janine incredulously, given they were talking about a spirit of some kind. "But all the research is, what? To find out who killed him?"

"Exactly." Annie nodded once. "I can't find anything. No police reports, no newspaper articles about a murder, nada, zip. The only things I have to go on is that I know it happened in '78, I have the victim's name, and... Well, there's a chance that George Thomas was involved."

"Thomas? Any relation to-?"

"Richard? His uncle." She nodded, answering the question before it was hardly even asked.

"Wow." Janine looked across the table at the books waiting to be searched for clues and answers. "Okay, where do I start?" she asked then, dumping her bags on the ground.

Annie almost laughed with the surprise of the offer.

"Um, if you want to look for anything about the owners of the Hall between these years," she said then, pulling forward a large leather-bound book and handing over one of her many pieces of paper full of notes. "I have almost a complete timeline, but there's a gap right here."

"Right around the time of the murder." Janine nodded her understanding. "I'm on it."

She smiled, digging right into the research without a moment's pause.

Annie sat staring across at her friend for a moment. First, completely stunned by how well Janine had taken her crazy news, and second, how willing she was to give up shopping and fun for dusty books and random research into a murder of all things. There was a reason why they were such good friends, Annie always knew it, but now more than ever.

"Annie?" said Janine then, not even looking up as she spoke. "This hot guy that haunts your house, he have a name?"

"Jack Green," she replied with the strangest smile on her lips.

Janine recognised the look the second she glanced up and saw it. Annie was in love, with the ghost apparently. It explained a lot, but was also kind of tragic. For now, she wouldn't say anything about that, there was time to deal with that particular hurdle later. In the meantime, they needed the truth, which hopefully the books in front of them could provide. One step at a time.

Chapter 24

It was starting to feel pointless and stupid, pouring over all these books and papers. Annie had been here over an hour and Janine nearly half that time. If they stayed too much longer, Shanice and Michael would start to wonder where they were, maybe even come looking for them. Annie didn't want to have to explain. It wasn't that she didn't love or trust her other two friends just as much as Janine, but they both had a tendency to be a little flighty and dramatic, where J was calm in the face of almost all things. She had taken talk of ghosts, murder, and the like without a hint of panic or drama. Annie was grateful for that. She would be even more grateful if they could find some evidence of what the hell happened at Bennington Hall in 1978 that was so significant and apparently difficult to uncover.

"Bingo!" said Janine suddenly, scribbling into Annie's notes, filling in a previous gap. "No luck with the seventies, but this name right here?" she showed her friend, pointing to 'Emilia Bradbury' on the page, owner of the Hall way back before the Great War. "Bradbury was her maiden name. She inherited from her father right around the time she got married... to George Thomas."

"No way!" gasped Annie, leaning over to see the entry in the book that said just that. "Well, that can't be the same guy." She shook her head. "The George Thomas that I know, he's like fifty or so. That's way too young to be Emilia's husband."

"Could be related though." Janine shrugged. "Fathers name sons after themselves all the time, especially back then."

Annie sat back in her seat thinking carefully about what she had just seen. It was completely possible the

Thomas family owned the Hall way back when, long before Eva would have even been around to know about it. Besides, it seemed that the Bradburys out-ranked the Thomas clan in society. If Annie understood correctly, they could easily have lived under the wife's name if they chose, at least for the time that they owned Bennington Hall.

Focusing back on the book in front of her for a moment, Annie flipped to the next reference to her home without any real confidence of finding anything. The top of the page stated 14th September 1978 and she ran her finger down the text, searching out the relevant article about Bennington Hall. Her eyes widened when she realised she had found it, the word 'murder' springing out at her too suddenly.

"Oh my God, finally!" she gasped. "'Police received an anonymous tip about a possible disturbance in the abandoned Bennington Hall on Tuesday night'," she read aloud in a quiet voice.

Janine leaned over to see and they both continued to read in silence then. There were no real details, just that a body had been found, and police were investigating a possible murder. The deceased was described exactly as Jack looked, including his clothes and the colour of his eyes and hair. Annie shook her head, feeling tears fill her eyes as she continued to read. It was so shocking to see it in black and white, the exact description of how Jack had come to die by a blade through his body. She heard it from his own lips, and yet somehow this was worse. She couldn't explain exactly why, but it hurt.

"This all has to mean something." Janine shook her head. "The connection with this George guy, and now proof there really was a murder?"

Annie nodded slowly, swallowing down the emotion that was thick in her throat.

Unleashing the Spirit Within

"We need to trace the family tree," she said suddenly, looking around at the shelves. "We don't have long before the others are going to come looking for us, but we have to piece this together now we've come this far," she told Janine desperately.

"Okay. We can do this," she agreed. "You remember those last-minute cram sessions we had before our finals? The amount we learnt inside a couple of hours was unprecedented, and we passed those tests with flying colours," she told her friend with an encouraging smile. "We can do this."

Annie nodded her agreement and dived out of her seat. Census records were all online these days, and there were half a dozen free computers across the room from where they were. They could do this. If she could just track George Thomas down his family tree from the old owner, they would have a potential motive for him wanting the Hall back for himself. She recalled seeing references to raves and squatters in the Hall up to the date of the body being discovered. It all had to fit together somehow and now she had Janine to help her solve the puzzle, maybe they could do it. She really hoped so.

* * * * *

It would be two days before Annie and Janine were alone together again. This was the last day the three visitors would spend in Bennington Hall. Tomorrow they left for the airport and flew back to New York, not knowing when they might see Annie again. It was painful to think about, and yet at the same time, there was an odd sense of relief in Annie, knowing she would have her home to herself again. She felt horrible about it, but she needed the freedom right now. Above all, she needed to talk to Jack.

Shanice wanted to go into town to say goodbye to all the friends she had made. That was pretty much code for kissing the face off her guy, Tommy, and they all knew it. Michael said he would go with her, as he would genuinely like to see Eva and some of the other people in town before he left. Janine claimed to have packing still to do. Even though they all knew she was the most organised amongst them and ought to have been done days ago, nobody argued. Annie stayed back with Janine because she already knew the plan. They needed to talk about the research they had done, that which had continued for Annie on her own computer when they got back here, and was now as complete as it could be without outside help.

"Did you find the connection?" asked Janine the moment the door was closed on Shanice and Mike, their cab well out of sight by now.

Annie nodded, but didn't say a word. She grabbed Janine by the sleeve and walked her through the house, straight out the back door into the garden. They sat down together on the old swing seat and Annie pulled a wad of folded paper from the back pocket of her jeans.

"The old George and the current George? Definitely related," she explained, as Janine read her friend's scribbling and saw the truth of it.

It seemed George Thomas was in fact the great nephew of those that owned the Hall before the First World War, which would certainly give him a reason for thinking he had some right to the place. It would be motive enough for some to kill, and actually, as it turned out, he would have been old enough.

"He was eighteen," said Janine, reading carefully. "When Jack died, he could've been here. He could've..."

Unleashing the Spirit Within

"I know." Annie nodded. "I can't find any proof. There's nothing else about the 'potential murder' anywhere that I can get to."

Janine sighed and continued reading Annie's notes. She had a lot of information, but none of it was definitive proof of anything at all. Richard's uncle was the right age to have been around when Jack was killed, and if he knew he had a connection to Bennington Hall he might've had a motive to commit murder, but only if Jack owned the house. There was nothing to say he ever had, and the way Annie described the guy, she couldn't imagine for a moment he ever did.

"Doesn't add up, does it?" said Annie sadly. "I so wanted to be able to tell him what really happened, J. I want him to... I want him to have peace."

Tears were filling her eyes and Janine's heart broke for her friend. Annie was such a good person, when all was said and done. She wanted others to be happy, those she cared for, and hated to see the people she loved suffer. This Jack Green, the man who apparently haunted her house, he had clearly come to mean a lot to her. Janine knew some might find that crazy, but strangely she could understand it. Maybe it was because she knew Annie so well. Maybe it was just because she was open-minded enough to believe that it was possible to fall for a spirit that was hardly even there.

"Hey, come on," she said, putting an arm around her friend and pulling her close. "It'll work out. Just tell him what you know so far. He might even be able to piece it together from there. I mean, he has to know something about what happened, right?"

Annie wasn't sure about that. She never had got out of Jack just exactly how much he did know about his own death. He recalled the actual moment of dying with shocking clarity that had made Annie feel genuinely sick, but he never spoke of who was there, why he was even in the Hall that fateful night.

Wiping her cheeks dry with both hands, Annie took her papers back from Janine and found them stained by her own tears. So much for all her research, maybe the only person who could help her fill in the final gaps was Jack himself. At least tonight she would be able to ask him. This silly deal they made about him keeping hidden for as long as her friends stayed in the Hall would be broken once they were gone.

"Are you sure you're gonna to be okay?" Janine checked.

"Yeah, I will be," Annie promised, forcing a smile. "And I don't want you to think I'm not glad you came here, J, any of you. I couldn't tell Mike and Shanice about all this, I wouldn't know where to start, but that doesn't mean-"

"I know," her friend assured her. "I know you love them and trust them. I do too, but this is big, and a lot for anybody to take in, believe me. I won't say a word."

"Thanks." Annie smiled a little more genuinely this time. "For everything, Janine, thank you."

They hugged then, and Annie looked over her friend's shoulder up at the back of the Hall, wondering how much Jack knew of the research she had been doing these last two weeks, wondering what answers he might have himself that she could never uncover alone. Tonight, she might just find out, once and for all.

Chapter 25

Anastasia arrived home from the airport where she had waved her friends off and watched their plane leave for New York. Her heart ached, and not just because she had no idea how long it would be before she saw them again. She felt bad because a part of her was glad they were gone. She loved Shanice, Michael, and Janine, every single one of them in different ways that she couldn't begin to explain. They were her family, but right now, she needed them to not be here.

The only way to figure this whole thing out was for Annie to talk to Jack, a spirit she couldn't summon up until her friends had gone home. Now here was the moment, and Annie had the shakes.

Walking through to her own living room, she opened up the door and smiled at the sight. It looked just as it should. George hadn't broken anything or even needed to force the door. Anastasia had tidied up shortly after chasing him out of the Hall and now it was as she left it before her friends arrived two weeks ago, almost as if no time had passed at all.

Taking a deep breath, Annie went to the centre of the rug, tossed her jacket onto the nearby table and kicked off her shoes. It was odd, when it came to the very moment of calling Jack to show himself again, she almost felt as if she couldn't do it. Her hands were shaking, her heart thumped in her chest. Annie would say it was because she was nervous to try and talk to him about such a serious topic. Jack never seemed to want to discuss how he died, except for that one occasion all out of the blue when he told her the way he was run through with a sword. It was so much more than just the subject matter that was making Annie feel strange about seeing Jack again.

Valerie Sells

The last time he was here, they had been so close, and when he reached out to touch her, she felt his fingers against her skin. It ought to have been impossible, and that required as much explanation as anything else. Maybe she would start there, build up to talk of what happened to him years ago, potentially at the hands of George Thomas.

"My friends have gone home," she said into the empty air around her, turning a full circle as she spoke. "I watched the plane take off. So, now it's just you and me again. Jack?"

"I heard you."

Annie couldn't control the smile that spread across her face as she turned to face him. The sight of him only made the shivers running through her body all the worse, or better, depending on how she chose to think of the reaction she was experiencing. Of course, he looked the same. Had he been absent for two years rather than two weeks, he would still be as he had always been, and Annie felt stupid for expecting anything else. Pushing her hair back off her face in some kind of nervous gesture she couldn't explain, she finally spoke again.

"I don't think I realised how weird it would be not having you around until you, well, weren't around," she admitted, feeling dumb just saying it.

Jack smiled, or maybe smirked would be a better word, but it was getting to the point where the two seemed to merge one way or the other each time Annie saw him.

"I was always around, love," he reminded her. "Just 'cause you couldn't see me, I could always see you."

"I figured."

"Gotta say, nicer when I can be here... or as much as I'm ever here," he considered. "Conversation's something you miss when you're, well, whatever you wanna call this," he said with a shrug, exhibiting his skill of walking through things unhindered as he phased through the side table.

"About this incorporeal thing you have going on..." Annie began then, knowing she had to deal with that point before anything else.

Jack seemed to be quite willing to avoid the issue and changed the subject without a care.

"Your friends are a riot, ain't they?" he said, wandering around looking at the pictures on the walls like they were just so interesting, even though Annie knew he had seen them a million times before. "Good folks, I s'pose, but bloody hell they get loud when they drink and all. Mind you, I had enough mates like that back in the day. Nothin' wrong with havin' a good time, I s'pose, though your queer fella could use a taste-transplant when it comes to music. All those squawking girlie-girls give me a headache."

"Jack!" Annie snapped at him, causing him to turn sharply and look at her.

Her face was like thunder, which was ironic given it was his party trick to bring on the storm sound-effects at a moment's notice. Jack sighed.

"Sorry, sweetheart. Not s'posed to call 'em queers anymore, right? I didn't mean-"

"It's not about that!" She rolled her eyes, moving closer to him. "Jack, I can't... What happened that last day before you disappeared?" she asked desperately, needing to understand that before anything else.

Maybe his murder ought to be more important, perhaps it was selfish to put her own needs first, but Annie couldn't help it. She had to know what happened, and she hadn't realised quite how much it mattered until she saw Jack again.

"Didn't disappear. You asked me to make myself scarce," he corrected her, but Annie's severe expression soon made him get to the point. "I don't know, love." He sighed heavily. "Wish I could tell you. 'S never happened before, and believe me, I spent years enough tryin' to effect bloody change. Up to now, all I can touch is myself. In my own little bubble stood here, I might as well be real as you are," he explained, proving his point by patting himself down as if looking for something in his pockets, his hands not passing through his own body in any way at all. "But reach out for anything else..." he demonstrated, his hand going towards the lamp, fingers phasing through the shade.

"Except me," said Annie, taking one more step forward, putting herself as close to him as she had been once before. "You touched me, Jack. I felt it."

"I know," he confirmed with a single nod, emerald eyes locking onto hers with that intense gaze that made her knees weak. "Can't explain it, but I felt it, as much as you did."

"Has to mean something, right?" Annie smiled bravely, even as her heart beat so hard it threatened to burst out of her chest.

"Not enough," he told her, turning away. "I'm not here, Anastasia. I'm not a person, not like you. I'm not anything. Wish I knew what I bloody was so I could do something about it."

"I wish I could help more," said Annie, wanting to laugh and cry all at the same time. "I... I wish we could be... I don't even know what I wish," she admitted, putting both hands over her face as all the mixed-up emotions threatened to overwhelm her.

Jack didn't know what he was supposed to say to her.

As much as he managed to touch her before, he had no faith in his ability to hold her right now, to bring her any comfort at all. She was like no other woman he ever met. If he had known her in life, things could have been so different, but as it was, they could never really be anything to each other. It was bloody tragic is what it was, but their fates were sealed. He was stuck here as this ghost-like figure, maybe forever. She was destined for great things, Jack was sure of that, if only he could convince her of it.

"Sometimes wonder," he said quietly then, "these last two weeks especially, started wondering if maybe this was why I was left here like this."

Annie let her hands fall away from her face. She hadn't been crying, though she still looked like she was trying hard to keep the tears at bay. She looked curiously at Jack and he gave her half a smile.

"Maybe you were the point, love. Never known anyone like you, that's for sure. Maybe... maybe I was supposed to. Who's to say?"

"Maybe you had to meet me so I could tell you what you need to know," she said then, sniffing back her tears because this was more important than self-indulgent wailing. "Jack, when George Thomas was here, you weren't happy. Now a part of me thought maybe you were just trying to scare him with your thunder-and-lightning tricks. To get him out of the house and protect me. That'd be flattering, but I don't believe it."

"Why not?" he asked her, neither confirming or denying she was right.

"Because you know better than anyone that I can handle myself," she stated plainly, smirking the way he usually would. "I could've dealt with him without your help, and you know it. You reacted out of anger at seeing that asshole in this place, in *our* place. You know him from the past, when you were both much younger."

The look on Jack's face was a picture. The expression was mixed to say the least. Annie would like to think he seemed proud of her deduction skills, as well as a little surprised about the conclusion she had come to. One thing was for sure, he was confirming with that look that she was right.

"Wouldn't say I knew him exactly, but yeah, I met the little toad once," he sneered.

"The night you..." she began, changing her mind too suddenly. "Your last night?" she said, instead of the 'd' word that stuck in her throat.

"That's the one," he confirmed. "What do you know about it then?" he checked, head tilting to one side as he stared at her.

Annie took a deep breath and without even referring to the copious notes she made, she started to explain.

"Not exactly what happened, that's for sure. George was here the night it happened, I know that for certain. Pretty sure he had some part to play in what was done to you, maybe even did it himself. His motive was the house. As far as I can tell, his family used to own the Hall but lost it. That part's sketchy," she admitted. "The point is, he was trying to get it back, and somehow thought it would help to get rid of you."

Jack smiled slowly, sadly, He shook his head.

"Was never about me, love. Not really."

It pained him to talk about it, or so she thought at first. The more Anastasia stood there staring across at Jack's sad expression, the more she knew it wasn't himself he was feeling hurt for, it was her. He didn't want her to have to hear the gory details, but she was ready and she had to know. It was driving her crazy just wondering.

Unleashing the Spirit Within

"Tell me, please," she urged him. "I can handle it if you can."

He smiled at that and nodded slightly.

"There was a poker game here. Used to do that sort of thing, just bust into some abandoned place for a rave up or a decent game of cards. Couldn't tell you why, just something people like us did sometimes. My cousin, Trev, he knew a fella runnin' this high stakes game and... Well, he was in a bit of bother, needed the cash. I only come along to keep him company, I s'pose, 'cause I was bored and fancied my chances of makin' a few quid," he said, smiling slightly, eyes looking off into nowhere as he recalled the day so long ago, people that would be aged by now if they were alive at all.

"So, there was me and Trev, this bloke, Tim, running the whole thing, and three or four others I never met before. Couldn't even tell you their names now, but we were a right rabble between us, including that George. We were all drinking, some more than others, smoking a bit of this and that. Every hand was gettin' sloppier, even me, and I was being careful how much I had. Can't win at cards if you can't count, right?"

"What happened, Jack?" Annie prompted when his story stalled in details that weren't important anymore. "Was it George?"

"As if he'd have it in him." He rolled his eyes at the very idea, seemingly leaning heavily back against the wall, thumbs in his belt loops. "You're not wrong about him wanting this place though. Hadn't a clue at the time, but I found out later. In all your book reading and runnin' about, love, you found the name of who your gran won this house from, didn't ya?"

"Yes." Annie confirmed with a nod. "Timothy Whitelaw was... Oh my God!" she gasped, one hand shooting to her mouth. "Your cousin's friend who ran the game?"

"The very same," Jack confirmed with a wry smile. "Beautiful and smart - you'll go far, sweetheart."

Anastasia didn't feel very smart right now, only confused. The man that owned the Hall before Rachel was there the night that Jack died, but that didn't explain what George Thomas had to do with anything, or how the murder had happened exactly.

"I know, few blanks to fill in still," said Jack, coming closer, trying to meet her eyes in amongst the lines of confusion on her face. "See, I had no idea what was happening that night. All I knew for sure was I was getting legless a whole lot faster than I should be on the booze I was putting away. I blacked out somewhere along the line, in a room we both know well," he said, looking oddly cocky for a guy recalling such a grim tale. "One minute I was waking up wondering when the lorry ran me over, and the next..."

He looked down at his own body and Annie knew what he was picturing - the blade showing itself through his chest. Somebody made sure he was so out of it, he wouldn't know what happened when they ran him through. All he hadn't said was who it was and why they felt the need to do it.

"Never suspected old Tim for a second." He shook his head, glancing up again to look at Annie's shocked expression. "George wound him up, had him smoking the old wacky baccy 'til he couldn't see straight. See, I just thought he was a dirty little toe-rag of a drug pusher, that's all. Turns out he had a plan. Thought old Tim owned the Hall, didn't he? Believed the drunk fool when he started saying he did anyway. Had to be one of the least stable blokes I ever met my whole life," he said, shaking his head. "Reckon George thought he could get him to sign over the house, even top himself and leave it to him maybe? That bit never did come clear, even when Tim tried to explain. He bought this place a few years back after winning the bloody lottery, if you ever. Spent his whole life drinking but never enough to take him out of the world. Once he come into money, since apparently gambling was the way he kept himself in booze, well, he thought it was his duty to buy this place and die in the house where he committed his terrible crime. Got a right bloody shock when he found me sat in here waiting for him," he told Annie, eyes sparkling with something akin to devilment.

She couldn't blame him. He had come face to face with the man that killed him and been forced to hear the explanation for what he had done. Jack couldn't enact revenge upon Tim, or even George who seemed to have caused the tragedy. He could only stand by and watch.

For fully five minutes, Anastasia couldn't speak, she could hardly breathe. All this time trying to find out what happened to Jack and now she knew. The real shock was realising that he had known himself all along, and the strangest part was that he was still here. In ghost stories and the like, spirits hung around purely to learn the truth of their demise, and then they were free to go. Jack had known what happened ever since Tim Whitelaw lived here, and that was before Rachel ever owned the place. Annie was confused.

"You knew this whole time?"

"I did, and I didn't keep it from you to be a pain in the arse, sweetheart, I just... I didn't want to burden you with it. 'S not a pretty story and you're too good to be... to be caught up in all this nasty stuff. The truth is, the man that took me out of the world was never in his right mind, and now he's met his maker anyway.

"As for George Thomas, he colluded in something, but he's not actually a murderer either. Your gran was all for havin' him hung, drawn and quartered when she found out the whole story," he said, smiling fondly when he mentioned Rachel. "Stayed in thick with the old goat on purpose, I reckon, just to see if she could play him at his own game. She was trying to get some sort of confession out of him, I reckon. Never really did know for sure."

Annie's mind was reeling as way too many facts hit her all at once. It was awful knowing how Jack had come to die, but a relief at the same time. He knew the truth and he had dealt with it somehow, she supposed because he had no real choice in the matter. There really wasn't anybody that could be blamed for what was done, it was all a tragic mistake, but that didn't mean George Thomas wasn't on her personal hit list. He was a despicable wretch for what he had put so many people through. Her mind spun to Richard and how under his uncle's thumb he was. It made her worry for his safety, but right now, Jack's focus was her.

"I don't know exactly what he's capable of, love," he confessed, suddenly even closer than he had been before, so much so that Annie jumped a little when he spoke. "Part of why I scared him out of this place that night he broke in. Can't be sure what he was looking for, unless he thought maybe your gran was onto him. He never touched her, I can promise you that. She died peaceful and natural, I swear she did. Bothers me what he might do to you though, and I know you can handle yourself, but I..."

He stumbled over what he meant to say as Annie glanced up and met his eyes, unshed tears shimmering in her own. It was this perfect moment of clarity when they looked at each other then. They were finally on the same page, they both had all the information, except for one fact that sprung to Annie's lips unbidden.

"Jack, I think I lo-"

"No," he said fast, cutting her off unceremoniously. "Sweetheart, I don't doubt you think you mean it, and bugger me, if I couldn't just as easy say it back, as barmy as that sounds. I don't know for certain, but I reckon we get confessional here, that's me done. Nothing else makes any bloody sense, if any of this ever did."

His hand went towards her cheek and hovered there. He so wanted to touch her again and Anastasia was aching with a need for him to do so. Neither knew if it were possible, but she was willing to take a chance if he was. After all, though the words had not been spoken, they had all but confessed they loved each other just now, that her love was all his restless spirit had been waiting to experience before he could leave this plane of reality for good. Annie pushed herself forward, eyes closed, every ounce of concentration on this moment. She made contact.

Jack was bowled over by the sheer force of her kiss. For a man who had felt nothing real in almost forty years, it was a revelation, and even in life he was sure he had known nothing like it. Brief as the moment was, it meant everything to him, and he was sure it would've taken his breath away if he had a reason to breathe.

Annie was full on crying when they parted, unable to hold it in anymore. It was so unfair, to be so close and still so far. Seeing her tears broke whatever remnants of a heart Jack still had. If he were still alive, the pain would doubtless kill him in a second.

"I'm sorry, darlin'," he whispered, and then he was gone.

Annie yelled his name into the space left behind, sinking to her knees as she cried like her own heart was breaking. She knew he wasn't gone for good, not yet, but he might as well be. They could never be together, she had always known that, but it hit her all over again like a punch in the gut right in this moment. The tears just kept on coming and coming, and there wasn't a thing she could do to stop them.

Chapter 26

It was strange being in the house knowing another person was there and yet not. Annie had been living like this for weeks and months now, but it seemed all the more peculiar after what had happened between her and Jack.

The slightest amount of concentration and she was back in that moment, his lips on hers, like ice and fire all at the same time. It was something she was sure she would never be able to explain for as long as she lived, any more than she could properly put into words how she felt about the spirit that haunted her house. She had almost told him she loved him, and if she had, Annie knew that would've been true in a sense, even if it did seem ridiculous to admit. It wasn't that Jack didn't want to hear it or that he didn't feel for her in his own way too. He feared leaving her forever, and now that she knew her love for him might cause such a thing, Annie was almost too afraid to think about it. Unfortunately, it was hard to think of anything else.

Michael called late in the night to tell her they all got home safe. Annie had said she wanted them to do that, screw the time difference, otherwise she would worry about her friends. It was good to hear Mikey's voice and she started crying all over again just as soon as she put the phone down. There was certainly no chance of sleep tonight, she hadn't even bothered to try. Instead Annie sifted through so many papers and research that no longer mattered, checking which could just be binned and which probably ought to be properly destroyed. She was at least half way to completing her task when something caught her eye and made her stop.

The deeds to the house had ended up in amongst the other research. Annie wasn't sure how they came to be muddled up, but now she was looking more closely at the information included, it made her frown. The deal with the house way back when it was owned by Emilia Bradbury was complex to say the least. She had inherited only because there was simply no-one else in the family to take it on, no male heir in the form of sons, cousins, or nephews. Annie had to think they were pretty prolific about having girls or just that the family got very small and she was the last left standing to take it on. The rules after Emilia were very clear, that only a male heir would do, the eldest son of the owner, always and forever.

Shuffling her papers around, Annie suddenly had a sickening thought. If George Thomas was so determined to have the Hall, believing he was the rightful heir, he would have to be the eldest son of the last surviving member of the family with a claim. Annie knew that couldn't be true, because Richard had distinctly said his father was the older sibling.

Anastasia felt as if her stomach dropped straight through the floor as she found the family tree that she had hastily sketched in the Dalton library last week, confirming that Richard's father, Jeremy, had indeed been older than George. If he found out he had to be the oldest in order to inherit, could Richard's vile uncle really be responsible for the death of his own brother? Annie hated to think it, but she was already certain he could be. After all, he was responsible for Jack's demise in his way, and for what had become of old Tim Whitelaw.

"Richard!" she said to herself, a gasp of panic behind her friend's name as she realised why George might yet keep Richard close to him, controlling him the way he did.

The Hall wouldn't fall directly into the hands of

George now Jeremy was gone. If he managed to argue his case through the court, it would default to Richard, his elder brother's son. He had messed up his own plans in so many ways and Anastasia had to wonder if Richard was supposed to be killed with his parents. If that were the case, George might very well still be plotting against his nephew. Annie's blood ran cold. They were together in London now, away from anyone who cared about Richard, away from the safety of home.

"He's dangerous," she said to herself. "Oh, God! Richard!"

She scrambled to grab her phone and speed-dialled his number, hoping against hope he might pick up. This late, there was every chance he had switched his mobile off, or at the very least would sleep through the ringing. Even if it had been a decent hour, Annie didn't hold out much hope of him answering. After all, when he left they hadn't been on the best of terms. Now she so desperately wished they were, more than she ever had before.

"Oh, for God's sake!"

She threw her phone down onto the rug when it went straight to voicemail. This was not the kind of thing she could explain via text, that was for sure. There was nothing else for it. Annie was going to have to go to London and find Richard. Of course, she had no idea where to even start looking, but Annie knew someone who would, someone in town who always knew everything about everybody. She couldn't imagine Eva caring if she turned up on her doorstep at six in the morning. She would be up already, preparing food for the cafe, just like always.

Annie ran to her bedroom to pack a bag. There was no time to lose.

Valerie Sells

* * * * *

Richard Thomas couldn't sleep. It had been a problem for days now, and he knew why. Part of it was the stress of being stuck in London with only his uncle for company. It wasn't as if Richard had an abundance of friends at home in Bennington Town either, but there were at least friendly faces and people who said 'hello'. Then there was Annie. She was a bright light in his dull little world, a force of nature that he had loved getting the chance to meet and become friends with. Perhaps he was a fool to ever think she could see him as more than a friend, pathetic little drip that he was. At twenty-eight years old, he had no real life of his own. The death of his parents had derailed his life's plan, and the only way to get back on track seemed to be to follow in Uncle George's footsteps. He hadn't known the man well in the beginning. The more he knew of him now, the less he liked him, but it seemed too late to get away and start again at this late stage.

For a while, Annie had made him think that things could change. She came into his life like a gift, and Richard saw a whole new world open up before him. With her to show him how, he felt at last he could be a whole person, the man that he wanted to be. He was different with her, more himself than he had ever been since the day his parents died. What a fool to think she could care about him, Richard saw that now, and yet he could not get her out of his head. Anastasia Addams had taken up residence in his mind and heart, there seemed to be no way of getting rid of her. If he were completely honest, Richard knew he wasn't trying as hard as he might.

Switching on his phone, he was surprised to find a missed call logged there. Of all people, it was her, his

Unleashing the Spirit Within

Annie. Only she wasn't his at all. Richard wasn't sure that she was anybody's girlfriend exactly. When he asked, she seemed to clam up as if she felt guilty for admitting it. If she didn't have a man in her life, she probably wanted one that was far different to Richard himself. Some suave, sophisticated gent, or perhaps just the rough and ready type, the bad boy that adventurous girls like her would love immensely. Richard couldn't be either of those men, he could only be himself, and he doubted that would ever be enough for someone with the life and spirit of Anastasia Addams.

Tossing the phone aside, he turned to the window and looked out over the city that was coming alive for a new day. London was a great place and he knew he ought to be happy to be here, but he wasn't. With Annie at his side, he might have been. Richard had an idea at one time to bring her here, show her all the sights, from the Tower to Buckingham Palace, St Paul's to St James's. Things she had never seen and places she only knew from pictures and films, he wanted to be the one to show her. The day he was going to offer her the chance was the very same when she had so vehemently denied any feelings for him, stating most definitely she had no romantic interest in him whatsoever. Richard didn't want to tell her that she broke his heart, it sounded too pathetic, but something fractured in him when she looked so severe and spoke so strongly against him.

"Get over yourself, Richard!" he told himself firmly, fist thumping against the wall as he leaned into the window.

Unfortunately, it just wasn't that simple.

* * * * *

Valerie Sells

The train wasn't going fast enough.

It was all Annie could think at first, and then when she started to go over it in her head, all that she must tell Richard, wondering at how she could ever explain it to him, she wished the journey would take forever. He never did speak all that highly of his uncle, but to tell him George had caused an innocent man to die, that he might even have had a hand in his own brother's demise, Richard's own father, it was almost too much. Too much for him to hear, undoubtedly, and almost too much for Annie to even begin to explain, but she must. She had no choice if she wanted to ensure her friend's safety, and she truly did.

Grabbing her phone from her bag, she tried to call again. This was the sixth attempt and still it went to voicemail. Her throat constricted every time she thought about leaving some breezy little message. This was all too serious, too deep, way too much for a voicemail. This had to be face-to-face and it had to be now.

Who knew what George was planning next. Maybe nothing, maybe something terrible. It pained Annie to think about it. She couldn't lose Richard, she just couldn't. Jack was already disappearing, quite literally, from her life. Richard meant too much for Annie to lose him too. She wasn't sure she had realised quite how much he really did mean until now.

The train wasn't going fast enough.

* * * * *

Laughter echoed through the empty halls, a twisted, painful, cackling sound, though there was no-one there to hear it. He couldn't cry. Perhaps that would have been the ultimate irony, if he had not already realised a crueller twist in his fate. To be left behind in this form, to fall in love for the very first time with someone he could never have, never hold, that he must leave behind the moment she confessed her feelings and he reciprocated in kind.

It was a bad joke, a punch in the gut after all he had already been through, and yet when Jack stopped to really think about it, he knew this had to happen. To trade all that he had suffered, being alone in this house, unable to effect change, a literal ghost of what he used to be, she made it all worth it. That had to be the point.

Life gave him the short end, always, right up to his demise. Death brought him a freedom and grace he never knew before. It brought him Annie; a kindred spirit, for lack of a better term. He had to know her to be given this gift, this love he had never known in life. Maybe it was worth it.

"Who am I kiddin'?"

Shaking his head, he wandered through the wall, appearing once again in the room where he first showed himself to her.

"Anastasia is everything I ever wanted, and no matter how short the time or weird the circumstances, I got her. She was mine, and now she'll be somebody else's to love."

His hand ran along the top of the fireplace, or at least it seemed to. Wouldn't be long now. She would go and find Richard, sort things out, make sure George Thomas didn't hurt anybody else. She would love the man that had been in her life even a little longer than Jack, and would remain for a whole lot of time after he was gone. It was how it had to be, and somehow, he had known it, almost from the very beginning.

Humming to himself, Jack faded out of sight for now.

His melody was a song he had learnt from Annie's joyful sing-alongs, and his voice echoed in the room a few moments after he was gone, with the lyrics of Joey Ramone's 'Don't Worry About Me'.

Chapter 27

Anastasia had never been to London, at least she couldn't recall it if she had. New York was a big city so it wasn't as if she wasn't ready for bumper-to-bumper traffic and people streaming by in their droves, but it was still different. Honestly, Annie wished she was here to just experience the place, see the sights. Instead her mission was very specific and potentially dangerous.

Eva had known exactly the hotel that Annie should go to in order to find Richard. He and his uncle always stayed in the same place and it had been mentioned in conversations often enough that Eva recalled it. She recalled so many things, and Annie had never been more grateful for that fact.

Consulting her phone as she exited the underground station, Annie wasn't convinced she had worked her journey out properly at all. So much for the assistance of the internet, there was no obviously large hotel around here as far as she could tell. Annie turned around and then consulted the map again. It took a while to realise she just needed to head down the street and around the corner.

Of course, when she got there Annie wasn't sure what to do. Asking for Richard's room number wasn't going to get her anywhere. They wouldn't tell her anything unless she lied and said something like she was his sister or his wife. There was every chance they would know that couldn't be true. At best, they would call his room and he would refuse to see her. There was certainly no way Annie could ask a hotel receptionist to give a man a note that said his uncle might be a murderer!

Stepping into the revolving door, Annie took a deep breath and let it out as she headed into the hotel lobby. It was a pretty fancy place, probably expensive. She had never doubted that George and Richard had money, which made their living in Bennington Town ever more strange to her. Maybe that should have piqued her curiosity from the beginning. Now she realised George had been hanging around this whole time to be close to the Hall, trying to win it back somehow. It was sad to Annie that a man would spend his whole life on a mission to get a house that couldn't really matter that much, but feeling sorry for George Thomas would be like having sympathy for the devil, and that was impossible.

Anastasia contemplated the front desk of the hotel, but then turned away. She chose a seat in the lobby and picked up a magazine from the table. Maybe the best thing would be to wait it out until Richard appeared. If he was here for work, he was probably in and out to meetings a lot, and with a little luck he would come by without George. If not, she would just have to make some excuse to get him alone. Annie figured she probably had plenty of time to think about it as she faked perusing her copy of Marie Claire. If the hotel staff asked what she was doing, she could just say she was meeting someone. It wasn't a lie, it was just that the guy she was meeting was exactly expecting her.

No matter how she thought about it, Annie was coming up blank on excuses for why she was here. If she had to face Richard in front of George, all she could say was she came to visit, which would seem eccentric at best. She had no other reason that would fly, and honestly, it would take all her strength just to be civil in front of the old tyrant that had caused the death of Jack, and potentially Richard's parents too.

It was almost an hour into Annie's pointless turning of magazine pages and thinking very hard about her options when one of the lifts opened its doors to reveal a familiar figure. Annie hadn't a thought in her head as she literally threw the magazine down on the table and rushed towards Richard. Other people turned to look at the supposedly crazy woman who just dived across the lobby and threw herself into a guest's arms. None were as shocked as Richard himself.

"Annie?" He frowned as he hugged her more by instinct than anything else.

"Oh my God, Richard!" she gasped, practically squeezing the life out of him, though he couldn't mind at all.

Honestly, he was as emotionally bowled over by her being here and holding onto him, as he had been physically by her rushing into his arms. Still, as much as he was savouring this moment of closeness, Richard refused to yield so easily. There was a reason why he hadn't seen Annie in a while, why he had left without so much as a goodbye. For all her friendly behaviour, she didn't feel as he did. She had made that abundantly clear and he could not let himself forget it. Holding her a few seconds longer, savouring the moment and breathing her in, he eventually pulled away and painted a serious expression on his face.

"What are you doing here?"

"That's a big question today," she told him, looking pretty grim-faced herself now that he looked at her properly. "Damn, I've missed you," she said then, a hint of a smile breaking through.

Richard might've been flattered if he didn't know better.

"Really? You missed me?" he questioned, shoving his hands in his pockets, all contact between them severed in a second as if it had never happened at all.

Annie felt her heart drop to her stomach. She had

almost forgotten how badly she hurt him before. In all the serious drama of murders and such, she just hadn't thought. Of course, it mattered that she hurt his feelings, but she had apologised for that and he said it was okay. Naturally, Annie wasn't so dumb as to think he was over it in five seconds flat, but she had hoped by now he had seen sense. Maybe she was wrong.

"Richard, c'mon," she urged him, trying to keep her voice in check with so many people wandering around them. "I said I was sorry about before and I meant it."

"I'm sure you did," he said, sighing heavily, hand going to his forehead as if he felt a headache coming on. "Look, I'm sorry too. I shouldn't have expected that you of all people would be interested in me. I mean, who would be, right?"

"Don't do that," Annie urged him, hand on his shoulder as she made him meet her eyes. "You're a great person and you know it, and it's not that I... I mean..." she faltered when he stared down at her, bright blue eyes boring into her own, it almost took her breath away. "I... Richard, I came here for a reason, and it's important. Can we maybe go somewhere not in the public view?" she asked, glancing away to see at least six people watching them. "I really have to talk to you," she repeated desperately.

Richard couldn't imagine what this was all about. Annie had been so insistent before that they could never be more than friends, and yet now she was following him to London and throwing herself into his arms in a hotel lobby. It didn't make a whole lot of sense, and maybe if he hadn't been so shocked to see her he would've concentrated more on finding out the reason for the impromptu visit.

"Annie, you can't just... I don't understand what's going on."

Unleashing the Spirit Within

"And I will explain it," she said softly, leaning in closer so he could still hear. "Do you have your own room here? I mean, you're not sharing with your uncle, right?"

"Of course not, he's down the hall from me," he explained just as quietly. "Actually, he's not even here at the moment. I'm supposed to be meeting him-"

"No!" said Annie definitely, and far too loudly, something she realised a second later. "Please, let's just go up to your room so I can explain."

He meant to tell her no, that whatever she had to say he wasn't interested. That would have been an out and out lie, and honestly, he wanted to know what had her so flustered. Maybe she had changed her mind about him, though Richard could hardly believe such a thing were possible. Women didn't run half way down the country just to come and tell a close friend they now wanted to date them, at least not outside of fiction. Besides, he couldn't really believe Annie felt that way in the first place, not anymore.

"Very well." He nodded once. "We'll go up to my room and you can explain to me what on earth is going on," he told her, leading her towards the lift he had just come down in.

Annie breathed a sigh of relief that he was at least going to listen to her. She still wasn't sure how she was going to explain herself. She had been thinking about it the whole way here, and nothing sounded right. Telling the whole truth meant revealing Jack's existence, and that might just be a leap too far. Annie struggled to think of a way to explain without including her friendly ghost, and knew it wouldn't be easy. Neither way was easy, given the circumstances.

They reached the eighth floor in less than a minute and Richard stepped out of the lift first, leading

Anastasia down the hall to his door. She watched him unlock it with the key card and then he ushered her inside ahead of him. Annie muttered her thanks, suddenly feeling very strange about being up here in a hotel room with a guy like this. She wasn't that girl, and Richard certainly wasn't that guy, but the implications of their situation weren't lost on her. Some that saw them come up could easily think they knew the reason why. How very wrong these supposed on-lookers would be.

"Okay, we're here in my room," said Richard, pocketing the key card and folding his arms. "What were you so eager to tell me that you came all the way to London on a whim?"

Annie was over by the window, looking out at the same view Richard had observed a hundred times, most recently thinking how he would love to show this very woman all the sights of the fair city of London. The irony wasn't lost on him that in some strange way that wish was coming true, because now she was here.

"I wish I knew where to start," she said, turning to face him. "Maybe you should sit down," she advised, glad that although Richard was confused, he did it anyway. "Um, I... What do you know about Bennington Hall?"

Richard frowned at the question.

"It's a very large, very old house?" He shrugged. "Your grandmother owned it, after winning a poker game of all things, and since her passing it has belonged to you."

"Anything else?" she pressed, already pretty sure that he had no idea about his own family's connection to the place, but feeling the need to ask anyway.

Annie met Richard's eyes once more and watched the confusion cloud their brightness. She was right, he had no idea what she was getting at, and was about to say as much when she relented and spoke again.

"Your family used to own it," she said quickly, eyes closing as she forced out uncomfortable words. "Way back, before the First World War, an ancestor of yours owned the Hall," she explained, coming to sit beside him on the edge of the bed.

"That's... Well, I certainly didn't know that," said Richard, shaking his head, eyes wide with the surprise of it all. "But that doesn't explain your sudden appearance here, Annie. You could have told me this when I returned-"

"I couldn't," she interrupted, a crack in her voice that he couldn't understand as her hand covered his atop his own knee. "Richard, I had to come, to tell you... Your Uncle George, he knows that the Hall was owned by your ancestors. I found out that he has been trying really hard, for more years than either of us have been alive, to get the place back."

Richard was utterly bewildered by the tale she was spinning. It made no sense. His family were not exactly poor but they were not insanely rich either. Saying they owned Bennington Hall years ago, it was possible, but the fact his uncle supposedly knew and never told him, that baffled Richard entirely. Surely, if George knew then so did his parents, and yet they never mentioned it, not even in passing. He shook his head.

"How do you know this?" he asked, making himself meet Annie's eyes. "I don't understand."

"I researched it," she told him truthfully, bypassing the news about Jack quite deliberately for now, because her story was already pretty unbelievable without adding a ghost to the mix. "I found out a lot about the house before I owned it, a whole list of people who lived there, and... and somebody that died there," she said shakily.

"Richard, a man was murdered in the Hall," she explained, reaching into her bag and producing a photocopy she had made of the article proving that what she said was true.

He took it from her, squinting at the too small text to read what it had to say. Sure enough, a body had been found in Bennington Hall in 1978, a suspected murder or possible suicide, the authorities didn't seem sure.

"But how did I know nothing about this? I've lived in Bennington Town for years. I know people that have been there practically their whole lives."

"Like Eva." Annie nodded, knowing exactly who he meant. "I don't understand either. I think there was a cover up. Nobody in town seems to know anything, it didn't even seem to make the papers there. I think it was covered up because... because George was involved."

"What?!"

Richard gasped in shock, humourless laughter escaping his throat a second later. He didn't always like his uncle very much, he knew him to be a cruel and thoughtless man at times, but he wasn't a monster. There was no way he was capable of murder, not at all.

"I don't like telling you this, Richard, but you know I wouldn't lie, especially not about something so serious, and not to you of all people."

"Do I?" he checked, practically throwing the newspaper article back at her as he stood up fast. "How well do I really know you, Anastasia? One summer of some vague kind of friendship and I'm supposed to trust your word when you tell me a man I know well, a blood relative of mine, killed a stranger in your house over thirty years ago? What do you take me for? A complete fool?"

"I don't think you're a fool, Richard!" she told him,

practically leaping up from the bed. "I am telling you the truth. George didn't kill anybody, but he was responsible. He set things up, he used people, manipulated innocents to make terrible things happen, and all in the pursuit of the Hall," she explained, right in his face. "I know it's awful to hear and worse to try and believe, but it is the truth, Richard. I have proof, and I would hope you'd believe that I would never tell you all this unless it wasn't what I believed to be true."

He looked down into her eyes and saw desperation there as well as perfect clarity. She meant every word she said, and Richard didn't doubt it. He had quite the ability to pick out a liar, it was sort of a requirement when one worked as a lawyer or similar. Of course, just because Annie believed what she said didn't automatically make it true. She could easily be mistaken.

"Show me your proof," he urged her. "I need to see it all and hear everything you know before I decide what happens next."

Annie nodded dumbly, seeing hurt in those beautiful blue eyes. This was just awful and she hated that she had to be the bearer of such terrible news. Of course, the only way to properly explain was to be one hundred percent honest. That meant talking about Jack. It also meant telling Richard what she suspected about his parents' deaths. Swallowing hard, she steeled herself for the conversation that was about to take place. She took not an ounce of pleasure in it. In fact, she was pretty sure it was going to break her heart.

Chapter 28

Richard was in shock, at least he was pretty sure that was what he was feeling, it was hard to tell. Nothing could ever hit him as hard as when he was told of the death of his parents, but the story Annie had relayed in the last hour came a worthy second on the list of shocks he had endured. He got up and crossed to the mini bar, grabbing the first bottle he came to without even looking at it and unscrewing the cap. He downed the fiery shot in one, gasping from the heat he really wasn't used to. It didn't help and he ought to have known it wouldn't, but he had to do something, anything to help.

"I'm sorry," said Annie, somewhere behind him.

He assumed she was still sat on the bed until he felt her hand on his back. She hoped to be comforting and kind, and Richard had a mind to let her, but honestly, he doubted she would be able to do anything right now to help him. His uncle was not a nice man, but what Annie was accusing him of, no, not just accusing, she had a practically water-tight case against him, his guilt plain to see when one heard all the evidence. The fact one of her witnesses was the spirit of a dead man, that was almost as hard to swallow as the dark truth about his relation and mentor, and yet he believed her.

"It's not your fault," he said too softly, unsure where his voice had gone to. "I just... It's so much to take in."

"I know," Annie agreed, moving around to his side and trying to see his face, hands gripping his sleeve. "Richard, I had to tell you. Honestly, as much as we're friends and everything, I wondered if you'd believe me, but I had no choice. You do believe me, don't you?"

He finally tore his eyes from some unseen spot on the wall and looked down at her. It was all so stupid and crazy. Perhaps the ghost story part was craziest of all, but he didn't doubt her. There was no part of Richard that thought he might need to call for professional help for Anastasia because she was losing her mind. He didn't need to question her or suggest she was lying in any way at all.

The worst part was how easy it was to believe when he really thought about it. George was ruthless in everything he did, and determined to stay living in Bennington Town despite how little sense it made for a high-class lawyer like himself. This explanation made too much sense, and the evidence on paper backed up every claim Annie was making. Even without her ghost story being true, there was a lot of proof that would need to be denied. It wouldn't be impossible, and yet it was easier to believe the horrible truth.

Richard swallowed hard.

"I believe you," he said, nodding his head. "I wish I didn't have to, but... but I do."

Annie's heart broke for him in that moment, and yet there was more to be said. She was tearing his life apart a piece at a time and Richard was the last person who deserved it. His knuckles were white as he gripped the empty miniature bottle in his right hand and Annie wasn't sure how he might react when she revealed her other suspicions, but they had come this far, he had to know everything now.

"Richard? If George was so determined to have the Hall for himself... I mean, your father was older than him and then you-"

"No." He shook his head definitely. "I know exactly what you're saying and I understand it, but George had no part in my parents' death."

"Okay," she replied. "But is this you hoping it's not true or...?

"I know it's not true," he confirmed without hesitation, even finding a smile as he looked down at Annie, albeit a very sad one. "There was no fault with the car, and no other drivers involved in the crash," he explained. "From what the investigators found, my father simply swerved to avoid something in the road, perhaps an animal or something. The car hit the side of a bridge and... well, the worst happened." He sniffed, clearly trying to hold in far too much emotion right now. "Some people survive so much worse," he said, so sadly that Annie started to cry herself.

Tears had been welling in her eyes this whole time, and now hearing this tragic tale, seeing this wonderful man try to hold it together through way too much, it made her want to cry like a child, and so she did.

Annie thought she was tough. In so many scenarios, she could be and was, but this was too much to bear. If nothing else, the relief of knowing George probably had no intentions of harming Richard was enough to undo her. Annie wrapped her arms around her friend, apologising over and over for everything he had been through. He hugged her back on automatic, not even thinking about what he was doing. His eyes had started to stare off at nothing again as his mind processed all he had been told and more that he remembered.

George had caused a death, whether he meant to or not. He had been ruthless and most likely part of a cover up. It was all just despicable, and he ought to pay for his crimes. Still, Richard wasn't sure what they could do about it. Keeping evidence from the police was a crime but they had no concrete proof that George was even present when Jack Green was killed. Most of this was circumstantial, except for the word of a ghost. That part was perhaps the hardest to swallow, though it might make sense of a few things. Richard's mind ran a mile a minute until finally it landed on a question he couldn't help but ask.

"Annie, is he the reason?"

She brought her head up from his chest and met Richard's eyes from the circle of his arms. They had never been this close and he had never looked at her with that much intensity. She wanted to ask what he meant by his question, and yet was pretty sure she already knew exactly.

Anastasia knew full well that the toughest part of her story to explain was Jack's presence in her home, that it would be the hardest to make sense of or accept. Richard had taken what she said as true because she was the one telling him, she supposed, or maybe just because it made a twisted kind of sense. It explained the rumours of a ghost and how she would know as much as she did about George and the past owners of Bennington Hall. She swallowed hard, eyes dipping to the floor a moment.

"I don't know," she told him, forced to meet Richard's eyes again when his fingers under chin made her look.

"You do know," he said definitely. "Annie, when I asked you if there was another man in your life, you gave such a vague answer," he recalled. "You speak of this Jack Green with such emotion and, well, it would make sense. After all the time you seem to have spent talking to him, hearing his stories of the past. When he was alive, I'm sure he would've been exactly your type of man," he said grimly, arm dropping away from her back then, fingers sliding from her face.

Richard turned away, feeling stupid. He was so torn up over George's crimes, so overwhelmed by Annie even being here, never mind the tale she had told him today. On top of all this, he realised that for weeks now he had been trying to win a woman away from a dead man. It would be funny if it didn't hurt so much, Richard thought, running both hands back through his hair and trying to get his bearings.

"I don't know what I feel about Jack," said Annie somewhere behind him, her voice betraying the fact her heart seemed to be breaking. "He's... I know he's not even really there, but he seems so real. We have talked, a lot, we have so much in common and... and then he said he loved me, and in that moment, I almost said it back. I know how it sounds, Richard, believe me. For the longest time, I've thought I was going crazy, falling in love with a ghost. It's like a bad soap opera plot, but I can't help it," she cried.

Richard hated that she was so upset, hated that he couldn't be of much comfort. He was hurting too much himself, over her, over George. He didn't know where to begin. His eyes caught the clock on the wall and he knew he was going to be in trouble for missing his meeting as it was. Of course, George had a great deal more to be admonished for. If he started a fight, Richard had already decided he would finish it.

"Richard..." Annie reached out to his arm, but he turned back to face her before she quite made contact.

"I have to figure out what I'm going to do about George," he told her. "I'm not sure going to the police would help, he'd just wriggle out of it. Your eye witness isn't going to count for much as it stands."

"No, I know that," she agreed, a little bemused by the shift in conversation back to his uncle's crimes. "I really didn't know what to do, Richard. All I knew for sure was I had to get here, find you, make sure you weren't in danger. I couldn't stand the thought of anything happening to you," she impressed upon him, grabbing his hand in both of hers. "I am so, so sorry."

What her apology was supposed to cover, neither of

them was entirely sure. Sorry that she loved Jack when the kinder twist of fate would have been for her to fall completely in love with Richard. Bringing him this awful news and no real solution as to how to handle it or fix anything. Just sympathy because the last thread of family he had was being completely cut away by the awful truth she had to impart today.

"I will have to face him," said Richard then, jaw set and eyes ablaze with anger and determination both. "When he gets back here, I'll have to, and it has to be alone, Annie. You can't be a part of this."

"But I already am!"

"No." He shook his head. "I mean, yes, you are but... but I have to do this," he told her determinedly. "Can't you understand that? I have to be the man in the situation, stand up for myself, like I should've done years ago!" he practically yelled in her face, though it wasn't his intention. "You really think my parents would want me to look up to that scum if they knew what he was? What he'd done? Of course not!" He shook his head again, looking down at Annie's tear-stained face and softening in a moment. "You have made a difference, Annie. You do, don't doubt that for a minute," he promised her, knowing he wouldn't be even half so bold as he was right now if not for her influence these past weeks, her proving to him over and over that his life could be more. "But I have to do this myself," he said definitely, his free hand going to her cheek.

All Annie could do in that moment was wonder why she couldn't love him more. Maybe she could. He certainly deserved it. Richard was like no other man she ever met, and was proving now that beyond the foppish exterior, there was the heart of a lion. He would not let what his uncle had done stand, not for a moment. If the police couldn't play a part, he was still going to do something, anything he could to see justice done. She only hoped that when he faced down George, he came out of it unscathed. It scared her half to death to think he could be harmed.

"Richard," she said more softly than she intended, leaning into his touch. "You have to be careful. Knowing what he could be capable of, what he's done..."

"I promise," he said, nodding firmly, aching to kiss her but sure that it would be a mistake.

It came as quite the shock, to both of them actually, when she suddenly pushed herself closer and crushed her lips against his own. Richard didn't waste a moment of the chance he had been given. His hands held Annie's face as he responded to her kiss with all the passion he felt.

With the emotion stirred up today, it was unlikely this would mean anything later, just be chalked up to panic and experience, but that didn't mean Richard would ever forget this feeling. He held on to Anastasia for as long as he could, and it was only when she finally pulled away to breathe, he realised maybe he had gone too far. He changed his mind when she reached out to fix his messed-up hair and found a watery smile underneath all the tears.

"You're a hell of a man, Richard Thomas," she told him definitely. "Don't ever doubt that."

He appreciated the sentiment, even if he might've preferred other words and at any other moment but this one. She gave him so much confidence, helped him remember the boy who wanted to see the world and fight for justice, instead of the pathetic person he had become lately, ruled over by his uncle, down-trodden by anyone who cared to try. Anastasia inspired Richard to be the best version of himself, and damn it, that was exactly what he was going to be from now on. The first step was facing George, and though he was not looking forward to the fight at all, he was ready for it, more than he had ever been ready for anything before.

Chapter 29

The waiting was awful. Anastasia had never been a patient person. From childhood, she had just wanted to be doing something all the time. Long journeys made her antsy and waiting for things just didn't work for her. She wanted to make things happen and then get on to the next adventure. She was not made for sitting around wondering, but on this occasion, she had no choice.

Richard was determined to face his uncle alone, confronting him with the story Annie had told and the evidence she handed over without pause. She trusted that Richard would not be swayed by any fine words on George's part. He had seen through the old devil, and he was going to ensure things were dealt with properly. Richard didn't seem to think going to the police with the proof they had would do any good, but George wasn't getting off scot free, on that he had been most certain.

Annie was glad somebody else had a plan. She was so emotionally involved in this that her own good sense and logic had all but flown out of her head. She had no doubt Richard was having plenty of conflicted feelings right now, but he seemed able to handle it. Annie felt kind of bad that it came as a surprise. She should have known better. For all that he seemed a little wimpy at times, Richard had a good heart and a strength inside that saw him through the hardest of times. Losing his parents, it was a tragedy that such a person should suffer that, and so young. Annie couldn't imagine what he had gone through, since she never really had parents to lose. Her father had died when she was so young and she had chosen to part from her mother and step-father since she knew she couldn't miss people who had hardly been there for her at all, not in any way that really counted.

All the family Richard had left was George, and now

he had to face that man and the awful truth of what he really was. That meant he was quite alone in the world after today, but Annie wouldn't allow that to stand. She was going to be whatever Richard needed for as long as he needed her. It wasn't just a debt she felt needed to be paid, though she had felt terrible having to tell him the truth about his uncle. She wanted to be with him, his friend at the very least, the family he was missing. Whatever else might happen, Annie couldn't say, couldn't even think about it yet. It felt like a betrayal somehow, even though she and Jack could never really be anything to each other.

Her hand went absently to her lips as she thought of Jack Green and the brief kiss they had managed to share during their last meeting. In her head, she heard his words of love, felt the overwhelming swell of her heart begin again. She was going to say it back, she felt as if she needed to, and yet Jack seemed sure those three little words would send him away forever. It would be both a blessing and a curse. To free him of his half-life, it was the humane and decent thing to do, but selfishly, Annie didn't want him to go. She wanted to hold on, find some miracle of a way to bring him further into her life, back into the world, even though she already knew that was impossible. Jack's entire non-existence in her life was ridiculous and inexplicable enough. She couldn't expect more than they had already shared. It wasn't fair to anybody.

Checking her watch one more time, Annie grumbled to herself for being so stupid. She was quite aware of how long it had been, since she had her eye on the time on-and-off for hours. The sky had turned dark beyond the window, the sun sinking fast behind the city scape. Richard had been gone for hours, and Anastasia was starting to get worried.

He had insisted on going to find George before he tried to come back to the hotel. They had a rented office in town where his uncle was supposed to be. His meeting was due to be over around ten minutes before Richard left to make the short journey. He was determined he would find him there and have this whole thing out with him, once and for all. Annie asked what he would say, what he would do. Richard confessed he hadn't a clue, but somehow, he was sure it would come to him when he had George in his sights.

Anastasia looked towards the door, recalled the moment when she made Richard promise to be careful and hugged him tight. She had planted a kiss on his cheek, mindful of initiating anything else after the last time. She still couldn't quite figure out what that kiss had been about and yet she had been the one to start it. There was no question that it had been a very good kiss, but in the moment, it was hard to determine what it really meant. So many more important things were at hand tonight.

Getting up to pace the room like a caged animal, Annie had never felt so very useless. She wanted to go after Richard, make sure he was okay, but she didn't even know where the office was. Hind-sight was 20-20, she thought, as she realised she should have asked, just in case. She was just considering whether she should try to call Richard or the police or something, but as soon as she pulled her phone from her pocket and contemplated her options, the beep of a key card at the lock got her attention. She rushed at the door, reaching it just as it swung open and there he was, her Richard, utterly drained, tear-stained, and bleeding.

"Oh my God!" she gasped, her hands at his face and then going to his ripped shirt as she checked him over, not knowing how best to help.

"I'm fine," he said flatly, running a shaky hand back through his messed-up hair. "It's nothing much," he promised, even as Annie picked up his hand in both of hers and observed his bruised and bleeding knuckles. "He moved. The wall was harder than his face would've been," he said, smiling slightly in spite of everything.

Annie felt like laughing and crying all at the same time. She had been the cause of this, in part, anyway. Whilst it was true enough that she hadn't made George the bad person he was or asked Richard to go and fight with him, she had been the one to uncover the truth and share it with her friend.

"I should've gone with you," she insisted as she led him over to sit down on the edge of the bed.

Immediately, she started rifling through the bedside cabinet and her own bag to find anything useful - tissues, plasters, antiseptic. There wasn't much to be had, but her make-shift first aid kit came together in the end and she turned to find Richard leant forward with his elbows on his knees and his face in his hands. He made no sound or movement and she wasn't sure if he was crying or about to explode in anger. Still Anastasia wasn't afraid, not of him, she couldn't be.

"Richard?" she said softly as she crouched down in front of him, trying to remove his fingers from his eyes.

"I'm sorry," he replied, looking exhausted as he faced her. "Sorry for you and for me... For this whole unholy mess that's unfolded around us."

"It's not your fault," she reminded him, uncapping a bottle she had grabbed from the mini bar and pouring some of the contents on a tissue to clean up his hand.

Richard barely reacted even though it stung like hell. Taking a swing at his uncle had hurt, in all kinds of ways. His hand throbbed, his heart broke. The old man was a git at times but he never completely believed he was a monster, until the confession came. George swore never to speak of this to anyone else, told Richard he could say what he liked, he would never be able to get him arrested for his crimes. Richard knew that was probably true, and so he bent the truth just a little. He said there was a witness, someone who could give evidence if needed. It was a half-truth at least, since Annie's friend Jack would be the perfect candidate, were it not for the fact he was the victim of a crime and already dead. It was enough to rattle George at least, the thought that enough evidence might exist to see him sent down all but frightened the life out of him.

"That conniving little bitch," he had said of Anastasia, and that was when Richard lost control and hit him.

The first time, George dodged and Richard hit the plaster of the wall beyond, but the second time his uncle wasn't so quick. After a brief struggle, he left the older man with a bloody nose and a lot to think about. Richard Thomas wasn't an obviously frightening man, but angry as he was, he had made his threats and meant them. If George ever came back to Bennington, his life wouldn't be worth living. If he ever, *ever* tried to contact Anastasia or go anywhere near the Hall, Richard would take every piece of evidence they had, and use all the skills and tricks George himself had taught him, to see him locked up for just about any charge he could have brought.

There was a time when George might have laughed off such threats from his wimpy nephew. Not now. Richard knew too much, and thoughts of Anastasia only served to make him stronger, more confident. George had played on Richard's fear of being alone and abandoned for so long, now that no longer existed. He had someone else in his corner and it made him prepared to fight, come what may.

"Am I hurting you?" asked Annie then, snapping Richard back to the here and now.

"No," he said, shaking his head, hardly aware of what she had been doing until she mentioned it.

He glanced down at his hand and found it clean of blood, the grazes covered by plasters. She had her hand to his face now, tending the wound from a glancing blow George had managed as he fell to the ground.

Anastasia was so close, so beautiful, and so inspiring. It was true enough that Richard could never have stood up to his uncle the way he had without knowing she was on his side

"Richard, please, talk to me," she urged him, backing away a little to meet his eyes.

His hand came up to her face, fingers running through her hair as the strangest smile formed on his lips.

"Let's go home," he urged her. "I know you want to know what happened and I will tell you but... but I just want to get out of here and... I want to go home," he repeated softly.

Anastasia couldn't argue with him, she didn't want to, and yet she had to know one thing before they left.

"He won't follow us?"

"No." Richard shook his head definitely, hand still cupping her cheek. "I made it plain that he should have someone else get his things out of Bennington. If he ever shows his face again, his life as he knows it will be over, we were clear on that."

Annie smiled a watery smile and nodded her head.

"Then let's go home."

Valerie Sells

* * * * *

Annie was glad to realise that Richard had left his car at Dalton station. It was bad enough that their train journey home had to be in veritable silence, since even so late in the day there were other people around. Theirs was not a topic of conversation that ought to be overheard by just anyone.

The car ride from Dalton to Bennington Hall afforded Annie enough time to ask the questions that wouldn't leave her. What George had said, how Richard had threatened him, how he could be certain his uncle would not just form some new plan of attack. He told her all she wanted to know in the shortest sentences possible, but Annie couldn't blame Richard for that.

Today, which was about to become tomorrow by the time they reached home, had perhaps been tougher on him than even on her. Yet there was still one more hurdle, one more emotional wrench to face tonight.

Richard wanted to meet Jack. Honestly, Annie hadn't seen that coming, but quite out of the blue in a brief silence as they came through town, he confessed as much.

"I owe him an apology, on behalf of a man who will never give it himself," he said nobly. "It can't really help or take back any part of what George did, but I want to say it anyway."

Annie agreed in theory. She could do no more than that, since there was no guarantee that Jack would show himself with Richard present. Actually, Annie felt a little strange knowing the two men in her life were about to meet each other. If she were honest, she loved them both in different ways. Her feelings for Jack had certainly blinded her to how much Richard cared and how much she might yet feel for him. Things were so confused and messy, the journey to this point had been so long, and Annie wasn't even thinking of the trip back from London, just this whole debacle that seemed to last all summer long.

"Are you sure you need to do this?" she asked, as Richard pulled the car up outside the Hall and shut off the engine.

Honestly, Richard wasn't sure how to answer that. He knew he should do this, make this apology, face the man whose demise had been at least partly down to his family. At the same time, he had another reason for coming here to see this Jack Green of whom Annie spoke so fondly. He was, for all intents and purposes, a ghost, and yet Annie loved him. There was a morbid curiosity in Richard that would not go away. He needed to see what all the fuss was about, he supposed. Needed to look this non-entity in the eye, man to man, for want of a better phrase, just once before the chance was lost.

"Let's go," he said, reaching for the handle and getting out of the car.

Anastasia took a deep breath and followed suit. She walked up to the front door and unlocked it, letting them both inside. Richard followed as Annie automatically headed for her usual living room. The thought had occurred to go to what she called Jack's room in her head, and yet she couldn't quite do it. His original painful death had been there. If he really did leave her forever tonight, she wanted it to be somewhere with better memories, for both their sakes.

"Come in," she urged Richard when he hovered by the door.

He had never seen this room, no-one had, not even Annie's closest friends. It had been hers, shared only with Jack up to now, apart from when George broke in the other night. Now it was time to let Richard in too.

They stood together in the centre of the room, and Annie's hand reached for Richard's own. She spared him a smile and then turned her eyes to the ceiling.

"Jack?" she called. "We need to talk to you. Please?"

At first, it seemed as if he wasn't going to put in an appearance. Annie was ready to yell for his attention again and Richard was about to question the sanity of the pair of them, when suddenly a figure formed in front of them. Annie smiled at the sight of Jack, she couldn't help it, but Richard didn't notice. He was too busy staring at the strange image of a man, dressed in black and yet somehow glowing with an ethereal whiteness. It was the strangest thing to see, and even stranger when the man spoke.

"Well, don't I feel special then?" he said, smirking. "Visitors comin' two by two now."

"Jack," said Annie, his name coming out like an admonishment. "Be serious."

"Got a feelin' there's gonna be little chance to be anythin' else in this little gathering," he replied, eyes flitting to the joined hands he could see before him, then back up to Richard's face. "You decide you wanted to come and see the freak show then, mate?" he asked him, attitude just a little bit over-done, Annie thought. "Name's Jack Green. I'd shake your hand but..." He smiled painfully as he showed the way he could pass his fingers clean through a nearby table.

"I think it's safe to assume we already know everything we need to about each other, from what Annie has told me," said Richard then, a little colder than maybe he needed to be, but Annie could understand that.

Unleashing the Spirit Within

She squeezed his hand comfortingly and didn't even try to get Jack's attention back onto her as the two men stared each other down. Richard had come here to say something important and she needed to let him. Soon enough she would be alone with Jack and it would come down to her to make the decision to set him free. She hardly wanted to think about losing him and yet she knew it couldn't be long now.

"I know who you are," Jack confirmed, thumbs hooked in his belt loops as he appeared to lean back against a wall that couldn't possibly be holding him. "Richard Thomas, nephew of George. She told you what he's like then, has she?" he said, head tilting towards Annie though his eyes remained on Richard yet.

"Annie has told me everything," he confirmed. "And I... I came here to meet you, to offer some kind of apology. I know how ridiculous that sounds, believe me."

"'Bout as ridiculous as a dead man walking around like a shadow, I'd wager." Jack smirked, eyes sparkling like he was holding in a laugh at his own bad joke.

"Perhaps." Richard nodded once, refusing to acknowledge any humour in this situation. "Anyway, I wanted you to know I'm sorry for what happened to you, and for the part my family played. For what it's worth, I'm seeing to it that George doesn't hurt anybody else. With the evidence we have and the way I presented it to him, I can promise you this ends here."

"That it does, mate," said Jack, looking away a moment, "and I appreciate the sentiment, even if it can't make much difference anymore. Took guts for you to come here and say all that, 'specially holding onto our girl here," he said seriously, meeting Richard's eyes once again. "Maybe took even more to cut old George off at the knees. Hope you socked the old devil for me."

"He got what he deserved," Richard assured him, trying not to smile back but finding it hard, even as his right hand twitched, showing off the plasters that adorned his knuckles.

"I see." Jack nodded. "In the end, I s'pose we all got what we deserved," he said a little bitterly, his eyes shifting to look at Annie then.

She was going to cry and she knew it. This moment was too great and too painful all at once. The two men in her life that meant so much, that she thought might come to blows if they were able, were now smiling at each other, a truce of some kind seemingly forged.

"Well, I should go," said Richard, shifting awkwardly when he noticed the look passing between Annie and Jack. "I said what I came to say. You'll be okay?" he asked Annie.

"I'm fine." She nodded, reaching to hug him.

Richard hugged her back for as long as he could, though he was entirely aware of being watched. Annie knew Jack was staring too but couldn't mind much. For all that he meant to her, Richard mattered too. She couldn't give up one for the other's sake. She had no choice right now but to let Jack go, it seemed, and the very thought of it was breaking her heart. Annie needed whatever comfort she could get.

Richard let go of her then and turned to leave. He nodded a goodbye to Jack and then he was gone. Annie watched him leave and listened for the front door to click shut before facing Jack again. He was right behind her when she turned around, close enough to touch if such a thing were possible a third time. She hardly dare risk it.

"Sort of a gent really, ain't he?" he said of Richard. "Got some balls to go with it though, I'll give him that."

Unleashing the Spirit Within

He said it as if he were proud of the man he only just officially met, and yet at the same time, there was a sadness in his eyes.

To Annie, it already felt like a betrayal if she so much as considered having Richard play a larger part in her future. The betrayal of a man she barely knew and could never be with. It was ridiculous.

"Jack. Please, don't."

"Don't what, love? Don't act like we're having a normal conversation when we both know it's gotta be the last?"

Shaking her head had sent tears streaming down Annie's cheeks that Jack ached to wipe away, but he didn't trust that he could right now. He couldn't stand the evidence of his non-existence in this moment. He just had to stand there and watch her cry.

"I... I don't want you to go," she told him, sniffing hard, "and I know that it's selfish and awful of me. It's not even entirely true, because I want you to have peace, I do," she cried. "I just... It's crazy. It's only been two months, but I'm going to miss you so much."

Jack smiled at that, a sad smile but genuine at the same time.

"You're a hell of a woman, Anastasia Addams," he told her, eyes taking in her whole face for what had to be the last time, and they both knew it. "You're beautiful, you've got brains, you're honest and passionate, and you bloody amaze me," he told her, his fingers tracing her cheek without ever making contact, but close enough she could almost imagine he had. "It's been worth it, y'know? Everything I went through. The pain and torment, the being alone. I'd do it all over again to get this chance to meet you," he said with a genuine smile. "You're one in a million, love, and you're gonna be the best thing that ever happened to some lucky bloke I'll never meet. Unless of course I just did."

"Jack..."

She tried to speak, but no more words would come. Annie ought to have known he didn't need them anyway.

"I love you, Anastasia," he said, more honestly than he ever said anything.

The relief of letting out a feeling he had never really known until her was immense, and Jack doubted it could be equalled until she replied.

"And I love you, Jack. Always," she promised him faithfully.

There was a warmth that burst into his heart then. It spread through his entire being which had always been so cold before, even in the years when he had been alive. Knowing time was shorter than ever now, Jack concentrated all his effort to lean forward and kiss her lips one more time.

Anastasia tripped forward as he pulled back, the moment over far too soon, but it wasn't up to either of them anymore.

"Take care, darlin'," Jack whispered, as some unseen force seem to pull him away and cause him to fade out all at once. "Go live that life of yours, don't waste a second."

He tipped her a wink, still smiling widely as she started to lose sight of him.

"I promise."

Annie tried to be brave but failed miserably in the end, as finally Jack Green faded from view, gone forever.

Chapter 30

It was days since Richard left his home. For a place that was only half a regular house, just three rooms, it was crazy to think a person could survive bouncing around in there by himself without going mad. The truth was, Richard thought perhaps he had gone completely insane at some point.

Extracting himself from George's life was not an easy task, it left him a shell, no life at all when his job was removed. No life but for Anastasia, and her he had not seen since dropping her at home four or five nights ago. Quite honestly, Richard had lost track of time, the cycles of day and night, as he cried in unmanly fashion over his losses, and worked through piles of work-related papers. It had to be done, this seemingly pointless, boring process, until it all came to a close. Such was the situation Richard found himself in now. Everything was done and he woke to a bright sunny day that didn't at all suit his mood.

The light flooding in through a crack between the curtains, struck across his eyes. Richard flinched and shifted away. It hadn't woken him, since he was awake long before dawn. Sleeping did not come easily to a busy mind and his was certainly that. Cutting ties with his uncle was something that very definitely needed to be done, but it left Richard quite alone, without a family to speak of, without a job of his own. Alone. It was a feeling he had learnt to live with over the years, and yet it bothered him more now than ever before to have to accept it.

He got out of bed and padded across the carpet to the shelf in the corner. On it stood a framed photograph of those he loved most and had tragically lost far too soon. He smiled sadly as he traced the figures of his parents, a perfect portrait that made them seem like the happiest couple on the planet. The truth was they were happy most of the time, content with their lot even though it wasn't quite as great as it might have been. They had money, more than some, but were by no means rich, not like the family had been once upon a time, as owners of Bennington Hall no less.

"I wonder if you knew?" he asked the picture that was never going to answer, not able to give even a hint of the truth.

Richard looked inside himself for the answer instead. No, his parents had no idea they might once have been heirs to a fortune, the mansion on the hill overlooking this little town. If they had suspected, even for a moment, he was sure he would have heard the tale. They certainly could never have known what George was truly capable of. He had covered his tracks well, kept everything to himself, living a singular existence, never letting anyone close. If Richard wasn't so disgusted with his uncle, he might actually have felt sorry for him in his self-imposed lonely world.

Alone. The word echoed through his mind once more and Richard put the picture back on the small shelf, turning away from it a second later. He surveyed the room, ran both hands back through his hair. For one so organised in all kinds of ways, he had taken to living in a state of confusion the past few days. The rooms of his home matched his state of mind, messy and confused. There were papers strewn about, food containers abandoned in the corners, clothes left floundering in piles. None of it seemed to matter whilst he dealt with the issue at hand. Now all the work was done, everything he could possibly do to part himself from George forever and ensure the old man didn't try anything desperate or dangerous.

Unleashing the Spirit Within

Maybe now was as good a time as any to pick himself up, dust himself off, and start again. Richard Thomas had little choice but to try. His mother's apron strings had been cut for him, his father's guiding hand ripped away. He had thrown off the shadow of Uncle George, and that just left Richard standing. Alone, certainly, and yet perhaps he could be better off for it. Flung into the deep end of the pool, a man's choice was to sink or swim. Richard didn't much feel like drowning. After all he had faced in his life, he ought to be able to do much more than just drag his head above water. He had started to take control, and would continue to do so, he decided, before he lost any of the momentum he had built up so far.

Taking a deep breath, he strode over to the window and flung the curtains aside, letting sunlight flood into the room and cover him in its welcoming orange glow. Time to face the world anew.

* * * * *

It seemed insane to be mourning a man that died before she was even born. Anastasia knew it was something she could never truly explain to anyone, how she and Jack had come to care so much for one another, how she missed him so terribly now he was gone.

Only two others living in the world even knew of his existence as a ghost, a spirit, whatever he had truly been. Richard had not been back to the Hall since the night they returned from London, and Annie didn't feel able to call Janine for comfort. It would require an explanation of everything and that she had not been ready to give. Days later, she still wasn't sure she could bear to talk about it. She wondered if she ever would.

Valerie Sells

The house felt bigger, and suddenly so much emptier than it ever had before. Annie knew she could fill it with willing bodies and cheerful chatter as fast as she could call two or three key contacts in town. There was still work to be done, tasks that had been put on hold when her friends came to visit, and still had not been picked up again. She had her reasons and they were good ones, but nothing she could tell her neighbours in Bennington. She would have to make other excuses, though she still had no idea what they would be.

The sun shone in through the windows and Annie wandered over to look out at the view. The hills and fields beyond the Hall were beautiful in the summer sunshine. A whole world lay out there before her, a life that needed living. That was what Jack had told her to do, to go live her life and not waste a second. She hadn't taken much notice, she realised, having spent four days locked in the Hall sobbing for his loss.

"You must be so mad at me right now," she said, laughing to herself, automatically looking up as if she thought he could hear her.

Maybe he could. She talked to her grandmother sometimes, assuming she could hear everything. Anastasia believed they did know she was talking to them, that they were watching over her now, the both of them, maybe her dad too. It almost made her laugh to imagine the scene, Grandma Rachel, Jack, and her own father, perhaps sat around a table with cups of tea as they discussed Anastasia and the life she wasn't really living.

"You'd *all* be mad at me," she realised, shaking her head. "I have this life, this great life, with friends and a beautiful home and enough money to do whatever I want. Good things, stuff that helps people, and that makes me happy too," she considered with the first genuine smile she had worn for days. "I love you, all of you, and I'll keep on loving you and missing you, but if I don't live my life... Well, I'm letting you down if I don't live my life like I should."

Turning away from the window, Annie headed straight to the wardrobe and flung open the doors. She needed something to wear, and then she was headed to town. There were things to do, people to see, a life to live, and she wasn't going to waste another second.

* * * * *

Richard didn't have an exact plan when he left his home. Freshly showered, cleanly shaven, and dressed in dark jeans and a button-down shirt, he looked so much like the Richard Thomas the town knew, and yet he was a changed man. He felt he was walking a little taller, in spite of everything. He made sure he was, as he strolled down the streets he knew so well, and yet they looked different somehow as he passed through them.

Perhaps it was deliberate, though Richard suspected it was subconscious, when he realised he was headed for the far side of Bennington Town, up towards the church by now. A little further was the cemetery and then the final bus stop from where he could catch a lift up the hill to the house that overlooked his home town. Anastasia might not even be there, and if she were, she may not be alone. Richard stopped in his tracks as he thought a moment. Meeting Jack had been all very well. Facing the victim of his uncle's greed and making his apology, it had been the right thing to do. It was a whole different prospect to meet the eyes of that man again.

Jack wasn't just a hard done by victim, he was also a rival. He loved Annie in his own strange way and she loved him, though she swore she had no idea how to explain it. Richard didn't want to be jealous. It seemed so petty and ridiculous to feel so green over a dead man, and yet he couldn't help but wish his own relationship with Anastasia ran deeper.

They certainly had a connection that could never be broken. What they had faced together, it built a bond on top of the friendship they had already nurtured between them. He wondered how they went forward from here and yet dare not ask, at least he hadn't so far. Maybe today was the day.

Richard started walking again, with a renewed sense of purpose. He didn't have far to go when he suddenly saw movement out of the corner of his eye. The sight of her made him immediately turn and continue in a new direction, through the gateway, into the cemetery. She was stood at the foot of her grandmother's grave, a fresh bunch of flowers laid there before her. Anastasia was as radiant as he had ever seen her, even dressed as she was in a simple T-shirt and cropped trousers, her hair flying wildly in the light summer breeze. She turned bright eyes to meet his own and smiled, a look he suddenly found easy to return.

"Hi."

"Hello, Annie."

It was good to see each other again, and yet neither was really sure what to say after everything that had passed. Richard's eyes drifted to Rachel's shining new headstone and then the yellow roses Annie had clearly laid.

"They were her favourite," she said, having followed his gaze to the flowers. "It's one of the few things I know about her for myself, not through reading her will or talking to the people in town. I can still see her arranging yellow roses in a vase and saying how they made her so happy, how the colour always reminded her of summer time."

Richard swallowed hard, felt the emotion in her voice hit him like a slap around the face. It was idiotic to stand there, six feet away with his hands in his pockets. Moving closer, his arm slipped around Annie's back and pulled her close into his side. She let her head rest at his shoulder and hugged him back, glad of the sudden closeness and support.

"I've missed you," she whispered, words mostly muffled against his shirt.

"Missed you too," he replied, kissing the top of her head without a thought.

They stood in silence a while longer and then suddenly both seemed to realise it was time to leave. Their arms still around each other, they moved up through the gate and back onto the road. Annie looked towards the Hall and then back to town.

"You hungry?" she asked, looking up at Richard. "I was thinking we could get some food in town then go sit in the park. It's a beautiful day for a picnic."

It seemed like a crazy suggestion, too simple, too cheerful in the circumstances, but it appealed in ways Richard couldn't describe. Nodding his agreement, he let his hand slip down Annie's arm and clasp her fingers. People would talk and they both knew it, but though her eyes lingered on their joined hands for a moment, it made her smile, not comment.

Avoiding Eva's cafe was a deliberate act on both their parts, though not a word was spoken on the topic. They picked up sandwiches, bottled water, snacks and the like from a corner store they rarely used, and then headed on into the park. They sat down comfortably on the grass and ate in silence, at least at first. Eventually somebody had to bring up one of the many topics they had so far avoided. There was just no choice in the matter.

"Jack's gone," said Anastasia, quite out of the blue. "We talked after you left and... Well, he's gone now. For good," she admitted, glad to have at least got the words out without crying like a child.

Richard nodded to prove he had heard but didn't really have any answer to give to her admission. Jack was gone. Richard didn't know whether to be happy about that or sad on Annie's behalf. In the end, he supposed he was glad enough for the man himself. He had to be at peace now, and that was a positive if nothing else. No more or less than a person deserved, he supposed.

"Life has changed so much in the last few days," he said then, turning to meet her gaze. "Though perhaps it all started weeks ago, when this wonderful woman came to town."

Annie could hardly bear the soft look in his eyes meant only for her, or the beauty of the words he was saying. She didn't think she was all that wonderful herself, and she certainly didn't feel she deserved for Richard to think of her that way. It didn't change the fact that he cared, that he was inching ever closer until his lips touched her own. For a little while, Anastasia let herself sink into the moment, Richard's fingers tangling in the hair at the nape of her neck as he deepened their kiss. She wanted to let it happen, a part of her longed to, and yet she pulled back too soon with tears in her eyes.

"I'm sorry," she said, gasping in air, her hand shooting to her lips.

"No, I'm the one who should be sorry," said Richard, sitting up fast and shaking his head. "You didn't ask for this and... I'm sorry," he repeated, turning away.

Unleashing the Spirit Within

Annie put her hand to his shoulder just in case he thought about bolting. She didn't want that. Of all things in the world, she did not want Richard to walk away from her, not now, not ever, if she were honest with herself.

"It's not that I don't want to... to just let go and have this happen, Richard," she promised him. "A part of me wants that more than anything, but I was... Me and Jack..."

"I can't compete with a dead man, Anastasia!" he snapped at her, though he hadn't really meant to.

"And I'm not asking you to compete," she told him desperately, pulling on his arm until she had his full attention again. "Richard, please, after everything we've been through," she urged him, her hand going to his face, making him keep her gaze. "Please don't walk away from me now, I couldn't handle that. I just... I need a little time, to let everything settle. To see how things are going to go. Do you understand?"

Richard wanted to say he didn't, that maybe it would be easier if he just ran and never looked back. It might be the smarter choice in some ways, but it would break both their hearts if he abandoned her now. She was one thing that he knew was worth clinging to, worth sacrificing things for, even if the one thing he must sacrifice was his own heart.

Neither of them had really had time to catch their breath yet, to decide what they felt, what they wanted from each other going forward. She needed time, and maybe he did too. Certainly, they needed each other to lean on if they were going to find their way in the world, down this new path they appeared to be on now.

"I understand," he promised her eventually. "And I'm not going anywhere, Annie, not unless you're going too."

She smiled at that and reached to hug him. Richard held her close and let his eyes drift to the blue sky above. However things ended up working out between them, the fact they were going to be in each other's lives from here on out seemed to have been agreed without question. Fate had thrown them together, destined to stay that way. That was enough for now.

Chapter 31

"There wasn't too much to do construction-wise. The surveyor said we had no foundation problems or anything structural to worry about, which is amazing given the age of the place," Annie explained to Eva, with a smile on her face that had been missing too long up to now, at least her friend thought so. "What did need attention is pretty much done. The guys at the builder's yard have been so good to me. There's still a lot of cleaning to do and taking out anything unsalvageable on the top floor, but I have a lot of help and we're on target to be done by the end of September," she enthused. "I'm so bowled over by all the people that want to pitch in. I mean, they're just giving up their time for no money, even kids on their summer vacation. It's truly amazing!"

"You are the one who's amazing, my love," said Eva kindly, her hand over Annie's own on the table. "That old place was so tumble-down, even when your gran was there, God rest her soul. It needed so much work and look at what you've achieved already! Sounds to me like it's a veritable palace."

"You should come see it, and soon," Annie told her definitely. "I can't believe I've lived here all this time and you still haven't seen the place."

"Well, I'm always so busy here, aren't I? By the time evening comes, the busses have stopped running, and Sundays, I'll be honest, I can't be bothered to even be dressed up proper to go anywhere," she whispered, as if it were a scandal.

Annie laughed at Eva's words.

"You never have to dress up to come and see me," she told her, rolling her eyes at such an idea and continuing to giggle.

Valerie Sells

Richard was certainly glad to hear the joyful sound as he came into the cafe and found his two favourite ladies sat together. It had been a few weeks now since he and Annie decided to take things slowly with whatever their relationship was going to be from here on out. They saw each other almost every day and he had helped a lot with the Hall. At the same time, he looked into getting himself a new job, somewhere local, and today had been his first interview for a firm in Dalton. To come back and find Annie here, smiling and laughing like she hadn't a care in the world, it pleased him to no end.

"Might've known you'd be hiding in here, filling up on cake," he teased her as he came to sit down with her and Eva.

"You're just jealous that I can eat so much and not gain weight," she said with a wink.

"Ooh, I should say you don't have to watch your figure!" Eva declared with a grin.

"Of course not. She has me to do that for her," said Richard, at which Annie's eyes went wide and a blush rose in her cheeks.

She wasn't much for getting embarrassed, especially by compliments from guys, but Richard was different to any other man she ever met. Actually, Richard now was even different to how he had been before. He was still everything she liked about him, plus a new-found confidence that made him all the more attractive somehow.

As tragic and twisted as circumstances had got where George was concerned, it almost seemed to have done Richard the world of good. Annie couldn't help thinking all these things happened for a reason, her being here, meeting Jack, getting close to Richard. Somebody had to have a plan. It was too amazing to think it was all just coincidence.

Unleashing the Spirit Within

"Annie?" Richard prompted.

She seemed to be lost in a daze, though he couldn't really mind it. Her eyes were focused on him alone as she daydreamed.

"Huh? Oh, yeah. I was just telling Eva, she should totally come and see how good the Hall looks now," she said, snapping out of her hazy moment. "You'd drive her up to visit, right?"

"Any time at all, Eva," he promised. "Name a day and a time, I am at your service," he said, mocking a bow across the table.

"Oh, you're such a good lad, Richard." Eva smiled, patting his hand. "Let me see how I'm fixed and I'll let you know, okay? Now, I must get on."

She got up from her seat and hurried off to continue working. Annie watched her go with a grin on her lips that wouldn't shift. Eva was just the nicest lady, not quite a mother figure but certainly a kindly aunt or similar. Anastasia was very glad to have met her, glad to have met all the wonderful people of Bennington Town. It was a far cry from her way of life in New York, but in the last few months, she had come to think of this place as a home.

"So, how'd the interview go?" she asked, turning to Richard so suddenly he almost jumped with the surprise of the question. "You knocked it out of the park, right?"

"Since you seem to be feeling particularly Americanised today," he said, finding her equal parts amusing and adorable at the same time, "no, I couldn't really say I knocked it out of anywhere. I'm no baseball expert, but I think this might be what you would call a swing and a miss."

"Oh, Richard. I'm sorry," she sympathised, her hand rubbing his arm where it lay on the table. "What happened? I mean, how could they not want you? How could *anybody* not want you?"

That got his full attention, though he was sure Annie hadn't meant it quite the way it came out. She was talking about law firms wanting to employ him, not a person physically wanting him the way a woman might want a man. Still, the thought was in his head now and his eyes betrayed him when they met Annie's own. She knew that he thought about her that way, of course she did, but they agreed they weren't going to jump into anything too fast. They needed to regroup and Annie in particular needed to re-evaluate both her life and her feelings. She and Richard were close, there was no denying that. All the time they spent together, all that they had shared by way of conversation and such, and yet they weren't exactly dating. He would hold her hand sometimes. She hugged him when they parted ways. Kisses had been strictly pecks on the cheek since the day in the park when she pulled out of a pretty serious moment and said she wasn't ready. He wouldn't push and she still wasn't quite ready to jump. Unfortunately, it put them both on edge sometimes, when certain comments got made or they received significant looks from those in town who put two and two together and made nine.

"Um, yeah, I meant..." she began to explain, but he shook his head.

"I know what you meant," he assured her with a smile that was supposed to be understanding and comforting both, even if it was killing him by degrees to continue keeping his distance. "And I don't know exactly why they didn't want me. I got the distinct impression my name might've made matters awkward. George wasn't exactly a popular man amongst his peers, and though I did make clear that the whole reason I was looking for a job was to leave his business, it didn't seem to make much difference."

"That sucks," said Annie definitely.

"Yes, it does suck." He smiled as he echoed her phrasing that was so foreign to him.

"But hey, that's just one place," she said with confidence. "There are others."

Richard wasn't so sure he wanted to try any other places. He knew he had to. Without a job, he was on limited funds, and they would run out before long. Annie had promised him some days ago that if things got tough she could help, but he wouldn't hear of it. She meant well and he thanked her accordingly, but he wouldn't take charity from her of all people. He couldn't live with himself if he did.

"Anyway, happier topics, please," he urged her then. "Work on the Hall still going well?"

"Oh yeah," she agreed happily. "And I've also been thinking seriously about what I might wanna do with it when it's all fixed up and everything."

"Okay. Colour me intrigued, as you Yanks like to say," he teased her.

Anastasia said from the start she wasn't so sure she would live in Bennington Hall forever. It was far too big for one person and Richard knew she had been weighing up her options on what the place might become. A hotel, a spa, a tourist attraction. Whichever she chose would require a lot of research, money, and work to get it set up, but Richard knew she would be up to the challenge if anyone ever was.

"Okay, so, maybe this is crazy," she confessed, "but I was thinking about everything, the history of the Hall, and what happened years ago. What do you think about a rehab facility? Like a half-way house or something? I mean, it's big enough, and it's far enough from town that it shouldn't be a danger or a worry to anybody down here, but it'd be helping people, Richard. People with addictions and problems. I'd feel like I was doing something worthwhile with my grandma's legacy, and helping people like Tim Whitelaw, and..."

"And Jack?" said Richard with a knowing look. "Drink and drugs were part of his life too, you told me as much."

"Yeah," said Annie vaguely, unable to meet his eyes.

Richard took hold of her hand and got her attention back.

"You can mention him, Annie. I won't break from hearing his name," he assured her, kissing the hand he held. "And for what it's worth, I think your idea is a brilliant one. Bloody brilliant."

Anastasia smiled and leaned over to kiss his cheek.

"I think you're bloody brilliant," she told him, laughing at herself a moment later because it really did sound ridiculous in her accent. "And it's amazing to me that you don't think I'm a crazy person."

"Oh no, I do think you're crazy," he said with a wicked grin. "But I wouldn't have you any other way," he promised her faithfully.

In that moment, Annie couldn't help but wonder why she ever told him she couldn't date him or wanted to take things slow. There were reasons, she knew there were, and chief amongst them had been the very man they just spoke of. But hadn't Jack been the one to tell her to live her life? Hadn't he even said she was probably destined to make Richard a very happy man?

Anastasia shook her head, letting those thoughts fade for now. There was plenty of time to figure these things out later. They had all the time in the world.

"Um, I should really get back to the Hall," she said suddenly. "You wanna come with?"

"If you'd like me to."

They said goodbye to Eva and headed out together, Annie's free hand slipping easily into Richard's own without her even thinking too much about it.

"We can take my car, save catching the bus up," he told her, gazing a moment at their entwined fingers.

"Sure," she agreed easily. "Oh, I just need to stop off at the post office, pick up my mail."

They agreed to part ways at the corner. Annie went to collect any mail she might have while Richard fetched the car around. He was outside the door, engine running when she came out with a hand full of envelopes. He made some joke about feeling like her getaway driver, but Annie didn't answer, didn't even laugh. Richard didn't drive away, instead he switched off the engine and put a hand to her shoulder.

"Annie, is something wrong?"

"I don't know," she said, shaking her head. "Somebody sent us a letter."

"Us?" echoed Richard, taking the envelope she offered him.

He was frowning a little at first, face blanching entirely when he saw the handwriting. It was then Anastasia realised who must have sent the letter. There was really only one candidate that would address an envelope to the both of them and could make Richard look so pale so fast.

"George," she all but spat, the very name leaving a nasty taste on her tongue. "I thought you said you made sure he would never come back?"

"He hasn't come back, has he?" snapped Richard,

though he hadn't really meant to. "I'm sorry, I just... I never expected him to contact me."

"Apparently, he contacted *us*," she considered, staring across at the envelope in his hand. "Are we going to read it?"

"I suppose we should," he said, nodding his head, and yet he made no move to open the envelope at all.

Richard wasn't sure what to think. If George was writing to the both of them, there were a multitude of things he might decide to say. A confession or a denial, an apology or an excuse. Every possibility ran through Richard's mind in that moment, including the fact this could be a suicide note or last will and testament. Even after everything, he shuddered at the thought.

Eventually, his fingers moved to rip open the envelope and pull out the pages inside. He started to read, meaning to do so aloud for Annie's benefit and yet he couldn't. His eyes scanned down the page, taking in line after line of words he had not really believed he would ever see. Tears came to his eyes that he fought to blink away, and then he laughed.

Anastasia hardly knew what to make of it. Laughter in this moment seemed the most inappropriate thing in the world, even when Richard pushed the letter into her hands and encouraged her to look. She frowned as she took the pages from him and scanned over them just as Richard had done.

The letter was as heart-felt as anything Annie had ever read. It seemed almost impossible that George Thomas, the mean-spirited, conniving old devil, had written such words, and yet he had. He apologised for everything, he begged Richard's forgiveness, and assured him that all he had done had always been for the good of the family. He knew it was wrong, but he only wanted his dear parents and his brother to have everything they deserved. After his parents were gone, and then Jeremy and Susan, his focus landed on Richard. He professed to only be so hard on him because he was a constant and painful reminder of his much beloved brother. The loss of Jeremy seemed to have hit George much harder than anyone could have imagined.

"His life was so full of losses," said Richard softly, wiping a stray tear from his cheek. "I never thought of it that way. It doesn't excuse what he did, of course, but his motives were based in good intentions, I suppose."

Annie didn't answer, just continued reading and let out a breath she hardly knew she had been holding when she reached the end of the letter.

"He's gone," she declared at last. "He doesn't say where he's going, but he's promised you'll never see him again."

"As I asked." Richard nodded absently. "I'd like to think he's taken himself off somewhere nice, in Europe, maybe further afield, but I've got this awful feeling, Annie," he said, staring off out of the windscreen.

"He wouldn't..." she started, knowing when Richard met her eyes that maybe he was right.

She looked back at the letter in her lap. It sounded a lot like a goodbye, a very permanent kind of goodbye. It was one thing to be mad at George, to hate him even, but to think of him taking himself out of the world, it was too much. Annie knew it would be far too much for Richard to bear. His laughter before had been bordering on the hysteric. Disbelief and sadness combining in a small explosion of giggles that were so misplaced. Annie's heart broke for him.

"I'm sorry," she said, reaching out to put an arm around him. "I don't know what else to say, I just-"

"Don't say anything," he told her, swallowing down

the lump in his throat. "Honestly, Annie, I'm fine," he said bravely.

Anastasia wasn't sure she really believed that. He couldn't possibly be fine, but if he wanted them to act as if everything was okay, she wouldn't push. He never did push her when she urged him not to.

When Richard suddenly righted himself, pulling on his seat-belt and putting the car in gear, Annie followed suit and prepared herself for the journey home. She filed the letter away in her purse with so many others, and accepted the change in conversation when Richard asked her more about her plans for the Hall.

One way or another, George was out of their lives, and that was what they wanted. Whatever happened to him now was his business and not theirs. Annie was determined that Richard would never be alone just because his family had fallen apart. She had him and he had her, that was the deal now, come what may. Where they ended up, her house, his job prospects, it all faded into obscurity. Anastasia looked across at Richard and she knew, no matter what else, it was the two of them against the world now. That was just how it was supposed to be.

Chapter 32

It almost seemed apt that it was so dark. Even with all the curtains tied back and the lights turned on, this one room seemed so full of mysterious shadows. It didn't scare Anastasia now, if it ever had before.

A man died in this room, suffered in agony and passed away, unnoticed by the world at large. It was a sad story, but strangely it had a happy ending. A spirit left to wander, he had continued in pain and loneliness, until she came along to meet him. She showed him what love could be, and perhaps what Jack Green had never known was that he had done the very same thing for her.

"You set me free," she whispered into the empty space around her, speaking to a man she believed watched over her from above now. "You said you were trapped here until you learnt what love was, from me," she said softly, almost laughed at how silly it sounded, and yet she was serious again in a second. "You taught me too, y'know? Without you I... I wouldn't be me. Not the way I am now, not as happy as I am now," she told him, smiling brightly.

It occurred to Anastasia that she wasn't even speaking exclusively to Jack anymore. Her grandmother played a part too. She would never have come to own Bennington Hall if not for Grandma Rachel. Never known Jack, Richard, Eva, or so many other friends and acquaintances she had made here. A whole new family somehow, in a world she barely knew existed before.

"I made a home here," she whispered, as if realising it for the first time somehow. "Not in this room or even this house, I don't think, I just... I found this sense like I belong somewhere, with somebody. You gave that to me, the two of you, and I could not be more grateful," she promised both Rachel and Jack.

Valerie Sells

Annie walked a circle around this room, stopping by the window to look out a moment. The trucks were arriving, all full of building supplies, fixtures and fittings. Work was starting today to turn this place into the Wickfield Green Rehabilitation Centre. It seemed like a fitting tribute to rename the Hall after its two most important inhabitants. At least they were the most important to Annie.

"I hope you're proud, Grandma," she said towards the slowly lightening sky beyond the window. "And thank you, so much. I don't know what I did to deserve your kindness, but thank you."

Getting up from the sill, Annie retraced her steps to the door, a distance she had walked back and forth over so very many times before. Still, when she stopped and turned to look back into the empty room one more time, she recalled one day in particular. The wind blowing and thunder cracking overhead, as Jack made his presence felt long before he ever showed his face. She saw him stood there now as clear as anything, even though it was months since he had disappeared for the final time.

"It's my turn to leave now, Jack," she told him, a single tear creeping down her cheek as she swallowed hard and fought to keep her composure. "I won't be needing this anymore," she said, unfastening the chain around her neck, on which the key to this very room had hung for so long.

The weight of it gone from her chest felt strange and yet it was a relief in a way. She would always remember Jack, with or without a physical memento, and there was no way to move on with him literally hanging around her neck.

"Rest in peace, Jack," she said softly, leaving the key behind her. "And keep watch over all the people that pass through here. They just need a chance, a helping hand, the same as we did."

Anastasia moved quickly as she left the room then, down the stairs and to the front door where one bag was waiting for her still. The rest were packed into the car, all the belongings she might need for her trip. So many other things were in storage for when she figured out where her life went from here. All she knew for certain at this moment was that Bennington Hall was no longer home, it was just a place she had lived.

Outside, she found her real home, the welcoming arms of a man she loved so much.

"You okay, sweetheart?" asked Richard as he hugged her tight, his breath visible in the cold air of an early frosty morning.

"Yeah," she promised, planting a kiss on his lips. "I'm good."

He smiled as he pushed her hair back behind her ear and just took in her face, rosy cheeks, teary eyes and all. She was beautiful and incredible, and Richard Thomas hadn't a clue what he had done to deserve her, but Annie was here in his life and she loved him as he loved her. They were starting life anew after so very many trials, so much loss and pain.

It still hurt to think of what his uncle had done, taking his own life. Richard had felt somewhat guilty when the news of George's death came to him, within a week of the letter that seemed so much like goodbye. The old goat had met his maker, and left behind one lone nephew, his sole heir.

Richard hadn't wanted the money. He was eager to give it all away, knowing that much was earned through less than decent means, more aware of how easily money could corrupt. In the end, he had put much of his newfound fortune into Bennington Hall's transformation. He and Annie gave all they could afford of their money, keeping back just enough for an adventure of their own, a round the world trip. This was their chance to see all the places they had ever dreamt of, and figure out their true place in the world. They were ready to embrace the future, whatever it might bring.

"Oh, my dears!" Eva exclaimed as she rushed to hug them both tightly. "I am going to miss you so!"

"We'll miss you too, Eva," she was promised by the both of them as they took turns in bidding her farewell with hugs and kisses.

"We'll send pictures and postcards," said Annie definitely. "From every place, all the time. You'll be sick of getting mail long before we ever get back!" She laughed.

Eva laughed too, but tears streamed down her face all the same.

"I doubt that, my love," she said with a brave smile. "But you two go and live your lives, have all the fun you can, and don't spare a thought for anybody else. You deserve all the joy and happiness God has given you. I for one couldn't be more pleased for you," she swore, a hand reached out to each of their faces.

"You are kind, Eva," said Richard with a nod of thanks. "And if it's at all in my power, I will ensure Annie enjoys every moment of our *vacation*," he teased the woman in question with a word he would never usually use himself.

"We're never going to get to go on this vacation if we miss the flight out," she realised, suddenly noticing the time on Richard's watch.

There was a sudden rush to get into the cab and leave, the driver instructed to go just as quickly as the winding, hillside road would allow. Eva waved them off, comforted by Tommy who was heading up the contractors working on the Hall. He would see to it she got back home safely, and that meant Annie had nothing in the world left to worry about.

"I do love you. You know that, don't you?" she told Richard, her eyes trained on his own as all the feeling she possessed for him poured out like the brightest light.

He smiled across at her and slowly nodded his head.

"I know," he promised her. "And I love you, Anastasia Addams, like I never loved anyone else in my whole life. You make me so happy, I never knew it was possible."

She smiled too at that, though the tears that had been welling in her eyes so long were forced to escape at the sweetness of his sentiments spoken so truthfully.

It almost seemed wrong to feel so free and happy when so much tragedy had come into their lives in the past months, and yet Annie couldn't feel guilty. She believed in fate and destiny enough to know that this was right, that although she had no idea where in the world she was supposed to be right now, she was certain that Richard was meant to be by her side.

Turning to look back at the Hall one last time as the car headed on down the hill, Anastasia Addams watched the old house slide away from view and she sighed.

"I thought coming here was a dream," she said looking out into the darkness giving way to dawn. "When I left New York, it seemed like a fantasy."

Richard watched her expression, the almost child-like innocence that came over her beautiful face as she gazed out of the back window, long after the Hall was gone from sight. Even now she was still a dreamer, though reality had dealt her some harsh blows, and she had borne witness to enough of Richard's pain too. Annie talked of the world with as much wonder as she ever had or ever could, still dreaming of a better life, a better world.

"And now?" he asked, pulling her close in his arms just as soon as she turned forward in her seat.

"Now I know I was right," she said, smiling and kissing his lips. "It's felt like a dream being here in Bennington. Not quite real. So much, almost too much," she considered, happy expression breaking down just a moment before it slowly returned. "But it's led me to this, to you and me, and our future. We have a new dream now, together, a future that hasn't been written yet. That's why I don't think there is a single thing in the last year that I would change, not for anything in the world."

"Agreed." Richard nodded, returning her kiss. "We have a lot to thank old Bennington Hall for," he said as he held her close and Annie leant her head comfortably against his chest.

"Yes, thank you," she whispered.

Perhaps she wasn't really speaking to the building she had lived in these past months, the pile of bricks and mortar and stone. Instead, she liked to think of it as thanking those who were no longer there, who had helped her so much, and now lived on in her heart, always.

"Thank you so much."

About the Author

Valerie has been an administrator all of her adult life, but has always dreamed of being an author of novels. She cut her teeth on fanfiction but is now finally sharing her original works with the world. An avid reader, writer, and self-proclaimed nerd in all the best ways, she wants to find people who love to read the kind of things she loves to write. Valerie lives in the south of England with her ever-supportive family, dreaming up new characters and plots, and Tweeting about her adventures in writing - @Valerie_Sells

Printed in Poland
by Amazon Fulfillment
Poland Sp. z o.o., Wrocław